The Core

GLORIA FOSTER

GLOBAL
PUBLISHING
SOLUTIONS

THE CORE by Gloria Foster
Published by Global Publishing Solutions, LLC
923 Fieldside Drive
Matteson, Illinois 60443
www.globalpublishingsolutions.com

Library of Congress Control Number:
2021918594
International Standard Book Number:
978-1-7372244-6-4
E-book International Standard Book Number:
978-1-7372244-7-1
Audio International Standard Book Number:
978-1-7372244-8-8

Printed in the United States of America

For my readers

THE CORE

He never knew
That
Something was
Changing
His spirit.
He didn't
Even know
When he left
That it had
Affected
Him
And
Even
Controlled
Him.
Her
Magic.

The Core

Gloria Foster

Contents

Preface

The Core is the second book of The Woman's Soul series. The first book, The Mind, was primarily all about Sheila Leclaire's uphill battle with depression and the childhood trauma that affected her. The other characters of the first book included her friends Valencia, Allie, and Mary and her guyfriend, Jonathan. More focus on the characters is set forth in The Core as well as how the ladies are affected by various issues. Additionally, the novel explores Allie's tumultuous life and what is hidden in her past.

Prologue

7:45 p.m.

I'm not going anywhere.

I hear a voice. It is familiar. I crease my eyebrows; I am confused. I look around while I feel the hair at the nape of my neck rising. There is so much air in the room. I don't understand where it is coming from.

I stand up from the bed and close the window. I draw the curtains. After locking the restroom door, I look around the room and sigh. She always leaves a mess behind.

I walk towards the kitchen to get a garbage bag. I have to start cleaning, or the room will start smelling like a junkyard. I would not like that. I walk back to the room and start with the other end of the bed. I know what I will discover there, and I have been shocked about it.

I pick up the glass bottles quietly and remove the ashes from the carpet, as well as the side tables. I see an entire pack of pills, and I throw it in the bag as well. I have to help her in any way I can.

I sit there for a while and think. There is so much I could do to help her get through what she is going through, but I chose to remain calm and let her live it the way she appears fit. I know that my eyes might start tearing up. But there is no time for that right now, and I have to get back to cleaning.

I stand up from the floor and start to pick up the pile of clothes lying on the floor. I will never understand how she became a messy person. As far as I can remember, she was pretty organized. That was one of the best traits about her.

I pick up the clothes and throw them on the bed. I settle myself on the bed and begin folding them one by one. I really can't figure which ones are clean and which ones aren't. They all look pretty much the same to me, so I just fold them and place them on the bed.

8:30 p.m.

I have already vacuumed the carpet. Now I have to freshen up the bed and make it smell better. I spray a lot of air freshener in the room and switch off the lights. I stand at the edge of the door and take one last look at the room.

I shut the door behind me and walk outside.

9:45 p.m.

I am beginning to feel hungry. I switch off the television and look in the fridge. It is not much here, so I decide to cook. After all, she will come home, and she will be hungry. There is no way she would do something for herself, so I might as well make something for the both of us.

11:15 p.m.

I am through with my dinner and also fed the baby. But she isn't home yet, and I won't be able to sleep until she gets home. I have the baby in my arms, and she is sleeping soundly. I walk to the baby's room and put her in the bassinet. I kiss her forehead and exit the room.

11:25 p.m.

I resume knitting the sweater that I had been working on for the past week. I keep checking the time, and it's getting late.

11:50 p.m.

I am pacing and knitting. It's almost midnight, and she's not home yet. She is never late. Even with all that she is into, she is never this late. I try to keep my calm, but I can't seem to stop pacing.

12:20 a.m.

I can feel my heart sinking. I know something is wrong. I say a prayer and wish really hard that it is fulfilled. I don't think there is any more space for things to go more wrong at this point in my life. I crack my knuckles and scratch my head. I breathe in deeply and walk back to her room.

12:30 a.m.

I walk in and survey the room, looking for a spot left unclean, but I find nothing. So, I involve my time with rearranging her dressing table. I move the perfumes to one side and her makeup to the other side. I wipe the dust off her jewelry and start placing it inside her drawer.

But the drawer doesn't open.

I am trying hard to open the drawer, but it seems to be stuck because of something. I bend down and look at its left.

Nothing.

Then I turn to the other side and find something sticking out. It is small, but it looks like the corner of an envelope. It makes sense because the drawer can easily get stuck because of paper.

I try to pull it out more, but it takes a lot of effort because it's just a tiny piece. I manage to get a little more of the envelope out but realize that there must be something inside the envelope.

I open the drawer and insert my fingers in the tiny space enough to clasp the envelope between my fingers. I hold it tightly and pull it out.

The envelope, along with the drawer, comes out. I catch the drawer from falling, carefully take the drawer out, and put the envelope on the dressing table.

I open the envelope, and I discover an entire bundle of letters.

I quickly collect the letters. I hurriedly place the drawer back and take the letters to my room. But I had no time to read them.

1:30 a.m.

Suddenly my heartbeat sounds louder than the sirens surrounding my home. I feel a chill run down my spine.

I hear the doorbell ring.

"She wouldn't ring the bell. She has keys."

I tried to muster up some calmness and walked towards the door. I don't know why my heart is thudding and why I'm sweating.

I unlock the door and look at the police officer who is standing out there in front of me.

I gaze into the nothingness trusting it would devour me some time before the news would.

A Step Back

"200 or nothing."

A tall, broad man looked at the woman who was staring right in his eyes. She was small with piercing eyes. Her voice was sweet yet stern enough for people to know not to mess with her.

The guy opened his mouth to protest, but he knew there was no point in doing so. He reached into his pocket, produced 200 bucks, and handed them down to the woman. She smirked and then licked the thumb of her left hand to count the bills which she had just received.

She bent down to securely put the money in the safe. Then she walked over to the back divider and brought out a large bag with packets in it.

She drew nearer to the guy who took the bag from her instantly, turned, and began to leave.

"Have fun with your goods," she said.

A deep voice filled up the room as the tall, broad guy left the garage.

"Phew, Angela, you are a real scare," he said.

Angela looked around and saw Frank, her boss, surveying her from the far end of the garage.

"That gets the job done. Doesn't it?" Frank laughed.

Angela reached down into the drawer and brought out a bottle of whiskey. She poured two glasses and handed one to Frank.

"Feel free to go home. You've been good."

Angela raised her glass at Frank and chugged down the whiskey in one go.

"See you tomorrow, Frank."

"Mhmm," he said.

Angela put the glass down on the concrete slab, grabbed her bag, and exited the garage. The walk from her "workplace" to her home was not long, but she preferred taking the long way home. She liked her peace and her own pace. Plus, she didn't want to "do stuff" at home because of the possibility that her activity would be found out. She had, at last, come to discover a little peace.

It had taken her a long time to be happy, and she was finally getting there. But she didn't realize that her happiness was as short-lived as the effect of the "stuff" that she took.

Finding out the truth had been severely hard on Angela. When Emmanuel walked out on her, she had been calm—as if she was waiting for more. She had been normal. She went to work and tried not to think a lot of the situation that had been presented in front of her then. She was in denial but did not know it.

It was all getting too much for Angela to bear. She had no way out of it. At least that is what she thought for the most part. She did not want to talk to her mother about it. She was afraid that she would give her nothing but judgment, and Angela did not have any space for any more trauma in her life.

She had walked home from work that day just so that she could feel something. As soon as she reached home, she dropped on the bed with her eyes staring at the ceiling.

Her head kept spinning—weaving thoughts of what could be and what could have been. She wanted everything to stop. No more thoughts. No ideas. No suffering.

Suddenly, her baby started crying. Angela shut her eyes and clenched her fists. She was frustrated to her core. It seemed like everything in the universe wanted to piss her off, and lately, it was succeeding.

She walked to her room, picked the baby up, and tried to quiet her. As she began pacing in the room, she hummed a tune to calm her. Gradually, the baby started to quiet down. There was serenity all around Angela.

In that harmony, she found the peace that she was yearning for.

As she put the baby down on her bed, she picked up the phone and dialed the one number she had been dreading to call for the longest time.

"I'm coming to D.C.," she said.

"You're always welcome, dear."

With a daughter in her arms and only two bags, she had a mind full of thoughts, but Angela flew to where she believed would be safety.

Forever Caught

The clock had struck 10, and Miss Charlotte was waiting for her daughter to return home. She was worried, but she also knew that Angela knew what she was doing. What Miss Charlotte didn't know was that her daughter had caught herself up in deep, deep trouble.

Miss Charlotte would turn off all the lights at night, but she would not put her head against the pillow until her daughter made it home.

She knew that Angela had been suffering a lot lately, but she didn't realize that her coping mechanism was way worse than she thought it would be.

All of a sudden, she heard the sound of her arriving, and Miss Charlotte got up. She turned on the lights and was glad to see that Angela had come home. But she was also furious. She did not like these late-night shenanigans of hers, and she had been pretty clear about it since she relocated to D.C.

The events in Philadelphia were never revealed to Miss Charlotte. She just knew that Angela had gotten divorced and that she couldn't stand being there alone with just her daughter. Miss Charlotte was aware of how much Angela loved her husband. She did not have the heart to tell her daughter no. She didn't want to.

Even though that night had been quite rough on Angela, it was hard on Miss Charlotte also. She couldn't quit thinking about how she would manage with Angela and Allie. But she kept her calm. That is what she was the best at.

"You shouldn't be coming home so late," she said.

"Shh, mom. One day I might not come home at all."

"Angela Rose! You need to get a hold of yourself! You have been nothing but useless from the moment that you have moved here. I hate to break it to you, but the baby that lives with us is your daughter. And she needs you!"

"Mother, please, I don't think I can—"

"No, Angela! Enough is enough! How selfish do you have to be to leave a child just months old to someone else? How does it not bother you knowing that your baby might be crying for you, and you are never there for her? This is what I was scared of from the moment that you called me telling me that you were coming here for good. I knew you were going to turn this around and act like this is too much for you to handle. That is not the point, Angela! You need to start taking some responsibility, especially for your daughter. You are not a child anymore!

Angela's ears were ringing. She had seen this coming, but she didn't expect her to get upset so soon. It had hardly been three months since Angela had moved back with her mother, and her mother had already started to throw around fits of anger here and there.

Every day was a struggle to avoid her mother to retain her peace. But it was short-lived, and she was aware of it. She needed a way out of the hurt—an escape, a getaway. And in the search for hope, she had ended up in an endless tunnel—a pit that she had jumped in knowingly. But she wasn't sure she could get out of it anymore.

If she were to get out, she knew she wouldn't be getting out of it alive.

Angela's eyes began tearing. She didn't know how to respond to her mother. She just left the room and went to bed contemplating everything happening with her lately. Her head was banging. Her heart was thumping loudly. Her eyes were burning.

She shut her eyes tightly. She thought of the one person that had been continuously following her, and she slipped into oblivion unknowingly.

I can feel it.

Someone is following me.

I can feel it.

It's not safe for me.

I can feel it.

Someone is closing in.

I can feel it.

Why aren't my feet running?

His hands are on my throat.

Should I let this grasp completely take me under?

I want to scream but can't.

There is no voice left inside of me.

I should have stopped.

I am forever caught.

Sometime later, Miss Charlotte found herself sitting on the sofa trying to hush the uncontrollably crying child in her arms and talking to the officers who seemed to be explaining things to her. But she could not take it. It was too much for her.

"Suspect."

"Murder."

"Victim."

"Addict."

It was all a blur. But she thanked the officers for speaking with her despite being confused about what had happened to Angela.

As soon as they left, she packed her bags, turned to the baby, and said, "We are going to start a new life together. I promise."

Good News

While peering out the living room window, I see the view that shows a blanket of snow. Although the beauty of winter in the Northeast causes those who have relocated to warmer climates to make trips back to experience the snow, it seems to be for only that reason. They would instead continue living where they are because it is much more sun than here.

I appreciate the sun, especially on a snowy day like this, but I would like to have more of it like far-away golden, sun-kissed California with all its beauty—the breathtaking views such as the stunning mountain ranges and the calmness of the ocean waves. I am energetic on the warm days of spring, despite the rain, and also the hot days of summer. With the heat of the fireplace and the snowy day making me kind of lazy, I drifted off into a midday nap.

The striking sound of a clapping noise unsettled the stillness in the air. SLAP!

"No, you won't haul off and hit me!" Allie cried.

"Keep my name out of your mouth," Reginald's girlfriend said.

"You slut!" Allie screamed.

"You did not know that Reginald was lying to you," she said.

"Reginald, she slapped me!" Allie said.

"What are you going to do about it?" Allie asked.

"That is between you and her," Reginald said. "You should not have followed me here."

"What? What did you say, Reginald? I am your wife!" Allie screamed.

"Better yet, don't say anything, Reginald," Allie said. "You're NOT sorry. I knew that I would eventually catch you."

"I am not sorry, Allie," Reginald said.

"Yea, because she has you under her spell," Allie said. "Get out of my life Reginald. Don't ever call me. Ever! You are low! Stay out of my life! Stay out of my life! Stay out of my life." Allie yelled as she turned and walked to her car.

"Woah! That was woozy," I said as I awoke to the telephone ringing.

"Hello," I said.

"Hi Sheila," Valencia said.

"Hey, Val," I said. "I just had a crazy dream about Allie and Reginald. She was in an argument with him and some woman who he was cheating with. Allie followed them. She told him she was through with him and to stay out of her life. The woman slapped Allie. Reginald said that he wasn't sorry that she caught him. And, to make it worse, he didn't do anything about the woman slapping her. What is up with that, Val?"

"Wow!" Valencia exclaimed. "That dream was crazy. And you know what?"

"Don't tell me it's true, Val!" I shouted.

"She is going to call you," Valencia said.

"Great. How is she managing being alone?" I questioned. "I have not heard from her in a while now."

"Yea. She is great! You know that it was a matter of time before that would happen," Valencia said.

"True," I said.

"She is really happy," Valencia continued. "She has her life together now. It is almost like she is alright now that she is not with him. She did not need to be chasing up after any man that was below her. She is better than that. He was the scum of the earth.

He probably has found his match. She slapped my Allie—I should wring her neck."

"Val, why do men do that?" I questioned.

"Well, here is the real deal with Reginald," Valencia explained. "He is jealous. And, he is a sick man. He has low self-esteem. He downright hates himself. So he cannot show anything but hate towards others because of that. The woman that he is with does not have anything going for herself. So she is no threat to Reginald. With that woman that he is with now, he is controlled. She has so much control over him. It is rather odd."

"But Allie is so pretty," I said. "She has her marketing firm."

"He is jealous of her—the way she looks, her life. She is high class. He could not find anything wrong with her," Valencia said. "And, that woman that he is with controls the heck out of him. She says jump. He says how high. There is something strange about her, Sheila."

"It sounds like it, Val," I said.

"Val, before I took a nap, I was thinking about California. It is beautiful as ever out there," I said. "How is the weather today?"

"It's in the sixties," she said.

"Thinking about California is only warming my soul Val," I said. "It's frigid here."

"Well, I have some hot news," Valencia said.

"Really!" I said.

"I am now Mrs. Xavier Alexander," Valencia said. "I eloped."

"That's wonderful, Val!" I exclaimed. "I've got to let you go, Val. Jonathan is on the other line. You better hold onto Mr. Alexander."

"I am going to Sheila," she said, "I'll tell you about him later. We'll chat later, Sheila."

"Hello, Jon," I said.

"Hey," Jonathan said. "What have you been up to?"

"I've got great news!" I said. "I just spoke with Valencia. She has eloped."

"That is awesome," he said. "You could be next."

"You better stop playing, Jon," Sheila said.

"Alright," he said. "What else has been happening?

"Well, I had an awful dream about Allie," I said. "Some woman slapped her. And, lo and behold, I find out that she has indeed left Reginald."

"Good riddance," Jonathan said. "I bet she is doing great now."

"That is what Valencia said," I said. "She told me that Allie is going to phone me to tell me."

"Cool," Jonathan said.

"Valencia also said Reginald's woman has some type of hold on him," I said. "She is controlling."

"Wait. Why are you telling me this girl talk?" Jonathan questioned. "Valencia is going to be mad that you are telling me what you all talked about."

"No. She won't," I said.

"I'm just playing," Jonathan said. "She got roots on him?"

"Yeah, Jon. Something is strange," I said.

Valencia

It's just jitters.

Valencia poured herself a glass of chilled water and gulped it down in a go. Her tireless pacing across her study room did nothing to relieve the pounding against her chest and the thumping in her head.

She rested her palms on her forehead and gave her temple a brief rub, but the pain didn't relent. With her eyes squeezed shut and temples getting a futile massage, she walked from her mahogany table to the shelf against the wall.

The short distance between the two fixtures seemed smaller than ever but was only a footstep apart.

"Don't worry. He's a good man."

The mere hint of it ran shivers down her spine.

"Why do men do that?" The pointed question seemed to challenge her decision. Her steps quickened; her pace hastened; her toes lightly grazed against the mahogany table but went unnoticed. For a moment, she wanted to place every man in the same category and denounce any association with that breed.

"All men aren't the same. They can't be the same. Jon is a nice fellow. I don't know him well, but he strikes me as a good man. Hands down he is a good man."

The mention of Jon somehow assuaged her growing disgust for Reginald.

"Is Xavier a good man?"

Valencia halted at the bookshelf and scoured through the books. She touched the books with her fingertips and thought about where she was going with her life. She stood there and took a deep breath.

"Stop overthinking all this. I've known him for some time. I can't be wrong. Your gut can't be wrong. My gut told me he is the right one."

With her trust in her gut, she looked at the books, and her eyes fell on one.

"The male brain," she read out the title loudly.

"There I go! It looks like I have all I need to get through with this."

It was not what she needed to feed her brain with right now. She found herself picking out that book.

"How does the male brain function?" The plethora of thoughts rushed through her mind, and she was once again in a whirlpool of questions. "If only I knew," she answered.

She opened the first page of the book. The words danced in front of her eyes as if everything was hinting to her to have second thoughts.

Male. Brain. Psychology. Neurons. Unknown.

The words boggled her mind, and she was forced to think about the uncertain, the unspoken, and the unwanted.

She placed the edge of the book on her chin and recalled the time she first met Xavier. Although she had eloped with him, fear bulged in her heart. She started to question everything that she had done with Xavier in the time that they had spent together. Though she knew that she had eloped with him after much thought and consideration, she couldn't stop herself from thinking whether he was the right choice for her.

"This is because of what happened to Allie. I know. It's clearly my reaction to that. I'm sure about it."

"But I can have second thoughts. It's my life after all. So why not?" she said speaking from her inner subconscious.

"Why am I questioning all of it now? This is not the right time to think about it." She was making a failed attempt to appease her brain. As she tried to hush away all the thoughts, she remembered when she and Xavier had their first date. She blushed as her lips curved into a smile. She tucked her locks behind her ear as she sprawled her legs on the couch she was sitting on.

"Oh, Xavier!" she exclaimed when she said his name. She could see all the past moments she spent with him in front of her eyes strung together like a sweet and romantic movie.

For a fleeting moment, she got lost in her thoughts. She forgot about the hovering questions and reminisced the time. But it took just one more thought to yank her out of her daydreams—the thought of Allie.

Poor Allie! She would have given marriage a second thought had she known that the love of her life would betray her like that. "Nobody ever knows what life has in store for them," exclaimed Valencia. "What if life had the same for me?" she asked.

She felt a shiver running down her spine; she had goosebumps. At that moment, she radiated heat. She rushed to look at herself in the mirror.

Clearly, she was scared to death. The thought had taken over her mind, and she refused to get it out of her head. She was in dire need of making it go away or maybe in dire need of talking to somebody about it. But she did not know who.

She thought of Allie and then Sheila, but her heart couldn't agree. Allie was pretty much exhausted by her own problems, and she didn't want to cause more trouble than Allie was already in. Sheila had her hands full with Allie at the time.

"Uuuuughhhh….." she said frustrated.

"Xavier." Her mouth solved her problem immediately.

"Yes. I think I should talk to Xavier about it," she said to herself while looking in the mirror. She knew the reaction wouldn't be good. She could only hope that things would turn out right for her.

"Hey, love!" Xavier's husky voice startled her, and she opened her eyes. He hung his car keys on the key holder and paced towards her.

Xavier was a man every woman would dream of marrying. His sharp jawline, round nose, beady brown eyes, and lean figure categorized him as one of the most wanted men; even men would often get envious of him. His curly hair only added to his charm and attraction. He spoke less and listened more.

With utmost grace, he came towards Valencia to put a soft kiss on her forehead. She smiled.

"What's up? You look unsettled," he said while scrutinizing her face.

"I knew he'd know." Her heart sank!

She then looked up at his face and said, "Why don't you freshen up? Meanwhile, I'll get dinner ready?"

"Sounds great," he said as he walked out of the room.

Valencia walked into the kitchen to heat dinner. She got the plates out and set the table. Xavier came back some ten minutes later. He took a seat opposite Valencia and breathed in the aroma of the food.

"Let's eat. This smells amazing."

Valencia smiled at him while nodding.

"So how did your day go," Xavier asked.

"Um," Valencia began saying but got interrupted as her phone started to ring.

She left the table and went to see who was calling her.

It was Mary.

Valencia turned to Xavier and said, "You go ahead and eat without me. I have to take this one."

"Okay but be quick!" he replied.

"Sure," she said as she exited the room.

She sat on the bed and picked up the phone.

"Hey," she said.

"Hi, Valencia. What's up?"

"Um. I really needed to talk to someone about this, and I couldn't think of anyone else except for you."

"That's cool. What is it?"

"Mary… I don't think I should have married Xavier. I mean I am having second thoughts about it. I know that it's foolish to think about it. I should be happy and thinking of all the good things that might happen, but I can't seem to get the thought of being disappointed out of my head. I don't think that I am confident about this. What should I do, Mary?"

"Val. Val. You need to slow down honey. First, you need to take a deep breath."

"Okay," she said while carefully listening to her friend who helped her to understand that everything she was feeling was valid.

"What's important is that you need to give yourself time and space to be able to figure this out. If you feel confused or think that something is bothering you, make sure that you communicate. Okay?"

"Yeah," she said. "Thanks, Mary."

"No problem love. Call me if you still need to talk."

"I will… Bye. Thanks, Mary!"

"Goodbye!"

As the line dropped, Valencia breathed a sigh of relief. She put her phone on the bed and got up to head back to the kitchen.

When she opened the door, Xavier was standing right there. Valencia's heart started beating loudly. She knew that he had overheard the conversation because of the still expression on his face.

"You want to talk about something," he asked politely.

"I think I should…" she answered.

Xavier gestured her to walk towards the table as he followed her.

"So?" he asked as he sat down.

"I'm not sure how much you have heard Xavier, but—"

"Tell me everything," he said.

After Valencia told Xavier what had happened with Allie and Reginald, she looked down and then continued. "I am sorry, but it's true. I can't help but think that something might happen to me too, and I don't want that. Life is difficult as it is, and I don't want to add the aspect of worrying to it."

Xavier reached out for her hand and said, "I know you are scared, and you have every reason to be. But a leap of faith can do you wonders, Val."

Valencia said nothing. She only nodded as if trying to convince herself.

"You take as much time as you need Val. We are going to be alright. I am with you."

She squeezed his hand and smiled. She knew she was with the right man.

Mary

"See you all tomorrow, kids!"

A sweet voice took over the room as the kids began forming a line and started to leave. A small, scrawny figure with eyes as deep as onyx smiled as she looked at the children one by one waving her goodbye.

Once everyone had left, she let out an exhausted sigh and nestled back into her chair. Things had been getting quite draining lately, and the only escape Mary could find comfort in was the classroom.

There was no day that Mary would not get up feeling tired, but that feeling would soon be overpowered by the pure joy that she would soon be surrounded by a group of children who loved being around her and she around them. She would wake up every day with the same purpose—to be with the kids. Most people would get tired of the monotony, but Mary loved her students beyond limits.

Mary had always been someone who adored being around children. Their cute smiles and eyes would take her breath away. So when she realized that she could never be a mother, the world around her literally collapsed.

She had only been to the doctor for a regular check-up. Her period was late for a month, and she wanted to rule out anything happening. After undergoing testing, her doctor broke the news to her. The idea of not being able to bear children was devastating to her. She was only 27 years old. It was everything she ever wanted. Knowing that she wouldn't ever be able to have kids of her own shattered her to her core.

The main reason that Mary had fallen so deep into the pit of grief was the mutual love her husband, Tobias, had for children. The two of them were pretty eager to have kids, but they also wanted to spend some time with each other. They loved each other very much, and the love they shared was quite visible. In general, people would be envious of the pair. They always looked like they had just found each other and were just in the "getting to know each other" and "want to do everything perfectly for each other" phase. So when they did decide to have children, his excitement was infinite. Tobias cleared space to make a nursery for the baby as soon as they began trying. He bought paints the next day, and the two of them argued on the room's color.

Just the day before Mary paid a visit to her gynecologist, the two of them finished painting the ceiling of the nursey. It was Mary's idea to paint a beautiful sky with neon paints, and the two of them dropped down tired after it was done.

"I can't wait for us to be parents, Mary."

She looked at his face—his wheatish complexion paired with deep, brown eyes.

The two of them were enjoying a perfect meal with wine. It was a great day. They kept talking and sharing jokes while laughing and munching on their food. By the end of the night, they got so tired that they ended up falling asleep in each other's arms on the carpeted floor.

Mary woke up in the morning feeling nothing but happy. Little did she know that her happiness was short-lived and that her heart would be broken within the next two hours.

When returning home, Mary was a tad bit glad that her husband wasn't there. She had no courage to face him. Or maybe she didn't want to face him.

The first person that Mary told about the news she received from the doctor was Sheila. She had always been closer to Sheila than her other two friends, and she knew that talking to her would come without any judgment.

Sheila was alarmed to learn how well Mary had taken the news. She was casual about it. But Sheila knew well, and she figured that her friend was in denial. She knew that suggesting she seek help wouldn't be the smartest thing to do at the time. So she kept her mouth shut. However, she was scared about Mary getting hurt worse.

But it was inevitable of course. Mary was totally fine for the first week. She talked to Tobias about what the doctor had said. Of course, he was distraught, but he didn't want to show it in front of his wife. He knew that she was going through enough, and he didn't want to add to it.

On the other hand, Mary began thinking that Tobias was drawing away from her. He had started coming home late, and it had been over a week since the two had shared a meal together. Mary had been trying to keep it all together. But that only lasted for so long.

After three weeks, Tobias opened his eyes that morning to banging and crashing. When he turned to his side, he realized that his wife wasn't there. He rushed through the house with his mind making up weird scenarios. When he reached the nursery, he didn't know the hell that would be lying ahead of him when he opened the door.

He tried to back off and leave and pretend like he wasn't even there in the first place. But he didn't want to leave Mary behind. The truth was hard on him, but it was worse for her. Mary had always been the emotional one out of the two, but she had also been the one who had always been there for him. It was time for Tobias to do the same for her.

When he stepped into the room, tears came to his eyes. The crib was broken. The light bulbs were smashed. The carpet was covered with dust. Mary was trying to scrape the wallpaper off the walls when Tobias caught her and cradled her in his arms. Mary began fighting him off her, but he held on to her tightly until her loud screams became sobs.

Tobias carried her in his arms to the room and fed her food with his own hands. He tucked her to sleep and held her close to him hoping that she would be okay in the morning. But she wasn't.

Mary's day in bed turned into two days and then a week. All she did was lay in bed and cry. Tobias didn't want to accept that there was something wrong with Mary. He called her friends over to help her get out of it. However, nothing helped. She looked like a lifeless soul on the bed—not talking and not eating. Tobias knew that the matter was now out of his hands.

Mary was not pushing her husband away on purpose. She wanted to give her husband the happiness he had been eager for. She blamed herself for not being able to conceive. She went to therapy for over three months. That didn't work at first, but she started getting better slowly and gradually. It was the therapy that motivated her to start teaching kids again.

But even after things had gotten better, Mary couldn't fully forgive herself for how her being unable to conceive children had affected Tobias. In no way could she understand that she was not to blame, but she knew that it was costing her their marriage.

As she sat in the classroom, all she knew was the perfect day of teaching the kids. It had been a pretty long time since she and Tobias had been back to normal. Her heart was urging her to wish that she could somehow turn back time and make Tobias and herself happy again.

The Split

"Then what happened?"

Sheila inched herself closer to her friend, who was right now in a pool of tears. She wanted to hug her, but she also didn't want to interrupt her sobs. So she just sat there looking out of the window listening to her carefully.

Sheila had taken a flight to Dallas just to meet Allie. She knew that her friend was in a terrible state, and she wanted to be there for her. She was tired too, but she knew what was most important right then.

"I'll tell you what happened! Just let me. Just. Whaaaaaa!" She broke her sentence into a hapless cry. She was unable to stop herself from crying.

Sheila extended her hand and reached for Allie's back. While patting it down slowly, she assured Allie that she was there for her.

"You can't possibly think that it's your fault."

"Isn't it?" she asked.

Sheila looked at her confused. Her lips were slightly curved at the edges—an expression that openly conveyed how perplexed she was. "Why would you think that anyway?"

"Nothing. I don't know," she began saying when the tears started to roll down her cheeks again.

"It's okay. I'm listening."

Allie nodded her head. She had known that Sheila would be there for her no questions asked. She didn't have the energy even to explain the situation. She hadn't broken down with anyone yet. It was different with Sheila. She had to be honest about her feelings for once.

"I guess I saw this coming. I think your gut always knows. Don't you think?"

"I do."

"But… I guess I didn't want it to be true. I think. I just wanted to be happy. I thought that whatever it was that he might get over it. I thought that maybe, just maybe, he wasn't stupid enough to do that."

Sheila darted a look at her friend. She was constantly trying to push her hair back and wiping the tears off her face. Her eyes looked bloodshot, and the mascara was dripping down her cheeks. She looked flustered like she had imagined something very embarrassing. Her fingers were constantly fidgeting with tissue. She kept tearing it into small bits.

Sheila loved Allie. They had been friends for a very long time. They had been there for each other in their good and all of their bad times. They had crashed parties together, shopped together, and told each other what dress they looked their best in. They knew what each other's favorite colors were, styled each other's hair, and even helped each other to look good for their dates. Heck, Sheila was the one who had gone with Allie to pick her dress for her wedding. They had taken the day off, spent it in the most expensive bridal salons, and tasted expensive wine. The two had been practically inseparable. Sheila had seen Allie at her lowest, but this wasn't something she had expected of her friend. She didn't know a man could so hurt Allie.

She couldn't bear to see her friend that way, and it was bringing tears to her eyes too. She wanted to be there for her friend, but she didn't know how. She turned her face to the window and thought for a while.

After a good fifteen-minute span, she realized that the best thing she could do for Allie right now was to be there for her. Sheila took a deep breath and said, "Come on. You know that you are smarter than this."

"I know I am," she replied. "But tell me, is it so wrong to expect something as small as decency from someone, let alone your husband?"

Sheila shook her head. She knew that Allie was right. She didn't want to be suggestive. She didn't want to sound optimistic. So she decided to be empathetic.

She took Allie's face in her hands and said, "Okay, you can cry all you want. But you have to promise me this. You cry today for the last time. You waste something as precious as your tears over someone as low as Reginald, and you do it for the last time today. You can cry. You can scream—but all today. I can't let you lose yourself over someone who doesn't deserve you. Do you understand?"

Allie put her face down as her eyes began to fill with tears. She grabbed another tissue to wipe the tears.

Allie burst into small sobs. She was unable to fathom why she felt so helpless. She had been in love before, but nothing had left her this sore. Sheila only pulled her close as she wept and wept. She patted her back while telling her it was going to be okay over and over again.

Sheila gestured at the waitress to get her some water while Allie was still crying. Her sobs had gone meek, but she was still not out of tears. She sat back and put her hands on the table. After she let in a deep breath, she reached for the tissue and wiped off the tears which had completely smeared her face.

Sheila poured her a glass of water, pushed it towards her, and nudged her to drink. Allie resisted for a while but finally gave in after accepting that her friend wasn't going to back down anytime soon.

Allie didn't realize that she was thirsty until she took the first sip. She then drank it hastily and put it back on the table.

"How do you feel?" Sheila asked.

"To be honest… I'm hungry as hell." The two of them burst out laughing.

"That is so Allie of you," Sheila said.

"Yeah, I know," Allie said while still laughing.

"Let's get you some food, drama mama," Sheila said as she gestured to another waitress to come to take their order. "No, but seriously… How do you feel?"

"I feel empty," Allie answered.

Sheila waited on her friend to patiently complete her sentence. She wanted her to get everything out of her system.

"I feel like there's nothing that changed—like I always knew that something was going to happen. I think at one point I even fell out of love with him. This is just me mourning what I already knew. But at the end of the day, I am a human. And I too, like everyone else, like to cling on to every ounce of hope that I can find."

Sheila reached out for Allie's hand. She wanted to give her as much support as she could.

"What I didn't know was when I would be seeing him for the last time. I didn't realize it would all end so soon."

Sheila was amazed to see how wise her friend sounded even at her worst. Allie was a lot of things. She was intelligent, brave, understanding, strong, fun, and bold. But she was also very wise. She wasn't born smart, but she learned her lessons through dealing with life. She walked down some difficult paths and even after she would lose the battles, she did not let it stop her.

Allie had a big circle of friends and a club that loved her. She was jolly, fun-loving, and highly extroverted. She was beautiful both inside and out. She was one of those popular women who people would love without any effort, but she would always find her way back to Sheila.

While sitting there, Sheila realized why the two of them had been friends for so long. She looked at Allie and said, "Sometimes a moment is all you need?"

"Yes. It took me just a moment to realize that I had fallen out of love with him."

"How did you know that?"

"I was more in love with the memories that we had created than Reginald himself. I knew for a while that everything was not like it was at first. When he stopped being himself and when he stopped making efforts, that is when I knew."

"Wow, Allie. You are….really, really wise. You are so smart!"

"I know."

"And yet here we are."

"It's not that, Sheila. It just aches. It just pains me to know that he left me for another woman. What does she have that I don't?"

"No brain for starters."

Allie chuckled.

"There are so many things that are lovable about you, Allie. You are the strongest person and one of the bravest people I know. You are definitely the most powerful woman I know. You have been through so much, but you still choose to see the good side of life. That's something."

Allie closed her eyes as if trying to remember something. When she opened them, there were tears. Allie hugged her friend tightly. She was grateful that she was there.

Allie had not talked to Sheila about Reginald in quite a while. But now she was pouring her heart out. Allie loved Sheila with all her heart, and the best thing she liked about their friendship was how Sheila would give her the time she needed. Sheila would always know but would be patient and just let Allie know that she was there for her. That is all she would need to hear. That is all anyone needs to hear.

"Allie. You are beautiful, and you matter as much as anyone else who walks on this planet. You don't need anyone who doesn't realize what you are worth because the right one will walk in at the right time. Forget everything else."

Allie smiled.

"I know it's easier said than done. But until you are okay to get back on your feet, just know that I am here. And I will be here as long as you want me to be."

"Thank you, Sheila. You are a really good friend. Thank you for flying here for me. I don't know what I would have done without you."

"And she's back!" Sheila laughed.

"You bet I am. And anyone who chooses a nasty heifer over me can go and fall down the drain for all I care! I'm pretty. He doesn't deserve me. Tonight we celebrate!"

"Your freedom?"

"You know it, girl!"

The two of them laughed as the steaks they had ordered arrived at the table. Allie heard her stomach grumble and dived in, not waiting for anything in the world to interrupt her.

"You know what, Sheila?"

"Mmmhmm?" she answered, chewing on her first bite. "Gosh, this tastes so good."

"I think we should really start focusing on ourselves from today forward. We have let the troubles get to us and lost ourselves in the process. Let's do something that makes us feel better. How does that sound?"

"Sounds perfect. But tonight we party!"

"For sure!" Allie said, grinning.

Emmanuel

"I need my cigar." Those were the words uttered most from Emmanuel Patterson.

It was a bright, sunny morning. Emmanuel had gotten up that morning with only one thing on his mind. He had to talk to his wife, but when he rolled over to his right, Angela was nowhere to be found.

"She must be in the baby's room." He left the bed and walked towards the room.

His legs hurt with every step that he took. He had taken a pretty bad fall down the stairs just a day ago. There was also something with his head. He had been feeling dizzy a whole lot these days, and he figured that it was just something that came with old age even though he was just in his thirties.

Emmanuel and Angela had gotten married relatively young. The two of them had been high school sweethearts, and the popular couple was named Prom King and Queen.

They had gotten far from each other during college, but Emmanuel soon realized he could not live without her. So he showed up at Angela's dorm one day with a ring in his pocket and high hopes in his heart. Angela was so happy that she cried the entire night. The two of them went out for ice cream and decided to get done with the wedding as soon as possible. They agreed on getting married a month later right after they would graduate.

Within the next few hours, all their friends and family knew that the two were getting married. They looked into venues. Bridal magazines were being sent to Angela. What was just 30 days seemed like an eternity? Their patience was running thin. Every time they would go out to prepare their wedding shenanigans, they would miss each other terribly afterward.

The day arrived when the two would finally not be spending another moment away from each other. Emmanuel was the happiest he had ever been. He looked so husky dressed in a jet-black tuxedo. His brown hair was set with gel to one side. His blue eyes were glittering with joy.

As for Angela, she was throwing a last-minute look at herself in the mirror. She was draped in a v-neck, floral net dress that was low cut on the shoulders. The jewelry she had adorned herself with was the most delicate set anyone had ever seen. Her lipstick shade was as pink as the beautiful, warm undertones of her skin. She had tied her hair in a bun with bangs, which were effortlessly falling to her deep, brown eyes.

When Emmanuel saw his soon-to-be-wife down the aisle, his eyes were teary. He smiled to himself subtly but deep enough for his dimples to be shown.

As she stood there in front of him, he took one look at her and knew once again that there was certainly no one else for him but her.

"My Angel. You have and will always be the only one I have truly loved. Today I want to remind you of how grateful I am for your existence. If it weren't for you, I would have never been this happy. Today I take you to be my wife, love, happiness, best friend, joy, whole life, and the whole world. I love you with all of my heart, and I shall keep doing so until I take my last breath."

Emmanuel had always been the more serious one in their relationship. His approach was always practical. By him bringing matters into discussion, they talked about the future and planned what they might be able to do together.

On the other hand, Angela was the jolly one in the relationship. She would joke around, talk about things that would make the both of them happy, or drag Emmanuel out on dates to the most extraordinary of places. She was the light of the relationship, and Emmanuel would often consider himself as the boring one. But then he would look at her face, and with her always smiling, he would know that everything in the world was totally okay and that there was nothing that could possibly go wrong.

So when she stood there reading out her vows, everyone in the crowd was cheering including

Emmanuel. He felt like there could not have been a better world for him to exist in.

Pretty soon the two of them kissed their promise and were called husband and wife. They danced the night away, drank, and shared food with their friends and family, and then they entered the room tired but full of love.

"I can call you mine now."

"What do you mean? I was yours before today too."

"You were. But now no one can take you away from me. That makes me the happiest man on Earth. I love you, Angela."

Angela laughed.

"When did you turn so romantic?"

"When I met you," he said as he planted a kiss on her cheek.

Angela reached for his hand and brought it close to her lips and kissed it. She then turned her face towards him and looked him in the eye.

"I love you, too."

Emmanuel extended his hand to caress Angela's cheek. He pulled her closer and kissed her cheek. The two of them then spent the night talking. They discussed everything from how they would work the expenses to what they would have for dinner the next day.

Everything was perfect.

Was.

Everything was gone now. The love. The promises. The closeness. It was all gone within the first two months of their marriage. Neither of them could recognize who they had become especially for each other.

"You don't even know what I like. Stop cooking for me!"

"I will. I don't care. I was just being nice, but I don't think you even deserve that!"

A continuous chain of bickering would repeat itself throughout the day. The two would then get tired, throw themselves in bed, and then wait for the day to be over.

They began avoiding each other at home to reduce the number of arguments. This resulted in the two dodging each other to their utmost. But they still held on to each other. Neither of them gave up their loyalty. Their relationship might have been going towards toxicity, but they did not want to give up their vows. As a marriage, it had become a truce where both parties were silently holding on to each other and hoping that they might get through this phase.

Angela worked in the nightclub, and Emmanuel was buying bar after bar. The wine tastings had gotten him so addicted that he became a sturdy alcoholic and came home drunk every night.

One day he came home with the widest grin on his face. He walked in straight to the kitchen where Angela was busy cooking dinner. He turned off the stove and pulled her into his arms. He moved her hand to his shoulder and while intertwining her other hand, he led the way and began dancing with her.

"You are in a mood," Angela said.

He was humming a tune and didn't stop. He leaned in closer and kissed her forehead. Angela had forgotten how it felt to be loved. Her face blushed, and she flinched a little.

Emmanuel put her head on his chest as they danced around the kitchen slowly.

"My dear today is the day I have bought the first bar outside of the United States. We are going to be rich."

Angela could smell the whiskey on his breath. She felt torn. She wanted to be there for her husband, but she also knew that he was up to no good. So she decided to stay quiet, stay settled, and compromise like she had been doing for most of their marriage.

Emmanuel cupped her face in his hands and brought his lips close to hers. That night the two of them sat at the dinner table and talked for a very long time. As midnight approached, the two of them went to bed satisfied. Angela made the most of it because she knew this moment was short-lived.

Emmanuel left in the morning before Angela even woke up. That was quite strange. Emmanuel got out of bed, made breakfast for himself, smoked his cigar, and left without a sound. He liked doing things his way, and disruptions were one of his biggest pet peeves. He learned to be discreet and cautious at a very young age because he did not like anyone telling him what to do—and that included his wife.

He was aware of the things that were happening in his home, but he didn't want to be a part of it. That was how he had always been. Running away from confrontations had always been his number one defense. He did not like talking about the things bothering him. He wasn't raised that way. He would bottle everything up until it would become too much, and he would then get ticked off about just a little thing. He would then explode out of nowhere. He was busy suppressing everything, drinking, smoking cigars, and keeping his head buried in work until now.

When Angela woke up in the morning, she felt dizzy. She thought it was probably because of the hunger and went downstairs to eat something. By the time she reached there, she realized that she had overslept. She had to go to the grocery store today. She quickly drank some orange juice, locked the door, and went on her way.

She had just taken a few steps outside when she felt like throwing up. Angela covered her mouth and ran back inside just in time. She could feel cold sweats covering her face, and she then felt hot. Her heart was thumping loudly, and she vomited in an instant. She took the day off work and called in sick.

She spent the entire day in bed, sleeping for some time, watching television, eating something, and then sleeping again. She didn't realize that when Emmanuel came home, he had nestled beside her. It took her a month to discover why she had these bad days and why she didn't get her period.

When Emmanuel learned about the pregnancy, he became more careful. He was a man of values, and he didn't want his wife to think that he was some sort of drunkard who wasn't fit to take care of a child.

That is when the two of them really began to work on their marriage. But it was already too broken, and not everything can be fixed. Nonetheless, they tried. While he became more careful and more patient, Angela became more attentive and more tolerant.

Nine months later, Angela was rushed to the hospital. Emmanuel held her hand tightly. She was having contractions and crying out of pain. Emmanuel felt nervous.

An hour later, a beautiful baby girl was born. Her face was shaped exactly like Emmanuel's face. Her eyes were the same color as Angela's eyes. Her lips were so perfectly shaped that they looked like a crescent. When the nurse handed her to Emmanuel, he looked at her, and his eyes filled with tears.

Emmanuel walked with Allie to his wife and kissed her cheek.

"What should we name her?" Angela asked.

Emmanuel looked at the baby. As she slept, Allie looked so peaceful. Her eyelashes were long and curly. She was so pretty!

"Allie," Emmanuel said.

Angela gave her husband and Allie a smile before she fell asleep. Emmanuel inched closer to her and said, "I will always love you."

Those were the last words Angela heard before she fell asleep.

When Emmanuel got up from the bed that morning, he had no memory of what he had said or promised to Angela. All he knew was that he had to leave.

He washed, did his hair, threw on a fresh pair of clothes, and then took the suitcase out of the closet. He felt nothing. He was about to make a significant change in his life, but he felt nothing.

Emmanuel cleared his throat as he reached the baby's room. Angela was sitting on the floor near the baby's crib. Her hand was on the crib, and her face was resting on it.

"Angela," he said.

Angela looked at him. She had been feeling some uneasiness. Their marriage was strained, but she wanted to give him the benefit of the doubt.

"Yea?" she answered.

As she got up and walked towards her husband, her eyes fell on the maroon-colored suitcase on the floor behind him. Her eyes began to tear. Her cheeks flushed. She fought back the tears and looked at Emmanuel as he looked at her with a grave expression on his face.

"Angela, I am leaving."

"Business trip?" she asked.

"I'm leaving," he said as his expression changed to a frown. Angela decided that it was better not to ask any further questions and nodded her head. This was bound to happen, and maybe she already knew that.

She could hear her heart beating loudly, and her tears had started making their way down her cheeks. She wanted to stop him, but she knew that it would not work. So she wiped the tears off her face and gathered the courage to look him in the eye.

However, Emmanuel had already turned his back on her. He was walking down the stairs. He was leaving.

Angela looked at the floor where he was standing just a few minutes ago. Her heart was pounding. Her mind was tangled. Yet, she was calm. She slid down on the floor and sat there hugging her knees.

Emmanuel had broken every promise, and she had been okay to forgive him. But this was one thing that she would never get out of her head. This was it. This was the last ray of hope—the last straw. This was the deal-breaker.

She sat there crying inaudibly. Emmanuel had broken her in the worst possible way, and she would not be able to recover from this.

"After all that time….. and it's betrayal," she sobbed.

Roots

"You are the prettiest bride I have ever seen."

While sipping in the words that he was drowning her in, her ears devoured the sweet sound of his voice. He was continuously complimenting her, and she did not mind it at all. She was enjoying this. This wasn't the first time that this was happening. There was nothing unusual about this. It was common—more of a routine. He would be talking, praising, and admiring her while she would sit there and relish it pretending to be flattered.

She sipped on her coffee as she was smiling slyly and recalling the events of the morning. She had gotten up before he could even open his eyes. She walked swiftly towards the restroom to change into better clothes. She came out wearing purple satin mini shorts and a tank top. She then walked in front of the mirror to do her hair. She dabbed her face lightly with compact powder, thickened her lashes with mascara, and put on the lightest shade of lipstick she owned.

She threw one last look at herself in the mirror.

"I look pretty damn fine."

Once she was done, she tiptoed towards the bed and nestled back in. She hovered lightly towards her husband's side and began caressing his face. This was what she would do every morning. He woke up. His eyes were piercing blue. He stared at her when she asked, "Are you alright?"

"Yea, I'm just exhausted. It's been a very busy week."

"Let's go out for breakfast," she said while running her fingers through his hair.

"Hmm," he said.

"What?" she asked with a hint of fury in her tone.

He looked up at her face like a scared little puppy and said, "Yes, yes, my love…."

She smiled as she pranced up from the bed and walked to the closet. He looked at her and dropped on the bed trying to close his eyes for the next few minutes.

"What do you want me to wear?" she yelled.

He got up alarmingly fast and said, "Could you ask that again, sweetheart?"

She felt slightly infuriated, but she had to keep her calm. So she said, "Honey, please... I don't like repeating myself."

"Yes, I know. I'm sorry, honey," he said and walked towards her. He pulled her towards him and kissed her forehead.

"Sorry," he said.

She giggled as she kissed him back and said, "Be more attentive next time."

"Yes, my lady."

She began fidgeting with her clothes, saying, "I don't know what to wear!"

He took charge and pushed the hangers here and there for a while before picking a pretty lime frock with orange polka dots.

She was looking at him keenly and not entirely satisfied with his choice. Her lips turned into a frown as she stared at the dress he had taken out for her. She rolled her eyes, and he began searching for something else for her to wear.

After some five minutes of scouring through her clothes, he picked a light blue frock with a round neck. It had pretty pink flowers on it. Her face lit up instantly, and he breathed a sigh of relief.

"Come on, let's get ready and go," she said.

He nodded as he walked from the closet and went to look for his clothes. He was tired, but he dare not say it. He wanted to stay in. But he was not sure of that anymore. He quickly made his way towards the restroom while thinking of everything at once. He washed his face and changed into a fresh pair of ice blue jeans and a pinkish peach shirt. He put gel in his hair and combed it perfectly. He sprayed on a whole lot of Old Spice.

She was putting the last layer of lipstick on her full lips and was happy that they were going out.

"Are we ready to leave?" he asked.

"Yep. Let's go," she said as she smoothed down her baby hairs.

He looked at her standing before him and looking extraordinarily beautiful.

"What are you thinking?" she asked while fluttering her eyelashes at him.

"You are beautiful," he said while studying every step she took as she walked up to him. He kissed her lips. He then grabbed her by the waist as they walked out.

As she settled in the car, he revved up the engine while still looking at her face as if he had been entranced. She knew that he was staring at her, and she loved the attention. But she didn't want to let him know that she was noticing, so she just put her hair behind her ears as she shut the door.

The two of them had been together for over three years. Yet the love, if anyone can even call it that, was still as strong as ever. She was calm and peaceful the first time that she saw him as if she was waiting for it to happen. For him, it was something different.

Her face seemed oddly familiar the first time that he saw her.

Or the first time he thought he saw her.

He could never put his finger on where he had seen her before.

It was quite strange that it had hardly taken a month for them to get married. The whole turn of events of them meeting each other, confessing their love, and deciding to get married without any delay was too fast. It was almost as if they had been put together by fate. It was too real to be coincidental.

They had gotten married among very few people despite her inviting all her relatives and friends. But for him, it was just his friends. After a relatively small wedding ceremony, they took off to Cameroon the very next day. Following their honeymoon that lasted for more than three months, they returned to the United States.

Their marriage was a happy one—at least for one of them. They were there for each other. They would support each other emotionally and financially. It was like a dream come true and a fantasy that was taking real-life form in front of everyone's eyes. They would go out, have fun, and then come back home with more memories to look back on. But in this marriage, the memories were just for one person to recall.

Their efforts to keep things going well for each other were always spot on. It was always easy for her because it was something that came very naturally. It was also almost the same for him with the only difference being his inner conflict. His spirit was dying over time.

Her plan to "let's go out for breakfast" was not spontaneous. It was preplanned. She wanted to go out and celebrate the fourth year of her meeting her husband for the first time.

Four years of patience.

Four years of yearning.

Four years of hoping.

Four years of *winning*.

Her mind took her back to the time when she met with her grandmother to learn the tips and tricks. She thanked her stars for being born in a place and in a family that had its roots deep in magic.

"You'll need patience, dear," her grandmother had told her.

She stayed quiet and just nodded her head because she didn't know if she had a choice. Her mind and heart were hell-bent on making him hers, and she was ready to do that regardless of what it entailed. She was ready to do it all.

And she certainly had to be very, very patient. She spent endless nights in pain waiting for her love to be hers finally. She would spend days worrying about what would happen if things did not go her way. Her days were spent in agony. But her faith in the spell was unwavering.

Things started going her way just like she had imagined. *He* started going her way.

She took her final sip of coffee and placed her cup down. She looked at him and was satisfied and happy that she would never again have to bear the pain of him not being with her.

She stared into his eyes as he said, "Lorelei, you are beautiful."

She let the words sink in before reaching for his hand and kissing it lightly.

"Oh, Emmanuel."

She looked at how he smiled.

Lorelei

"You'll need patience, dear."

The words rang through Lorelei's ears as she heard her grandmother tell her that she had to wait more. She wanted to cry. She wanted to scream and throw things, but she couldn't. She didn't want to throw unnecessary tantrums in front of her grandmother.

Lorelei had been getting her way from the day she was born. She had it all—clothes, friends, money, and resources. All she had to do was to say the word, and in due time, she would have what she wanted before her. She was living a luxurious life, and one person was behind all of it— her grandmother.

On the surface, Maeve and her family were normal like everyone else. But there was much more to them—especially Maeve. She was just a little girl when Maeve's mother began teaching her "some things that you need to get by in life." As time passed, Maeve became the most powerful mambo in all of Mississippi.

People from all over would come to Maeve to seek help, but she would only help the ones she really wanted to. People of all kinds would come to her—anxious, frustrated, angry, patient, tired, tetchy, restless, and skeptical. Everyone would go to her, narrate a series of events, and then tell her the reason why they wanted to make use of her "power." But Maeve was clever, and she wouldn't waste even a single breath on people she decided didn't deserve it.

She would send the people she cared less about to Neena, her daughter. Under her mother's influence, Neena showed much promise in her power. And when Lorelei came into the picture, Maeve directed all her power, love, and affection towards her.

Lorelei was a beautiful baby. She had the perfect complexion—the perfect balance between white and brown. She had big, green eyes and thick, black eyelashes. Her thick, brown hair was silky and soft to touch. Her lips were plump. Her body was slender. She had long legs. She was eye-catching beautiful.

Her beauty blossomed even more with time. On top of that, she was also intelligent.

Maeve would say to Lorelei, "You are made beautiful. Use that wisely."

Maeve took Lorelei under her wing beginning when she was very little. She would tell her how she should sit, what words she should use, what color dresses she should wear, and how she should walk. She would tell her how she should flutter her eyelashes and roll her curls while she laughed. She taught her everything.

Maeve loved Lorelei, and she was aware of the capabilities Lorelei could unravel with a few magic spells. She taught her how to cast spells on everyone—her teachers, her friends, and even her boss. Lorelei knew the spell to get everything. The only spell she hadn't learned and didn't know could work was the love spell.

She had met the love of her life a year ago in a grocery store. He was helping himself with some beers from the fridge, and she was just getting herself some essentials. When she darted her eyes to the left, he was standing there studying a bottle. He was humming a tune to himself and looking as handsome as ever.

Lorelei had stayed away from love. She had heard that "love is pain," "in the end it doesn't even matter," and "love is complicated." She was living a very happy life, and she didn't want to get into anything that would sabotage the peace. But curve balls are called curve balls for a reason, and even though she had planned not to fall in love, she had at first sight.

In the beginning, she could not even recognize the uneasiness that she started to feel out of nowhere. But after a whole lot of cursing herself, she gave herself a pep talk, and then gathering the courage, she decided to do something about it.

She pretended like she wasn't looking and bumped into him. She took a fall saying, "Ow!"

He was scared that he must have hurt the girl pretty bad.

"Oh my gosh!. I'm so terribly sorry! Are you okay?" he asked as he reached for her hand to help her up. His hand felt soft, and Lorelei didn't want the moment to end.

"I--- I feel fine," she stammered.

"I'm so sorry. It happened too fast. I didn't move out the way before you bumped into me," he said.

"Oh no, no, no. It was totally my fault. I didn't see where I was going. Please do accept my apology, Mr.?

"Patterson… Emmanuel Patterson."

"Ahh. Let's start over. Shall we?"

"Yeah, that would be great."

"Hi, Emmanuel. I'm Lorelei."

"Hi. And I'm sorry!"

They both then laughed and got into a big conversation. All of this was part of the spell that Lorelei had cast on to him as soon as he became suggestible to talking. She found out that he was married, buying bars across the country, and soon to be a father.

Lorelei burned with jealousy. She had gone home hurting with her heart feeling like there was a hole inside. She had never felt this way before, and it made her hate herself. This was something that she had never felt in her life.

She was unsure of what to do. She decided to turn to the only person she trusted with all of her heart. She called her grandmother and explained the events of the last few hours. She began crying on the phone. Maeve told her to visit the next day.

Lorelei spent the next hours in pain and misery, and as soon as morning approached, she made her way to her grandmother's house. Maeve had already prepared some stuff that she might need for luring Emmanuel.

The two of them sat down, and Lorelei did her best to remain calm but was raging inside. She didn't want her grandmother to think that she was making a mistake by teaching her a spell. She wanted her to know that she was ready.

Maeve knew that Lorelei was trying hard, and she felt nothing but proud. She was proud that she had taught Lorelei well, and she knew that she was capable of learning more. What she didn't know was whether Lorelei had enough patience to sit through the time it would take for the spell to work.

The love spell was the only spell that screamed "uncertainty." With the other ones, it would be easier to know how much time it would take for it to start working. But with the love spell, it could take just a day, two weeks, months, or even years. No one had the answer to it. Why? That's the thing about love. You can never enforce it because it takes time for the other person to adapt to it.

Once the spell was done, Maeve told Lorelei that she would have to be patient and spend some time with him. She told her that after he would be hers, they would cast a forgetting spell on him so that he would think that she was a complete stranger. Then no proof would remain that they had been together or that Lorelei had anything to do with breaking up the marriage.

Lorelei did precisely as she was told. And, in fact, she did have a lot to do with the breakup. She would meet with Emmanuel and whisper things in his ear to hypnotize him. She would tell him that there was no one but her for him and that she would be waiting for him in a bar once this was over.

It was slow and very painful for Lorelei to sit through, but it happened exactly like she imagined it would. Emmanuel left his wife and baby, and they got married the next month.

It happened just like that. Lorelei had won once again. But this time she had won her life by shattering someone else's life.

She went over to Emmanuel's house the night before she knew he would leave his family behind. Knowing he would freak out seeing her, she decided to cast a sleep spell on him. Lorelei was evil, but she was not wicked. She knew that Emmanuel still cared for his wife. Even though Emmanuel leaving Angela would be painful, Lorelei wanted her to hurt as little as possible because she had a baby to look after all by herself.

For a while, Emmanuel and Angela were still sleeping together despite cutting off every emotional connection with each other. Angela had just recently started sleeping in the baby's room.

Lorelei was aware of this and figured what better time to sneak up on her lover than the night when they both were sleeping apart.

She had carefully tip-toed up to the bedroom and hovered over Emmanuel. Before she started muttering the words, she heard a small creak of the door. She was alarmed and hid behind a curtain.

After she was sure no one was around, she cautiously surveyed to see whether there was anyone else in the room.

She breathed a sigh of relief and decided to get it over with soon. She quickly went over to where Emmanuel was in a deep slumber and closed her eyes. She spread out her palm, said a few words, and slid it across his forehead. She repeated the same words again but this time slid her palm across Emmanuel's eyes. She fluttered her eyelashes at him, bowed down, and whispered, "Meet me in the bar. I will be yours."

And she left.

When morning came, Lorelei got dressed and left for the bar. She had spent almost two hours getting ready, and she knew that by the time he would come there to ask for her hand, it would all be worth it. There was nothing that she had wished for so eagerly in the last few years, and she wanted to look her best when the moment arrived.

And it happened exactly how she imagined it would. Emmanuel entered the bar and swept her off her feet. Within a month, they had rings on their fingers and were walking at the airport with suitcases in their hands.

Lorelei had confirmed bookings for them both on a Tuesday afternoon.

"We're going to Cameroon, dear!" she announced with joy. Emmanuel just nodded.

They had to leave the next morning and had no plans to come back anytime soon. Emmanuel wasn't fully aware of what was happening. He didn't know that he had lost all capabilities at the hands of the woman he married, and he didn't know it was a problem. How could he? The magic was too strong for him to break free.

Lorelei had traveled throughout Africa, but she had never been to Cameroon, a place that she felt was always calling out to her. So when she got married to Emmanuel, it wasn't just one of her wishes that was coming true. There were two. She figured what better time to fall in love with a place and with the person she was in love with?

The two traveled safely and landed a day later in Yaounde, the capital city. They spent the next few hours settling in and then sleeping in because the flight was pretty long.

They began exploring the lakes and the wildlife reserves. It was all very beautiful. They even traveled outside of Yaounde towards the other parts of the country. They stayed in different hotels, tasted different foods, met new people, and wandered in the greenery.

Lorelei loved every moment. She loved every minute she spent outside of the hotel. Interestingly, Lorelei felt accomplished on Mount Cameroon.

She realized her true purpose. She was right in thinking that there was something different about

Cameroon. It was her place, the only place she could call home, and the only place where she could feel even the wind appreciating her for the sorcery she had done.

The day Lorelei climbed Mount Cameroon was the day she lost all senses. It was the day that she became even more powerful than her grandmother. It was a sudden surge of power that had hit her.

"Be careful, dear. Even with magic, there are limits," Maeve had told her. She remembered the words of her grandmother, but she would never be the same again because she had gained more power.

Maeve

"How do you control a man, grandmother?"

Lorelei had started asking questions against her grandmother's will, and she didn't seem to stop. Maeve was quite patient, but her granddaughter's questions were making it run thin. She wanted to tell her off, but she also knew what Lorelei was capable of. And she did not want her to throw everything away just because she would yell at her. Lorelei was a stubborn and wistful kid. And she knew that even if the slightest thing ticked her off, Lorelei would stop working, learning, and growing at all.

Lorelei looked at her grandmother closely and then let go. She knew that she was lost in some thought. She wanted to be a part of it. Luckily for her, she had mastered mind reading, and she could easily learn what Maeve was thinking.

In her head, Maeve was sitting with a group of women. They were all wearing the kanga and the gomesi. There was a fire lit in the center, and everyone seemed to be enjoying the conversations.

Maeve was beautiful. She looked like a goddess. She was shining alone in the midst of the women that were sitting there. Her hair had the most beautiful curls. Her face was chiseled. Her eyes were piercing. She was most definitely the center of attention, and she loved it.

Maeve was known throughout for her powers and wisdom. People from all over the world would come to her seeking advice, and she would be right in her suggestions almost every time.

Right by the fire, men and women were doing the Kpanlogo. They were dancing and having fun. The drums were quite loud, and people seemed to be zoned out with the music—all except one woman who was looking at a guy with desire in her eyes.

She wanted to do something about it, but she didn't know what. So she stood up from her place and comfortably seated herself next to Maeve.

"I gather you have come with a purpose," she said.

The woman began shyly and was unable to look Maeve in the eyes.

"Is it this one?" she asked her as she pointed at the man with the broad body. His naked shoulders were glistening as he danced with the rhythm.

The woman nodded.

Maeve laughed.

"How do you control a man," she asked.

"My darling controlling a man is the easiest task in the world. They are creatures hungry for love and attention. And if you are to give it to them, they are truly yours."

The woman nodded at Maeve. She wasn't sure what she was looking for right then. She only wanted to have a little fun. Maeve knew what the woman was after. She looked at her and said, "If you are looking for a little control, I might be able to help you with that."

Maeve shut her eyes and began chanting something. The words were unclear, and she was uttering them really fast. She opened her eyes two minutes later and blew on her left palm. Then she turned it to the man now sitting on a tree log.

Maeve looked at the woman and smiled at her. "Just a second more," she said.

Within a couple of seconds, the man came to the woman dancing. He extended out his hand gesturing for her to join in with him.

The woman blew a kiss at the guy. Maeve laughed as she looked at the two dancing and flirting all night. The events had reminded her of a time when she had been desperate to fall in love and make a man fall in love with her.

But she had always been a good girl. She was dedicated, and she was a quick learner. However, Maeve did not have the tolerance to sit through and put on a show just for a guy. She told everyone that she was self-sufficient and that she did not want to put on a façade to make a man fall in love with her.

"No matter what you say it should never be forced," she would tell everyone. With time, she found a better way to deal with it, and that is what she passed on to her granddaughter. Maeve turned around and looked at Lorelei. She had confidence that Lorelei would be as strong as her.

"Patience. It's all you need."

Bad Call

"Oh my gosh, I overslept!" Allie said to herself as she opened her eyes sleepily to turn off the alarm that had been continuously buzzing.

She quickly sat up. She had to start going over her schedule for today. She had gotten only a few hours of sleep today again, and she was feeling extremely exhausted.

It had been quite a while since Reginald had left. He told Allie that he was in love with someone else. Of course, she was strong enough to handle the mess, but she was tired of it. And the one thing she couldn't bear was sleeping alone.

There was always someone to accompany her at night. First, it was her grandmother. When she moved to college, it was her roommate. On the weekends, she would be with her friends. Her sleepover with her girlfriends later turned into Reginald sleeping over, and that of course became a permanent thing later. But is there anything permanent after all?

After Reginald left, it was nearly impossible for her to sleep for the first few days. She would stay up all night tossing and turning in her bed and was unable to get the necessary shut-eye that she had been yearning for.

She was feeling exhausted all the time. She was exhausted at work, at home, and with friends.

There seemed to be no escape from all of it because she might have gotten so used to the idea of Reginald in her bed that she couldn't sleep.

After giving her brain several pep talks, she was able to gradually close her eyes for a few hours. Allie just sat there on her bed while thinking about the direction her life had taken. She put her hand on her head. She was unable to break free from the chain of thoughts consuming her. She was already feeling sleepy, and it felt like she was just a second away from falling asleep again.

Just as her eyes were closing, her phone began to ring wildly. Alarmingly, she grabbed for her phone that she had put to charge before she went to sleep. As it turned out, she had forgotten to turn the switch on. And now her phone was just at thirty-five percent.

"Great. Just great!"

She rubbed her eyes to see who it was. The number was unknown. So she picked up the phone and waited for the person at the other end to talk first. But when there was no sound for the next minute at least, she said,

"Hello?"

Still nothing.

While feeling annoyed, Allie looked at the screen to see if the call was still ongoing.

"Who is it?"

Easing her forehead, she said, "Hello?" She spoke this time with a hint of sternness in her voice.

A sweet, high-pitched voice came through the other end.

"Hey. Is this Allie?"

"Yes. I am. Who am I speaking to?"

"You'll know soon enough, dear."

Allie frowned. She was unable to put the pieces of information she had received together.

"Umm… Can I help you?"

"Ha! I think you need to help yourself, dear."

Allie was taken aback. She was shocked. A stranger had just called her and was apparently very rude. Her frustration was reaching the highest level possible, and she was trying really hard to control it. Allie was never a morning person. She absolutely hated interacting in the morning. Everything that was happening right then was strange. It was too much for her to reply politely to snarky comments.

"I'm sorry? I didn't quite hear you there," she responded while trying her utmost to keep her cool. But it looked like the universe was hell-bent on pissing her off, and she knew she wouldn't be able to stay calm for much longer.

"I just insulted you. I guess you are way dumber than I expected you to be."

Allie's mouth opened like a fish as thoughts began circling through her head. With the last word that she heard through her phone, she knew who that was. She closed her eyes and was about to hang up the phone. However, the bickering from the other end was non-stop, and what she was saying now was quite hurtful.

"You can't even keep a man, and that's the most basic thing you can do! How stupid are you? You can't even do that. If you were so good, Reginald might still have been with you."

Allie said nothing.

"You know you are Reginald's biggest mistake. Now I know you're going to ask how I know that. So let me tell you. He told me that himself. If you didn't know that already, well now you know. Oh and one more thing. He never loved you."

Allie had already taken too much, and she didn't want to listen to this crap anymore. She didn't even want to argue or present her stance because she knew how low Bella could stoop. Hot tears were dropping down her cheeks, but she was silent. Allie had enough respect for herself not to let Bella know that she was hurt by what she said. So she just silently hung up the phone.

She threw her phone up on her bed, folded her legs up, and rested her face on her knees. The phone call had thrown her off completely, and she could not decipher how she should react to the situation. She just sat there sobbing silently and tried to push her thoughts away.

As the woman's words echoed through her ears, good memories when Allie and Reginald were happy together raced in her head. And she couldn't help but ask herself the same question over and over again. Why would Reginald say he never loved me? She lay there thinking of what she should do next, but she was smart. So instead of thinking, she started preparing for another phone call.

"Need to get things done meanwhile."

She found the strength and courage to pull herself up, take a shower, and prepare for work. She walked to the kitchen to brew herself some coffee. Then she went to the shower and turned the tap on.

Without wasting a single drop, she stepped in and let the water drench her completely.

Allie's escape from everything was most definitely showering. Regardless of what might be bothering her, she would always get into the shower and let the problems drift away. It would help her escape. Allie liked her peace. It was important for her to maintain balance, but she was a person who would hold in something long enough until someday it would just burst. That had always been the case.

But for the first time in her life, Allie could feel that there was more than just emotional drama that was bothering her. She could feel the pressures. She was chained under physically as well. It was getting really difficult for her to switch off the thoughts that were consuming most of her brain at the moment. She felt so exhausted that she decided to get out of the shower within ten minutes.

She wrapped herself in a bathrobe and dropped on the bed. She thought of why Bella would even call her. It felt weird. There had to be a motive behind talking to her since she had already "won" Reginald.

"As if he was even a catch."

She tried diverting her mind with breakfast and with then picking a dress for work. By the time she started working on her makeup, she was humming a tune like she had completely forgotten about the event that took course that morning.

Just as she was about to brush the first stroke of mascara on her eyelashes, her phone began ringing again.

Allie was totally aware of the phone call. She knew who was calling her. She just wasn't sure if she wanted to engage in a conversation with him, but she decided to answer.

She wanted to clear her side of the story one last time so that in her heart, she would know that she was never at fault. Forgiving someone else is easy, but forgiving yourself is not easy.

She grabbed her phone and looked at the screen. Her heart almost stopped.

It was Reginald.

Allie took a deep breath and picked up the phone.

"Hello?" she said with tiredness in her voice.

"My gosh, Allie. What the hell were you even thinking?"

"Great start."

"Why would you even do such a thing? I didn't know you could be so petty. Gosh!"

Allie felt furious. She asked, "What are you talking about? I do not understand a word you are saying."

"Wow. So you lie now too? What a disappointment," he said.

Allie couldn't suppress her anger any longer. Her entire motivation behind answering the call was to clear her side of the picture, but what she figured was going on here was way worse than she thought.

"I don't know what the hell you have heard or who said what, but it was your girlfriend who called me out of the blue ranting on and on. She was the one who was insulting. She was the mean one. I didn't even utter a word. I listened and hung up because that is what mature people do. And I will not listen to you blabber about irrelevant things either."

For a moment, there was nothing but silence on the phone from both ends. Then Reginald said, "She warned me that this is what you would say. She told me not to talk to you because it would only create a bigger mess, but I am glad I did. It made me realize who you truly are."

Allie tried protesting but withdrew. She knew that he was too far gone.

"You know, Allie. You are a mistake."

And then there was silence.

Bella

"You know you are Reginald's biggest mistake. Now I know you're going to ask how I know that. So let me tell you. He told me that himself. If you didn't know that already, well now you know. Oh and one more thing. He never loved you."

Before she could utter another word, she heard the other end beeping. The line had already been hung. She still had a lot to say, but she was still happy. Allie's reaction was proof that her plan would work.

She smiled at herself slyly. She was happy that she didn't have to do much to aggravate Allie. She thanked her luck and her mother who helped her reach this point in her life.

Bella quickly rushed to the kitchen as she heard her stomach rumbling. She poured herself some orange juice and made an egg and ham sandwich. She then went back to the room and switched on the television.

She had to start more drama, but she wanted her stomach to be full when she called Reginald. Talking to him was easy. Thankfully, she wouldn't have to put in much effort since she had already taken the time to make the guy hers.

That is probably why she wasn't even worried about it and why she was so relaxed about it. But she needed him to call Allie and get done with it as well. So she decided to time everything perfectly.

Her mind drifted back when she thought about timing. That is what her mother always told her.

"Time is a thief. You have to be careful."

Of course, no one understands the words of wisdom that are passed on to them. One always has to go through something to fully believe something. This reminded her of her first boyfriend. She was only 15 at the time. Her mother had already given her the "talk."

Whether lucky or unlucky, the mother-daughter relationship was quite frank and open between Bella and her mother. Bella never had to ask her friends for any kind of help. Her mother would get it done for her before she could even wish for it. From buying makeup to finding the right color for her lips, there was nothing that she couldn't go to her mother for.

Prom was coming up, and Bella was running for Prom Queen. It was obvious she would win. No one could beat her mother's genes and tricks. But Bella still wanted to look pretty. She had every reason to. But she wanted to look pretty mostly because she was in a relationship for the first time. And what girl doesn't like doing a little extra for her man?

Bella and her mother went shopping a week before and bought a beautiful lilac dress with a deep v cut and a slit on the right. The neckline and off shoulders were adorned with silver stones. At the time, Bella was overjoyed thinking of the perfect jewelry she had to match her dress.

The bell rung at exactly 6.30 p.m. Bella breathed a sigh of relief. She wasn't just ready at the exact time, but he was punctual about his timing.

And just like in the movies, her mother took a picture of them together. Then she moved forward and whispered something in Bella's ear.

"Don't do it," she said.

And that was the only thing Bella's mother advised her against. But she was young and naïve.

A week later, Bella told her mother that she did not have her period yet. And that is when the entire story unraveled. There was a whole lot of yelling and screaming.

The very next day, Bella was taken to the hospital by her mother. She continuously told her that "Time is a thief." That one lesson was more than enough for Bella to always listen to and trust her mother.

After the two came home, her mother told her the truth about her marriage, her background, and her secret. Bella's eyes kept growing wide, and her mouth kept dropping open.

"Teach me, mother."

"Time, darling…" she said while looking up to the sky as if waiting for a signal. "It's all about time."

Bella's heart was filling with excitement and rage at the same time. As much as she was eager to start learning what she was capable of, her mother wouldn't even start with the basics because "the time wasn't right."

But she didn't speak a single word, because she was reminded of the mistake that she had just made.

She realized that her mother was a sorcerer. For a very prolonged time, Bella would just ask her mother when they would start. Her mother would only reply, "Soon."

After Bella turned 17, her mother squeezed her hand tight, brought it to her forehead, and uttered something. An instant surge of energy passed through Bella, and she knew that this was when her mother decided to start to teach her.

For the next few years, Bella put her heart and soul into learning everything that her mother was teaching her. Her mother would always be proud of her. She was happy that Bella was as good as her. The only difference was that Bella was much more patient than her mother.

On the very last day of her training, her mother sat her down and said, "Bella. You are resilient. You are brave. And you are very beautiful, my dear."

Bella said nothing. She just blinked her eyes at her mother. Her beautiful curls dropped on her chin, and she pushed them back. Her mother cupped her hand in her palms and kissed Bella's forehead.

"Use everything you own very wisely, my child. Only you are fully aware of your worth. You'll know what to do in time," she had said.

Bella hugged her mother and thanked her for all the wisdom she passed on to her.

"I'll always be with you, Bella. Remember that."

Those were the last words that left her mother's mouth, and when she woke up in the morning, Bella found out that her mother had peacefully died in her sleep.

The thought had brought tears to her eyes, and she didn't want to feel that pain. So she picked up the phone and decided that it was the perfect time to call Reginald.

She unlocked her phone and called his number. She waited for him to pick up the phone. The phone rang three times before she finally heard his voice squeak a weak, "Hello."

"Okay, plan in motion."

"Hi, Reg…." she said with her voice cracking.

"B? Are you okay, my love? Did something happen?" Reginald asked with genuine concern in his voice.

"N-noo. I'm f-f-fine," she pretended.

"What! Why are you lying to me? You are clearly lying. Come on, babe. Tell me what's up."

"Oh, it's nothing," she said, sniffing.

"Tell me still."

"Umm... I don't want you creating a scene. You know. I don't want you to think that I had anything to do with this."

"Just tell me, honey."

"Allie called me, Reg… She— She said some pretty mean things, and I felt really bad. Reg, do you still love her? Maybe you should get back wi-"

"Oh please. Shut up, B. You know I only love you. There is no one I want more than you. Don't worry. I'll talk to her. She needs some straightening out."

"Oh, no! You don't have to."

"Shush. You just relax. Okay? I'll handle the rest, love."

"Ok."

"See you tonight, baby."

"Okay. Bye."

She put the phone down, grabbed another ice cream tub from the freezer, and chuckled at the thought of what might happen next. She was aware of it. She was just waiting for the fun to happen.

It hadn't been long since Bella had met Reginald. But she had fallen head over heels in love with him the moment she had set eyes on him.

The funny thing was that they did not have any connection whatsoever with each other. They did not study together. They were not colleagues. They had just met by accident.

Reginald had a habit of stopping by a coffee shop every morning. He would stop at the café to get himself a mocha latte. And on days when he would feel giddy, he would also buy himself a brownie. They were heavenly!

Reginald got out of his car one day with earplugs in his ears. He was listening to a song and humming along with the tune. He was so lost in his own happenings that he hadn't noticed who was inside the café.

The woman had taken a seat in the café, and she was eyeing him from a distance. She was staring, and staring, and falling in love with his beautiful, big eyes. His hair was combed so properly. He was listening to "A groovy kind of love." He looked like the perfect package. He wasn't just attractive, but he also looked like the hardworking kind. It was not like it would matter in the long run, but things like that needed to be considered.

After a complete scan, Bella's eyes fell on his left hand, where she could see a glistening platinum ring.

"Why?"

But of course, it only took her two seconds to remember her mother's words.

And she made up her mind to follow in her mother's footsteps.

The rest of the story followed exactly like her mother's life. The guy might have been someone else's when Bella had seen him for the first time, but getting him to be hers required only time and patience.

Bella had learned the best of the magic from her mother, and there was no way that she would be losing out on this one. She spent six months perfecting the spells. Once she was done, she said a prayer to herself. And it worked better than it worked on anyone else.

She didn't even have to create a separate spell for him to forget the voodoo that was happening to him because every day would be a new day to him. He would have no memories of what happened to him. He would just know that he was married to Allie and that she turned out to be the bad person. He would think that Bella was the one who rescued him from her.

On the day Reginald picked up his things and moved to Bella's house, Bella felt a feeling of ecstasy inside of her. They had just finished their dinner, and Reginald had excused himself to sleep.

Bella had been feeling strange the entire day. She felt like something was calling out to her. She walked into the balcony with weird thoughts circling her brain. Suddenly, a chill ran down her spine, and she knew that there was a presence there.

Bella stood there for a while trying to calm her breath. A moment later, she said, "Thanks, mother."

In Awe

Allie sat quietly on the floor. She was still unable to point where she went wrong. She wanted to get it off her chest, but she didn't want to talk to any of her friends. She knew what she would be hearing from them, but she didn't need any pep talk. She wanted someone to understand what she was going through. She wanted someone who would be able to impart words of comfort and even wisdom. She was getting tired of making every distraction an escape. She needed a place where there would be no judgment—a place where there was the truth. She needed to know.

The one person that she felt she needed the most right now almost brought tears to her eyes. But she didn't want to cry alone. So she stood up and walked into her closet. She picked out the easiest clothes possible and decided that she had to meet Miss Charlotte today. There was no way she could delay it.

She quickly changed, did her hair, and grabbed her things. As she turned the ignition in her car, she took out her phone to call Tina, her assistant. She told her to clear her entire schedule for that day and push any meetings to the next day since she wouldn't be coming in that day.

She then raced the car through the roads not taking a breather until she reached her desired destination. She parked the car and took a deep breath. She prayed that things would go smoothly.

Allie remembered the last time she was here, how she had come to find out another truth, how she had reacted to it, and how things went from there. While she knocked on the front door, she realized how much she loved Miss Charlotte and how thankful she was to her for everything she had done for her. She had always been her fallback. And she was here once again searching for answers.

She knocked on the door once very lightly as if she didn't even want to be heard. She just stood there holding her breath. She did want to go in, but she didn't. It was a dilemma that she was never able to resolve. The door flew open suddenly.

On the opposite end stood a short and stout figure with greyish white hair. She had light brown eyes. Her eyelashes had gone white. Beneath the wrinkly skin, she had a wide smile painted across her face.

Allie looked at her. Her eyes were studying her grandmother. She was wearing a yellow dress, and her hair was tied up in a bun. A sudden rush of emotions flowed through her body, and Allie realized how much she had actually missed her. Allie had just begun to say something when Miss Charlotte opened the door and gestured for her to step in.

"Thank you," she said in the lowest tone possible.

Miss Charlotte nodded and smiled at her.

Allie walked in and breathed in as she surveyed the house. She smiled happily as she looked around. The place looked exactly how she remembered it.

She nestled on the sofa very comfortably and left enough space for her grandmother to settle beside her. But to her surprise, she sat opposite her.

For quite a while, there was nothing but silence between them. Allie wasn't sure how to break the ice, and she kept clearing her throat.

"How are you, Allie?" Miss Charlotte asked her.

Allie didn't look up for a long minute because she didn't want to meet her eye. She also didn't have the words to tell Miss Charlotte how she was.

"Umm…" she began, clearing her throat. "I'm fine I guess. How have you been?"

"I've been good, dear. Just surprised to see you here."

"I just wanted to see you," she said.

Miss Charlotte only smiled. She didn't say a word.

There was silence again. But before it could get awkward, she moved toward Allie and put her arms around her neck. And before anything happened, Allie started crying.

"Tell me all about it," Miss Charlotte said.

Allie poured her heart out. She told her every event, every happening, and every problem that ever came between the two. Miss Charlotte was just patting her head and saying, "It's going to be okay."

Allie kept sobbing and said, "Where did I go wrong? What did I even do?"

Miss Charlotte knew that she needed to tell her the truth this time. She shouldn't be keeping Allie in the dark about this one.

Miss Charlotte said to Allie, "Wait here."

She returned after 10 minutes with a pile of paper in her hands. She sat down again and handed the letters to Allie.

"What is this?" she asked.

"Read them. You'll know."

Allie looked at the papers. They were letters. She unfolded one letter and started reading.

Angela,

I am writing this letter to tell you how unsuccessful you have been in your life. As a woman, as a wife, and as a mother, you are a disgrace. You are the absolute worst.

"I can't read this," Allie said.

Miss Charlotte took a deep breath and then began, "Allie. Your mother and father were both good human beings. Especially your mother. She did the best she could, but it wasn't her fault. Your mother and father were just different from each other. And someone took major advantage of that. That is the someone who wrote this letter. That someone is the mother of Bella."

Allie's eyes shot wide open.

"What do you mean?" she asked.

"Lorelei Patterson and Bella. Bella is your step-sister. Your father got under the influence of voodoo, and it was very powerful. You know that your mother got under the influence of heroin. She missed your father so much. You know that she was murdered, and we never knew why."

Allie's ears couldn't stop ringing. She couldn't believe what her grandmother had just told her. Her stomach started rumbling, and she started pacing in the room.

"I have to do something."

She couldn't comprehend the truth about Bella that had just entered her head. Her brain felt like it was on fire. It felt like there was a volcano eruption everywhere. She felt like the whole earth had somehow created a vendetta against her, and there was no way she could get out of it. She had come to her grandmother for nothing but peace. What she didn't know was that there was a much higher price to pay for it.

The thoughts in her head were contradicting each other. As much as she wanted to know more, she also didn't want to know more. It took her a moment to realize that she wanted to cry. But why did she? She didn't even know her mother. She answered herself quite instantly. She was understanding that this was something that resonated with her. She might not have known her mother, but she knew that what she was going through, her mother had already gone through. Then she knew that sometimes not knowing is the best thing in the world.

She stopped pacing and settled back in her seat. Miss Charlotte was staring at her face. Her expressions were calm and composed. She was sitting there waiting for her granddaughter to ask her whatever she had wanted.

Allie cleared her throat and began. "Tell me everything," she said as a tear rolled down her cheek.

Allie left Miss Charlotte's house at midnight. Her heart was racing. Her eyes were hurting. Her mind was spinning. She felt like she was more lost now than before she had come to her grandmother's house. She didn't know what to do. All she could understand was to go back home. She was sobbing as she threw her purse on the seat. She revved up the engine as her phone began ringing.

Allie was in no mood to even bother looking at the phone, but then she realized that she hadn't gone to work that day and that it might be important.

So she grabbed her phone and looked at the screen. It was Mary.

Allie didn't want to miss Mary's call. She picked up the phone not rethinking her decision for even a moment.

"Hello?" she answered, waiting for her to reply.

"Hey Allie, I have to tell you something important."

"Yeah, what's up?" she asked while wiping the tears off her cheek.

"I went to a witch doctor, and she told me that it was a curse. There was something that she did. It was something weird. Now I'm pregnant!"

"I'm having a baby!" Mary yelled.

"I can't wait!" Allie said.

After the phone call, Allie forgot everything and brought her mind back to the reality of the day.

Epilogue

I am seated opposite the witch doctor who isn't here at the moment. She excused herself ten minutes ago, and I have been studying the room ever since. It's small and stuffy with a lot of things spread here and there.

The ceiling has a small, pink-colored fan. I didn't know colored fans even existed. I wonder if it even works because it's not switched on for now. The walls are cracked. Some of them are orange-colored. Others are pitch black.

There are empty bottles everywhere, crumpled paper, and a lot of dust. There is a table right in front of me, and there are several bowls and mugs placed on it. There is a ball of yarn that has needles of all sizes sticking out from it.

I have been thinking about where I have seen the witch doctor before. She looks oddly familiar, but I can't seem to place where I know her from. I wish I could ask her how I know her, but I don't think I should.

I am recalling everywhere I have been in the last few days. I've tried to remember where I might have seen her, but it's all just a blur. I turn back to see the door, but there is no sign of her.

I think about the most random things. I know that I am hungry right now. There was a nice pair of shoes that I had seen while I was shopping.

I should have bought them. Somewhere along the way, I stopped loving purple so much. I like green better now.

"Why am I even thinking about this?"

"Is she making me think about this?"

"No," a voice from behind me announced.

I open my eyes and look back. She is walking towards me with her eyes staring into mine.

There is something different about her energy, and she is not like any other human being I have met. I don't know if that is a good or bad thing. I watch her carefully as she sits and makes herself comfortable in the spot opposite of mine.

Even though I'm not sure what I am nervous about, my heart is thumping. I am wondering if she can hear me.

"I actually can," she says.

I look at her. I don't know what to do, so I just smile at her.

"So what are you here for?" she asks me.

It doesn't take me a second to answer. There is only one thing that I have wanted for the longest time. The only wish that cannot be fulfilled by anyone else. I know that she is my only hope.

I clear my throat and say, "Revenge."

About the Author

Gloria Foster is the author of The Core and The Mind, the first book in The Woman's Soul series. The Mind received a 5-star review from Readers' Favorite and was a 2021 Screenplay Award Finalist in the Page Turner Awards. After she received a Bachelor of Arts in Mathematical Sciences from the University of Illinois at Springfield, Gloria started her own publishing company. You can visit her online at www.gloriafoster.com, on Twitter at @GloriaLFoster, and on Facebook at www.facebook.com/authorgloriafoster.

Thanks for reading! If you loved the book and have a moment to spare, I would really appreciate a short review as this helps new readers find my books.

Gloria L. Foster

P.O. Box 2043

Matteson, IL 60443

(312) 547-0368

gloria@gloriafoster.com

This *Book* is a *Special* *Gift*

from

____

To

____

Date

____

on the occasion of

____

TABLE OF CONTENTS

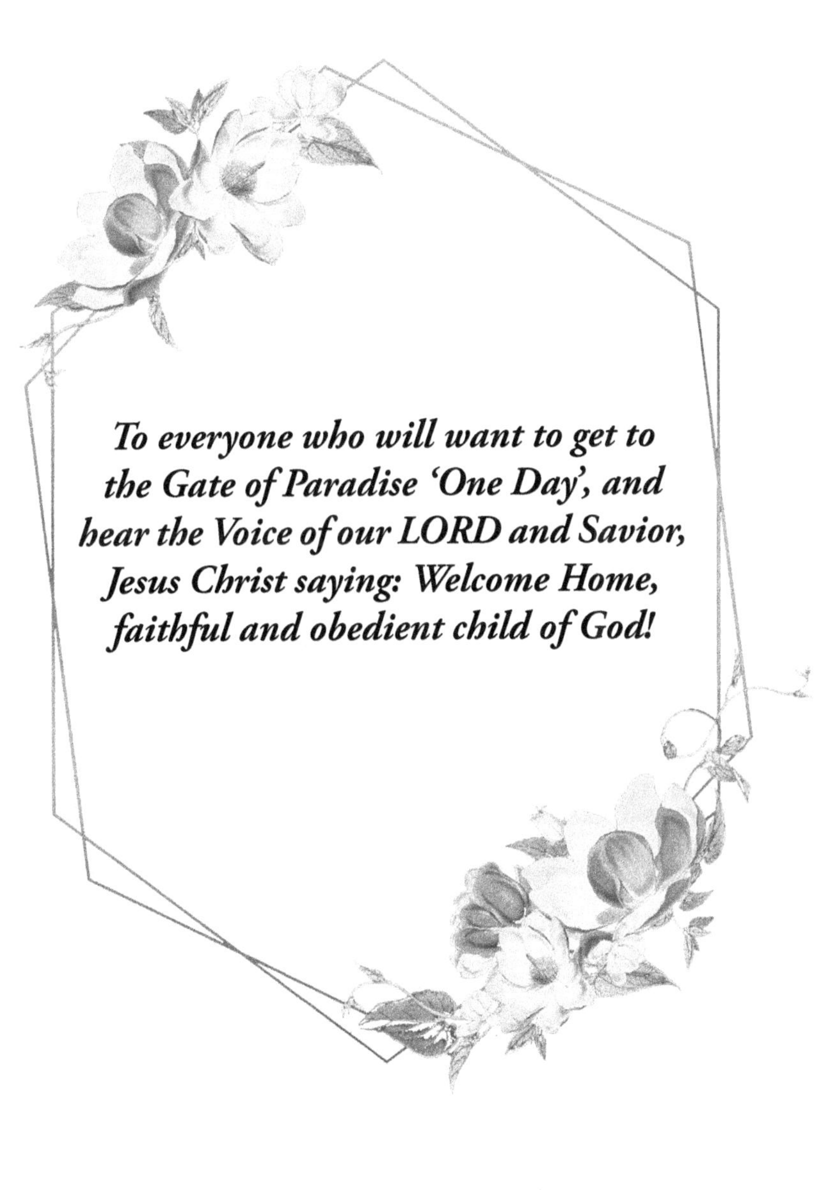

To everyone who will want to get to the Gate of Paradise 'One Day', and hear the Voice of our LORD and Savior, Jesus Christ saying: Welcome Home, faithful and obedient child of God!

PREFACE

Several scholars and prolific writers have written on 'Forgiveness.' But my primary purpose in this book is not to display a scholastic prowess, neither is it a production of an academic 'text book' for biblical students.

Its primary purpose is to be an inductive and in depth digging into the Scripture on **forgiveness**, with a focus on how divine and human relationships can be sustained; how to reunite broken godly relationships and how the wounds that are caused by unforgiveness can be healed. It is also aimed at bringing back peace, love and harmony into relationships, organizations, homes and churches where they are needed. This book is also targeted on how the body of Christ can live in oneness in line with the prayer of our Jesus Christ when he was leaving the believers, that his Father might bind them together as one (John 17:11).

In addition, controversial issues like conditions for forgiveness, revenge, praying for or against ones' enemies, unpardonable sin(s) and few others are addressed succinctly. So, this is an advanced Bible study guide on 'forgiveness.' The Scripture is allowed to speak more than quotations from mortal men. As a result, several scriptural passages are juxtaposed with the aim of grasping the truth on the beauty of forgiveness. The first time this book was written, it was titled Forgiveness. But it is here again published as 'Beyond Forgiveness.' You will find out as you read on why this is a befitting title.

The earnest desire of the author therefore, is that before any reader will drop this book, he or she would have seen the urgent need to forgive and make the necessary reconciliation with anyone he/she ought to, so that God's healing will follow as one continues to serve God with pure heart. May we as potential candidates of Heaven look inward and do away with the heavy load of unforgiveness that can prevent us from receiving warm welcome when we appear before Christ Jesus at the end of our journey here on earth.

Tunde A. Samuel

FOREWORD

How wonderful it is to have a concise, easy to read book on the difficult subject of Christian forgiveness - especially one that is supported throughout by applicable verses from the scriptures. Pastor Samuel has provided practical, step by step guidance on how to address this prevalent problem in the church. Over the years of my Christian walk, it has been interesting to observe so many Christians who excel in many aspects of adherence to God's word, but who still harbor ill will and resentment towards others. "Beyond Forgiveness" gives relevant examples of this in both the U.S. and Africa. Even though these cultures are quite different at times, the problem with unforgiveness is a common denominator in both cultures. After reading this book, I too, became convicted to examine my relationships to determine if there was someone to whom I hadn't granted forgiveness (for either actual or perceived wrongs).

I have studied the Bible along with Pastor Samuel for several years in the Louisville, Kentucky class of Bible Study Fellowship (BSF). It is amazing that he can balance family responsibilities, doctoral studies at Southern Baptist Theological Seminary and BSF (not to mention writing a book). Whether in the United States or Nigeria, he is and will be a blessing to all those he meets. Plus, it is my hope that "Beyond Forgiveness" will be life changing for people he may never meet.

Let the redeemed of the Lord tell their story (Ps.107:2)
God's blessings,

Bill Meyer, Teaching Leader
Bible Study Fellowship Louisville Men's Class
Louisville Kentucky

ACKNOWLEDGEMENT

My profound gratitude goes to God Almighty for His love, faithfulness, mercies and the generous grace He bestowed on me. He has forgiven me in Christ Jesus his Son, who shed his blood on the cross for the forgiveness of our sins. From the ash hip He lifted me and made me a co-heir and a beneficiary of His agape love with those He has redeemed. He has made me worthy to be called His dear son, to Him be all glory forever.

Big thanks to the entire members of my dearly beloved home church, 2nd Evangelical Church Winning All (ECWA) Amilegbe Kwara State, Ilorin, Nigeria. Being there as pastor for over six years was really another training ground. The wisdom and knowledge I have gained from my Seminary professors, especially the professors of my department in the Billy Graham School of Missions and Evangelism here at the SBTS is unquantifiable. Leaping on the shoulders of these committed men of God has enabled me to grasp the global perspective of world missions. I strongly appreciate the impact of my sub-group members at the Bible Study Fellowship (BSF) under Dwayne Hardin. Roger & Donna Scott together with the brethren at the Least, Last and Lost Ministry have been tremendously used by God to bless us in diverse ways. Only eternity can reward you in full for the seed of love you have sown into our lives. Brother Samuel Emadi (SBTS) and his colleagues have strengthened out helping hands in reading over the manuscript of the first edition of this book. Jean Plummer (member of my BFG, NAOBC, Louisville KY) and Linda Marie Wilke (Lyndon Baptist Church, Louisville KY) were also used of God for proof reading at one point and another.

Bill Meyer is the leading teacher of the Bible Study Fellowship International, Louisville Kentucky. Full of the Spirit of God, and with indiscriminate heart of love, he agreed to write the foreword of this second edition. In the spirit of love and mentoring, Prof. Tanimola M. Akande of the Department of Epid. & Community Health, University of Ilorin, Nigeria endorsed his words about the Book. There are individuals and families like Jack Gupton and his precious wife Judy, Tony Kennedy and his dear wife, Dewey Crawford and his wife, Mr & Mrs Dean Clark and several others whom God has used tremendously . The list of these types of men and women of influence has no end. But let me humbly say, God bless you all for the special roles you have played in our family. History will ever remain as canvas upon which the stories of your indelible impacts has be painted.

I am highly indebted to my dearly beloved Parents, Revd & Mrs. S. S. Alao. My Dad and Mom with the help of God provided atmospheres of love, wisdom and the knowledge of God for we their children were growing up.

God has made use of my darling wife, Peace, as an encourager and divine resource to tap from. Her God-given wisdom, Spirit-filled life and her immense contributions were the brain behind the success of this book. More so, her forgiving spirit is worthy of emulation as she has to forgive me times without number in this short voyage of our marriage and even in the course of writing this book, when a times I responded to her questions sharply and roughly in my attempt to pen down inspired ideas that run across my mind. Our children, Temple, Gospel and Miracle are parts of instruments God use for our daily brokenness. I remember one time when Peace and I made a mistake at a grocery store of which I once spanked Temple for the same thing in the past. Seeing that we did the same thing, the boy in a faint voice said, 'so children are not the only people that make mistakes.' By this I know I must be careful of my actions and reactions. We your parents make mistakes too. Thanks you guys for your support in all ways. Thanks to Urlink print media for taking the responsibility of bringing out this second edition in a unique way.

CHAPTER ONE
INTRODUCTION

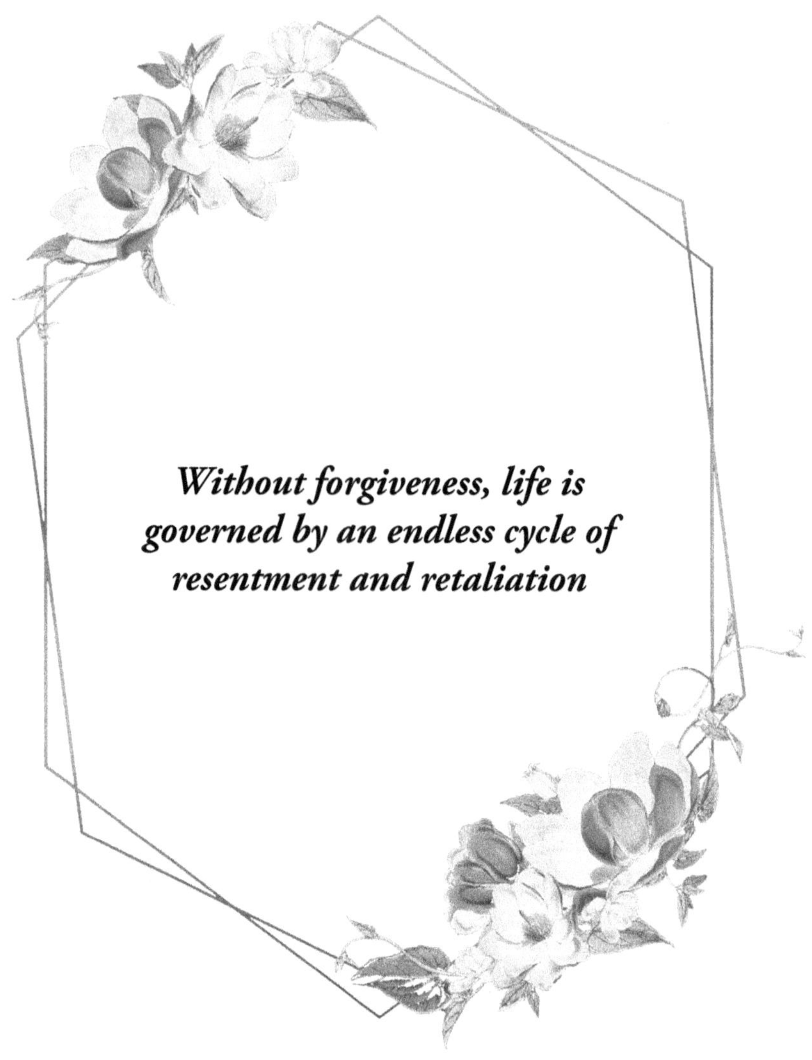
Without forgiveness, life is
governed by an endless cycle of
resentment and retaliation

CHAPTER 1 : INTRODUCTION

"October 12, 1984, at the extended family meeting, this was what he said; he called me a fool. Brothers, see the record here in this file by yourselves. I am not going to let it go just like that!" This was an expression of a deacon a short time ago when the conflict resolution team tried to resolve the long enmity between him and his brother.

"Stop wasting your time, pastor, because, even if you stay here to talk till daybreak, I will not agree. Nobody can settle this matter. Besides, I have made up my mind never to forgive him. When we get to heaven, we shall settle it there." This was an honest confession of a young woman a few years back.

"I will never forgive him until I pay him back in his own coin," said a spinster. "We have both engaged in sex times without number, and I have even committed abortion for him with a promise that we shall both get married one day. But now he is preparing for a wedding with another lady. If not forgiving him is the sin that will take me to hell, I agree! But I will never let him go scot free."

If not forgiving him will earn me a ticket to hell, so be it!
For I will surely deal with him.

One of the deadly diseases that has eaten deep beyond the flesh into the intestines, liver, kidneys, blood, bones, and marrows of the Church of God and the society at large today is unforgiveness. There are several conflicts and factions in the Church, the body of Christ, and the society at large due to this pandemic disease. For example, there are rivalries among political parties, political bigwigs, men of God, and members of the same Church, children of the same family, husbands and wives (which leads to a high rate of divorce). All these are results of unforgiveness.

The conflicting positions and multiplications of Churches these days are in some places not a product of revival, but of unresolved issues and unforgiving spirit among men of God. So some break away from their bosses or senior colleagues and become general overseers (GO) and superintendents of churches and ministries just overnight. Some members, due to this, also migrate from churches to churches. Unlike the revival of old, when sinners migrated from the world of darkness to the kingdom of light, today, it is migration from one church to another due to unforgiveness and unresolved conflicts.

Man as a social being has a relational ability. However, we live in a world that is full of relationship imperfections. And because of this, daily life brings lots of conflicts between spouses, parents and children, employers and employees, and the likes. If offence leads to resentment and resentment grows into bitterness, then anger, verbal outburst, and violence can result. However, life is an adventure in forgiveness. If people forgive one another, then healing, reconciliation, and restoration can follow. Without forgiveness, life is governed by an endless cycle of resentment and retaliation.[1] Therefore, the practice of forgiveness is our most important contribution to the healing of the world.

---

1 *Handout on Pastoral Theology (ECWA Theological Seminary, Igbaja, 2010).*

PRAYER

1. God, please open my eyes to see insightful revelations about forgiveness as I go through the pages of this book in Jesus' name.

2. Heavenly father, also help me embrace your stand on forgiveness as I read through this book in Jesus' name.

HOW GOD FORGIVES SINS

As far as the east is from the
west, so far has He removed
our transgression from us.

CHAPTER 2 :
HOW GOD FORGIVES SINS

There are so many "children of God" who for once have not enjoyed the riches of the forgiveness which they have received from God through the redemptive death of Christ. They do not have the knowledge of the unfathomable depth and the incomprehensible glory of this divine forgiveness. This is why they still go about carrying the burden of guilt which no longer exists, but which Satan and their ignorance of the Word of God impose on them. An inductive study of the Holy Bible gives us details of God's pattern for forgiveness. It is quite different from the way man forgives. For instance, man may *say it is over* when, in the real sense, it has just started. Man may say *I have nothing against you*, when indeed he has everything against you. In this chapter, we shall see in details God's ways of forgiving.

Men may still be judging you based on your past errors, but God does not see you in the light of that sin. He has forgiven you. When a sinner receives pardon from God, he is eternally separate from his past sins. To God, that sinful past does not exist anymore.

How does God forgive sins?

It is very important for us to have a good knowledge of how God forgives sins. In fact, the best way to understand God is to understand how He forgives. The sovereignty, love, compassion, justice, and other attributes of God are known to people. But they will be better appreciated when we understand how He forgives sins. You cannot help but love God when you appreciate this deeper knowledge of His forgiving attribute. God is love.

God is compassionate and gracious in forgiving sins

> *And he passed before in front of Moses, proclaiming, The LORD, the LORD, the compassionate and gracious God, slow to anger, abounding in love and faithfulness, maintaining love to thousands, and forgiving wickedness, rebellion and sin. . . (Exodus 34:6–7)*

Unfortunately, many people today only know God as a judgmental being. He is seen as One who sits far above us and is looking for loopholes or an excuse to release a thunderous anger on men for the slightest sins committed on earth. In the same way, some think of God as a sort of domineering master or monster who lords it over people. They visualize Him with a whip in His hand to afflict His erring children with sickness, suffering, and poverty. THIS IS NOT TRUE! God wants you to enjoy His blessings of happiness, sound health, success, and prosperity.[2] That is His will for you! This perverse perspective has not allowed many to enjoy the benevolence of God who is compassionate and gracious in forgiving sins. The Psalmist emphatically stresses this when he asserts,

> *The LORD is compassionate and gracious; slow to anger, abounding in love. He will not always accuse, nor will he harbor his anger forever; he does not treat us as our sins deserve or repay us according to our iniquities. . . (Psalm 103:8–10 NIV)*

---

2 T. L. Osborn, How to Enjoy Plenty (Abia, Nigeria: Overcomer & Co. Ltd ND), 28.

It is very important to know that God does not treat us as our sins and iniquities deserve. Truly, if God were to mark iniquity, no one is ever qualified to escape His wrath (Psalm 130:3). In fact, the righteousness and the holiness of the most pious saint here on earth are worse than a "filthy rag." God is not carrying a whip like a harsh master; neither is He looking for an opportunity to strike down His faithful and obedient servants at the slightest mistake or error they commit. Whenever any of His children falls into sin, God is always there reaching out His ever outstretched hand of love to lift him up, saying, "Come on, get up and let's go on."

For a righteous man may fall seven times and rise again, but the wicked shall fall by calamity. (Proverbs 24:16)

The steps of a good man are ordered by the LORD, And He delights in his way. Though he falls, he shall not be utterly cast down; For the LORD upholds him with His hand. I have been young, and now am old; yet I have not seen the righteous forsaken, nor his descendants begging bread. (Psalm37:23–25)

As a father has compassion on his children, so the LORD has compassion on those who fear Him; for He knows how we are formed, He remembers that we are dust. (Psalm 103: 12–13)

Therefore, contrary to the opinion of some, God is not an angry God who is busy watching out for the slightest opportunity to unleash His accumulated anger upon His faithful children just because they err. Rather, He is a compassionate and loving father. He is never a fault finder.

I want you to ponder this: If Old Testament saints who were under the rigors of the law had this understanding of the merciful and compassionate God, how much more should we who have been redeemed with the blood of His dear Son and are now under the grace!

God removes sins far away when He forgives

Have you ever sat down to imagine the distance between the heavens and the earth? The Apostle Paul hinted about three different heavens (2

Corinthians 12:2). Scientifically, I know that the distance between one planet to another may be millions or billions of miles. Astrologers might be able to give us approximate kilometers between the earth and the planets. But for the "third Heaven," I do not believe that any mortal man can give us the accurate measurement, because no one has ever gone there physically and come back. Have you ever thought about the distance between the West and the East, from the point of the rising of the sun to where it sets? The Bible compares the love of God for His children as he separates them far away from their sins like the distance between the heavens and the earth; and like that of the West from the East when He forgives. Another amazing fact is that; the West and the East never meet. This is great and truly amazing!

> *For as high as the heavens are above the earth, so great is His love for those who fear Him; as far as the east is from the west, so far has He removed our transgressions from us. (Psalm 103:11–12)*

> **It does not matter if the devil keeps bringing the sins to your remembrance. Once you confess and renounce them, God does not remember those sins anymore.**

God removes our transgressions and iniquities far away from us. What does this mean? This shows that God separates the sinner very far away from his sin when He forgives him. Men may still be judging you based on your past errors, but God does not see you in the light of that sin. He has forgiven you. When a sinner receives pardon from God, he is eternally separated from his past sins. To God, that sinful past does not exist anymore.

God casts sin into the depth of the sea

According to Prophet Micah, when God forgives, He casts the sin into the depth of the sea.

> *You will again have compassion on us; you will tread our sin under foot and hurl all our iniquities into the depth of the sea (Micah 7:19).*

From this passage, we see two things happening: God treads our sin under his foot, and hurls all our iniquities into the depth of the sea. It is like throwing a metallic object into the sea. You may agree with me that whenever a metal is cast to the depth of the sea, either decomposes there, or never comes up to the surface of the sea. Whenever such an object is sunk into the sea, it does not come out floating on the surface of the sea again because it has reached a state of permanent rest. This is exactly the way God treats our sins. Hallelujah!

God washes the sinner as white as snow or wool

Snow and wool are objects the Scripture uses to describe the way God forgives.

> *Come now, let us reason together, says the LORD. Though your sins are like scarlet, they shall be as white as snow; though they are red as crimson, they shall be like wool. (Isaiah 1:18)*

This means that, when God forgives, a clean slate without any record of wrongdoing is given to a man to begin anew. His past record of the evil committed does not exist any longer. He is a God of second chances and each person needs to respond to Him.

When God forgives, He remembers the sins no more

The way God forgives is different from the way man forgives. God does not remember your sins again when He forgives you.

> *I, even I, am he who blots out your transgression, for my own sake, and remembers your sin no more. . . For I will forgive their wickedness and will remember their sins no more. (Isaiah 43:25; Jeremiah 31: 34)*

David, the man after God's heart, grasped this astonishing truth when he said,

> *Remember LORD, your great mercy and love for they are from of old. Remember not the sins of my youth and my rebellious ways; according to*

your love remember me, for you are good, O LORD. (Psalm25:6–7)

Under the New Covenant, God said,

> *For I will be merciful to their unrighteousness, and their sin and their iniquities will I remember no more. (Hebrew 8:12)*

Do you really know what this means? He takes sins to a state of oblivion. It does not matter if the devil keeps bringing the sins to your remembrance. Once you confess and renounce them, God does not remember those sins anymore. Can you imagine that! What if every time we pray, God reminds us of every wrong thing we have done in the past? We wouldn't have any faith at all because of self- condemnation. And we would constantly be feeling guilty about our past with no confidence and boldness to come before Him and expect to receive anything from Him. If we have truly confessed our sins to God, then having confessed them once is enough. God blots them out immediately. And His promise is, "I WILL REMEMBER THEIR SINS NO MORE". (Hebrews 8:12). What rest comes into our heart when we realize that we've been truly forgiven and that we don't have to confess our sins again and again to the Lord.

A few years ago, and very pathetic indeed to say, I went for a particular ministerial training somewhere. Two pastors who were both old enough to be my father had a misunderstanding. The one who felt he was offended came to report the incident. I was privileged to be among a five-member committee that was to investigate and resolve the conflict. In the course of stating their cases, the other pastors who seemed to see the place where he had made a mistake, which to me was not even an offence big enough to be capitalized upon, prostrated on the ground and begged the one who came to report for forgiveness. But to everyone's amazement, this other pastor whose forgiveness was being sought brought out an old file with some documents in it. He opened it and said, "This file contains the names of all the people who had offended me since over fifteen years ago with dates, and today, your name and your offence enter my file." Right there in front of us, he penned down his name in the file. Frankly speaking, I became impatient as I rose and confronted him, saying, "Brother, if God were to be keeping the records of your sins just for two weeks, would you be able to bear the weight of the commensurable punishment?" What I said again offended him and he went about reporting me to some of my close acquaintances and told them to warn me seriously. Maybe my name and my offence have entered his book of records as well. Anyway, we had since then lost contact and I do not know how he is doing in the Ministry today, if at all he is still there. But the truth is, God is not a man, and He does not keep records of sins. Do you keep one?

Nevertheless, when anyone claims to have asked for forgiveness, and yet, he is still repeating the same sin on and on, such a person has not yet repented. In such a case, God can make reference to the sin as we can see in the life of the Israelites in the Old Testament. Moreover, when the Bible says that God does not remember our sin again when He forgives, it does not mean that God who is all-knowing has now become dementia and lost His memory, but it does mean that God will never bring up the matter to charge us for it again.

Nevertheless, when anyone claims to have asked for forgiveness, and yet, he is still repeating the same sin on and on, such a person has not yet repented. In such a case, God can make reference to the sin.

God changes the heart of the one He forgives

God engages in a positive heart transplant when He forgives sins. He gives you a tender and soft heart that hates sins or anything that is against His will. The prophet Ezekiel quotes God this way:

> *I will give you a new heart and put a new spirit in you; I will remove from you your heart of stone and give you a heart of flesh. And I will put my Spirit in you and move you to follow my decrees. . . (Ezekiel 36:26)*

God is just and faithful to forgive (1John 1:8–9)

About four years ago, a young Christian lady, who believes in sinless perfection, walked up to me and said, "Brother, why is it that your denomination preaches about eternal security of believers? Don't you know that you are only deceiving people, and this can lead them to hell?" I, in turn, asked her; "What is the criterion for losing one's salvation?" "When one sins, of course!" she replied. I asked again, "Since when have you given your life to Christ?" and she replied, "I gave my life to Christ over ten years ago." I said to her, "That is pretty good! But does that mean that since these ten years you have been living perfectly without making any error or had never sinned?" She was held spellbound for a while before she started stammering; eh!

Since she did not give me a definite answer, then I said, "Maybe you have lost your salvation already." "No!" she screamed "angrily" and said, "I reject that in Jesus' name." Anyway, I tried to convince her that it is not my denomination that preaches eternal security of the believers; it is the Bible, the living Word of God. In case you are confused too, well, I want you to know that your salvation is by grace (Ephesians 2:8), and its sustainability is by that same grace because it is God that works in you both to will and to act according to his good purpose (Philippians 2:12–13). Hence, our salvation and the keeping of it as well are by the perfect demonstration of the mercy of God. It is not of any man's personal ability, wisdom, carefulness, or charisma—knowing fully well that all man's good and perfect work of righteousness and holiness is like a filthy rag. To this, Apostle John, in his letter to the early believers, said,

> *If we say that we have no sin, we deceive ourselves, and the truth is not in us. If we confess our sins, he is faithful and just to forgive us our sins, and to cleanse us from all unrighteousness. (1 John1:8–9)*

No one can make any boast of being a "sinless-perfectionist," unless he wants to deceive himself. I believe that the true mark of a mature Christian lies in his ability to recognize and admit his imperfection as he continues to look up to God for His sufficient grace. If a man is born again, it does not mean he can never sin again.

But here lies the difference. When a true believer falls into sin, he does not continue in the sin. According to the Scriptures, any believer that sins can approach the Father who is just and faithful to forgive sins (1 John 1:8–9, 2:1–3). But anyone who claims to be born again and continues dwelling in sins has never accepted Christ (1 John 3:6–9 NIV/NLT). Anyone that keeps on sinning belongs to the devil. This is because hatred and distaste for sins are parts of the true signs of genuine conversion. Since this is not a book on eternal security, thorough justice cannot be done on the subject in this small book. But for anyone, to lose his salvation may mean the person has never gotten that salvation right from the onset. To this set of people, Apostle John says,

> *They went out from us, but they did not really belong to us. For if they had belonged to us, they would have remained with us; but their going showed that none of them belonged to us. (1 John 2:19)*

But for the true believers, this same John the Beloved quoted Jesus Christ saying,

> *My sheep listen to my voice; I know them, and they know me. I give them eternal life. And they shall never perish; no one can snatch them from my hand. My Father, who has given them to me, is greater than all; no one can snatch them out of my Father's hand. (John 10:27–29)*

I believe too like other brethren in living above sin, but I do not know of anyone who has reached that level yet. We're all still pursuing it (Philippians 3:12–14). The only perfect person I know is Jesus, and they crucified Him for it. And for others who say, "Well, we'll just go ahead and sin as much as we want because God will forgive us," I doubt if they have ever been born again. Because when you are born again, your nature is changed, and you cannot continue in the wrong pattern of life.

But anyone who claims to be born again and continues dwelling in sins has never accepted Christ. Anyone that keeps on sinning belongs to the Devil.

God forgives us in Christ

Just as God in the Old Testament forgave for His own sake (Isaiah 43:25), He equally forgives for Christ's sake after the crucifixion and resurrection of Christ. The Bible says that we are justified by the blood of Jesus Christ (Romans 5:9). When God cleanses us He justifies us too. That word justified means, 'Just as if I'd never sinned in my life and just as if I am perfectly righteous now.' How wonderful! We can picture our sins like many words written on a blackboard. Now that board has been wiped clean with a wet cloth. When you look at the blackboard now what do you see? Nothing. It is just as if nothing had ever been written on it at any time. That is how the blood of Jesus cleanses us - thoroughly and completely. It is in Christ Jesus that every sinner receives perfect forgiveness of sins. In him we have redemption through his blood, the forgiveness of sins, in accordance with the riches of God's grace (Ephesians 1:7;

Colossians 1:14). No sinner can receive forgiveness of sin from God until he comes through Jesus Christ. God made him who had no sin to be sin for us, so that in him we might become the righteousness of God (2 Corinthians 5:21). Salvation is found in no one else, for there is no other name under heaven given to mankind by which we must be saved—except the name of Jesus Christ (Acts 4:12). Just as God has forgiven us, he also wants us to forgive others who might have offended us. Someone rightly said, the people we need to forgive usually don't deserve it and sometimes don't even want it. They may not know they offended us, or might not care, yet God asks us to forgive them. It would seem outrageously unfair except for the fact that God does the same things for us that he is asking us to do for others. He forgives us over and over again and he continues to love us unconditionally.

Be kind and compassionate to one another, forgiving each other, just as in Christ God forgave you. (Ephesians 4:32)

What happens when and where God forgives sins?

The benefits of God's forgiveness are numerous and beyond measure (2 Chronicles 7:14; Psalm 103:1–5).

Two forms of healing

From the passages above, we can see clearly the two distinctive forms of healing that follow anywhere the Lord has forgiven sins and iniquities; the healing of the land and of the people.

Healing of the land

If my people, who are called by my name, will humble themselves and pray and seek my face and turn from their wicked ways, then will I hear from heaven and will forgive their sins and will heal their land. Now my eyes will be open and my ears attentive to the prayers offered in this place. (2 Chronicles 7:14)

Sin and iniquities always bring corruption and destruction to any land where they prevail. The sin of bloodshed, especially that of the innocent, sexual immorality and perversity of all forms, and idolatry rank high in this pollution of the land. For example, the sins of the inhabitants or occupants of Canaan defiled the land, and God, in turn, needed to purify it and bring in a new set of covenant people, the Israelites. The LORD said to the Israelites, "For all these abominations the men of the land have done, who were before you, and thus the land is defiled, lest the land vomit you out also when you defile it, as it vomited out the nations that were before you. For whoever commits any of these abominations, the persons who commit them shall be cut off. . ." (Leviticus18:28–29). And beyond any doubt, when any land is sick, its effect is quickly seen in poor fertility of the land, and the people work hard but without commensurate result. People remain lean and have nothing to show for their vigorous effort. This is because, when any land is sick, its inhabitants are also not excluded. Nevertheless, as the people of the land turn to God with sincere hearts of repentance, God will hear their prayers from heaven, He will forgive their sins and He will heal their land.

Healing of the people

Praise the LORD, O my soul; all my inmost being, praise His holy name! Praise the LORD, O my soul, and forget not all His benefits—

Who forgives all your sins, and heals all your diseases, Who redeems your life from destruction, Who crowns you with loving-kindness and tender mercies, Who satisfies your mouth with good things, So that your youth is renewed like the eagle's. (Psalm 103:1–5 NIV/KJV)

When you embark on an inductive study of the Bible, you will agree with me that the primary causes of sickness and disease are but Satan and sin. There was no mention of any sickness or disease in the Garden of Eden before the fall of man in Genesis 3. But glory be to the compassionate and merciful God who has been stretching out His hand time to time in healing right from Old Testament to New Testament.

The Psalmist exclaims that the LORD forgives all sins and heals all diseases. (Psalm 103:3)

✴ *Under the old covenant, God said, "I WILL TAKE AWAY SICKNESS FROM AMONG YOU … THE NUMBER OF YOUR DAYS I WILL FULFILL" (Exodus 23:25–26). "I AM THE LORD THAT HEALETH THEE" (Exodus 15:26). This word was spoken to about three million people (Exodus 12:37). EVERY ONE OF THEM BELIEVED GOD'S WORDS WERE TRUE. The result was, every one of them who needed healing was made whole. The Scripture says, "He [God) brought them forth, and there was NOT ONE FEEBLE PERSON AMONG THEIR TRIBES" (Psalm 105:37; cf. Deuteronomy 8:4; 29:5; 1 Kings 8:56). Can you imagine three million people all well and strong? If this were true in Israel, under the law, how much more for you under a better covenant that is ratified not with the blood of bulls or lambs, but with the special blood of Christ Jesus, the Lamb of the living God, which is without blemish (Heb.9:11–28; 1Peter1:18–19).*

✴ *In the New Testament, we see in several places where Jesus Christ only said to the sick, "Your sins are forgiven, rise and be healed. . ." Mark 2:1–5, 10–11).*

Beloved, God is still healing miraculously today if only you can put a total trust and faith in Him (James 5:14–16). Just as He forgives you your sins, He also has power to heal. The forgiving hand is the healing hand, and by His stripes, we were healed (1 Peter 2:24).

Several Bible scholars limited the interpretations of some of these scriptural verses on spiritual healing alone. But the truth is, if Christ healed physically in the past, He still has the power to heal today since He is the same yesterday, today, and forever (Hebrew 8:13). The subject Healing is a controversial issue in Christendom today. However, in my short time experience in ministry today, I have seen God healing people miraculously. It does not matter what position you hold unto, either you believe in the healing in the atonement of Jesus or not, one thing to me is certain, there is still healing in the name of Jesus. It is difficult for me to deny what I have seen God do face-to-face. Today, God can choose to heal; He can also choose not heal.

Redemption of souls

Salvation in Old Testament is sometimes synonymous with deliverance from death or dangers. This is why the Psalmist says, God forgives all your sins and redeems your life from the pit (Ps 103:3a & 4a). But in the New Testament, it is redemption of the soul. Frankly speaking, the salvation of your soul is the number one blessing you receive when God forgives you. This salvation is fundamental or contingent upon all other blessings that follow (Matthew 6:33; 16:26; 3 John 2).

Crowning with love and compassion

God is not judgmental as many of us take Him to be. When God forgives you, you automatically become the object of His affection, love, and compassion. He crowns with love and compassion when He forgives sins (Psalm. 103:4b).

Blessings follow God's forgiveness

Blessings and prosperity come along with forgiveness. The Psalmist continues by saying, "When God forgives, He satisfies our desire with good things" (Psalm 103:5a NIV). The same verse in the New Living Translation (NLT) says, "He fills my life with good things." Frankly speaking, there are many Christians with naive and parochial minds who never believe that believers should enjoy good things on earth because they see this as carnality or backsliding. But the Scripture is very clear on the prosperity of God's children. Examples:

> *Let them shout for joy, and be glad, that favor my righteous cause: yea, let them say continually, let the Lord be magnified, which hath pleasure in the prosperity of his servant. . . For the Lord God is a sun and shield: the Lord will give grace and glory: no good thing will he withhold from them that walk uprightly. . . Blessed be the Lord, Who daily loads us with benefits, The God of our salvation! (Psalm 35:27; 84:11; 68:19 KJV)*

> *You will show me the path of life; In Your presence is fullness of joy; At Your right hand are pleasures forevermore (Psalm 16:11).*

Indeed, all good and perfect gifts come from God (James 1:17). Hence, blessed is the man whose sin the LORD does not count against him and in whose spirit is no deceit (Ps 32:2). Similarly, Psalm 1:1–6 gives us the keys to enjoying a blessed life. This is quite different from prosperity that is acquired through gimmicks and manipulations. It is the prosperity that comes from God's blessing.

Refreshing and longevity

So that thy youth is renewed like the eagle's (Ps 103:5b). Not many people really understand the mystery of the life and nature of the bird "eagle." For example, eagles do not eat leftover food or a decayed flesh as the vultures do. No other bird can reach the height of flight that eagles reach when soaring, and even at a distance of kilometers up in the sky, eagles with their sharp eyes can sight an object at the ground level and pick it within seconds. More so, the eagle's strength is daily renewed. No wonder the Scripture likens the strength of those who wait upon the Lord to that of the eagles'.

> *Has thou not known? Has thou not heard that the everlasting God, the LORD, the creator of the ends of the earth, fainteth not, neither is weary? There is no searching of his understanding. He giveth power to the faint;*

and them that have no might he increaseth strength. Even the youths shall faint and be weary, and the young men shall utterly fall: But they that wait upon the LORD shall renew their strength; they shall mount up with wings as eagles; they shall run, and not be weary; and they shall walk, and not faint. (Isaiah 40:28–31 KJV)

For the righteous man whom the Lord has forgiven, and who has nobody in his heart that he refuses to forgive, he will stay fresh and green even at the old age. "The righteous will flourish like a palm tree, they will grow like a cedar of Lebanon; planted in the house of the LORD, they will flourish in the courts of our God. They will still bear fruit in old age, they will stay fresh and green, proclaiming, The LORD is upright; he is my Rock, and there is no wickedness in him (Psalm 92:12–14).

How do people receive God's forgiveness?

According to a missiological point of view, there are two categories of people on earth: believers and unbelievers. When a believer meets a fellow believer, they both need to encourage each other, just as iron sharpens iron. But when a believer meets an unbeliever, he needs to reach the unbeliever with the gospel, knowing fully well that every heart with Christ (born again and redeemed) is a missionary, and any heart without Christ (un-regenerated) is a mission field.

The way an unbeliever receives forgiveness of sin

- Through Jesus Christ (Ephesians 4:32).
- Through faith in His name (Luke 24: 47; Acts 10: 43).
- Through His blood (Matthew 26:28; Hebrew 9:22; 1 John 1:6–10).
- Through confession of the Lordship of Jesus Christ (Romans 10:9–11). Ideally, unbelievers need primarily to confess the Lordship of Jesus Christ with their mouths. And as well believe in their hearts that this same Jesus who came to this world and was crucified for the sins of the world rose from the dead. He is as well coming back again for his elects, and He is the son of the living God. By this they will receive forgiveness of their sins. And as they renounce those sins, they will be saved.

How does a believer receive forgiveness of sin?

Believers are those who have already received Jesus Christ as their Lord and Savior. They serve Him daily. What happens when they fall into sin? Know for sure that God is no longer wielding a sledge- hammer to crush believers for sin. So when a believer in Christ Jesus errs, he receives forgiveness of sins through the confession of his sin to God and asking Him for forgiveness. And after the confession, the believers renounce his sins and never to go back to it again. Apostle John, when writing to believers, said,

If we claim to be without sin, we deceive ourselves and the truth is not in us. If we confess our sins, he is faithful and just and will forgive us our sins and purify us from all unrighteousness (1 John 1:8–9).

Apostle James also admonishes us to confess your trespasses to one another, and pray for one another, that you may be healed. The effective, fervent prayer of a righteous man avails much. (James 5:16)

People who cover over their sins will not prosper. But if they confess and forsake them, they will receive mercy. (Proverbs 28:13NLT)

In a certain well-known denomination, a brother committed fornication, and knowing the various unscriptural legalistic rules and merciless approach the Church has for any member who commits such "unpardonable sin," he went straight and committed suicide by hanging himself. Notably, I am not against Church discipline for a sinning member. Neither am I encouraging brethren to go and sin. God hates and frown at sin. But please, you do not need to condemn or kill yourself when you commit a sin. What you need to do is to go to God repentantly seeking for His mercy and forgiveness. If He so much demonstrated His love for you by allowing His son to die for you when you were still estranged from Him and then you were His stark enemy (Romans 5:6–8), how much more will He not love you now when He has bought you with the blood of His dear son and has forgiven you (Romans 8:32–34).

Brother, God will not kill you because you fall into sin but will rather lift you up as you come naked before Him, confessing and forsaking your sin. Spiritual leaders must learn to know the place of God's grace, and this grace must be put first before legalism set up by men. It is by grace we are all saved and sustained, not by works and personal struggles (Ephesians 4:8). This is why the primary purpose of Church discipline should be for restoration and not condemnation.

The same Apostle John, the beloved, added:

> *My dear children, I write this to you so that you will not sin. But if any one does sin, we have one who speak to the Father in our defense, Jesus Christ, the Righteous one. He is the atoning sacrifice for our sins, and not only for ours, but also for the sins of the whole world. (1 John 2:1–2)*

Once in a gathering, as I explained the truth of the Scripture to the saints. A brother was there who really believed in sinless perfection and claimed that he was living by that standard on a daily basis. He walked up to me and said, "Brother! You are making this thing too cheap for people, and you are just giving them the license that will make them to be indulging in sins." Anyway, I have answered this type of remarks before, using 1 John 3:3–9. That somebody claims to be a believer does not make him one when he fails to live a daily holy life as befits a true believer. At the same time, not all that say, "Lord, Lord" (with ordinary mouths, while their hearts are far away from God) will enter heaven (Matthew 7:21f). However, this is the absolute truth of the gospel and the Scriptures. It is unchangeable and will ever remain eternally true. Jesus Christ is our "attorney general" who defends our cases to the shame of the devil, our accuser.

Moreover, while in prayer, the Bible admonishes us to confess our sins to one another so that our prayer will not be rendered void and ineffective. James, the Apostle rightly puts it this way:

> *Therefore confess your sins to one another and pray for each other so that you may be healed. (James 5:13–16)*

When asking God for forgiveness during prayer, it is best to be specific, and to say, "Lord, this is the sin. I've had a grudge against that person. I haven't forgiven that person. I've been jealous of that person. My motive in doing that was utterly selfish. I did it for my own glory, etc." You have to be honest. And after we have confessed all the sins that we know, we'll still have to pray like David, "Acquit me of hidden sins" - for we have all sinned in ways that we are not conscious of (Psalms 19:12).

You do not need to condemn or kill yourself when you commit a sin. Go to God repentantly seeking for His mercy and forgiveness.

Again, we receive His forgiveness when we forgive others. Jesus Christ elaborates this in His sermon on the mountain: "Forgive us our offences, as we also have forgiven those who have offended us. For if you forgive men their sins against you, your heavenly Father will also forgive you your sins. But if you do not forgive men their sins, your Father will not forgive your sins" (Matthew 6:12, 14–15). Therefore, according to these passages, receiving God's forgiveness is contingent on your forgiving others.

Believers and sin's consciousness

There is a need to understand the relationship between believers and sin's consciousness in the light of our righteousness in Christ Jesus. Many Christians suffer under the burden of condemnation of the devil or self-imposed condemnation. This is actually one of the greatest weapons the devil uses to keep people in bondage. He knows that the problem of sin has been dealt with, over two thousand years ago, and so he uses the weapon of sin-consciousness. He binds many with the thoughts that they are sinning even when they are not. These feelings of inadequacy, imperfection, and the imaginary guilty conscience make such people believe they are not qualified to do God's work or receive His blessings. A famous preacher once said,

Sin-consciousness is just as negative in its effects as sin itself. Sin-consciousness hinders your faith. For example, if a Christian who is sin-conscious makes a mistake, he will keep grinding and blaming himself

over and over, feeling bad even after he might have asked for forgiveness from God several times on the same sin. The more he does this, the weaker his faith becomes. That he did something wrong is not the problem; his problem is that he is more conscious of sin than of his righteousness in and through Jesus Christ.

On the other hand, if the Christian who is righteousness- conscious makes the same mistake, his heart will be sorrowful, but he will act on the Word, which says, if we confess our sins, God is faithful and just to forgive us our sins, and to cleanse us from all unrighteousness (1 John 1:9). Hence, as soon as he recognizes his wrongdoing and receives forgiveness, he continues his walk in Christ's righteousness. Notice that though the two men committed the same offence, it's their different knowledge and responses that consequently affects their faith-walk.[3]

Now, instead of focusing on sin, focus rather on what Christ has done on the Cross for you. On the Cross, Christ Jesus had paid all your debts. Powers and principalities of the dark had been disarmed. Death and its power had been crippled. There on the Cross the price for our healing had been settled long ago; and there Christ declared, "It is finished!" "Cross" consciousness is the answer to every sense of guilt the devil may bring your way. You must also be conscious of the fact that righteousness is the divine nature of God that is imparted into your human spirit when you are born again. This righteousness is a gift from God; you do not work for it (Romans 5:17; 6:23). Righteousness is therefore not just doing what is right. It is the divine nature at work in you. It gives you the ability to live right and please God. This is why no unbeliever can please God with any good work done with his Adamic nature, except he is first clothed in this righteousness that comes by grace from God (1 Corinthians 1:30). You need stop brooding over your past mistakes and failures. This will only fill your mind with grief, regret, and depression. No matter how ugly your past may be, as soon as you come to God for cleansing, He forgives you and you immediately become righteous in His presence. We are the righteousness of God in Christ Jesus. Hence, you become the righteousness of God, not because of what you have done right or that which you have not done wrong, but rather because of what Jesus Christ has done for you. He takes our filthiness away and covers us with his righteousness.

---

3 Rhapsody of Reality, A daily Devotional Guide: September 2008.

This gift of righteousness positions you right before God. The rating of the worth of your holiness and righteousness before God is never that which comes as a result of your personal struggles. You may think that the day you spent longer time studying God's word, prayed and fasted the most was when you were at your holiest state. You felt so close to God and seemed to be "touching" Him. All these are good. But you need to know this emphatically, that as long as you remain in this body of flesh, your best personal righteousness is not good enough to please God, because it is like a filthy rag (Isaiah 64:6). More so, we walk with God by faith and not by feeling. Apostle Paul says,

> *I no longer count on my own righteousness through obeying the law; rather, I become righteous through faith in Christ. For God's way of making us right with himself depends on faith. (Philippians 3:9 NLT)*

The righteousness that comes through faith in Christ Jesus alone is the only one that God recognizes. This righteousness declares us worthy and blameless before God and before the devil, his cohorts and the world. This is the reason you cannot please God by your works or rely on your human perfection to be approved by Him. The Lord Jesus came to set us free from our cultural and self-righteous mindsets to give us His own righteousness.

Righteousness is therefore not just doing what is right. It is the divine nature at work in you. It gives you ability to live right and please God.

PRAYER

1. Father, I thank you that in spite of all my short comings you still forgive me.
2. Please God, help me to stop sinning.
3. God, I refuse to be intimidated by recurrent accusations of my past sins as there is no longer any condemnation against me from you. Christ forgave the paralyzed man lowered on a mat through the roof
4. Thank you father for removing the burden of guilt and granting me peace.

IS UNFORGIVENESS PERMISSIBLE?

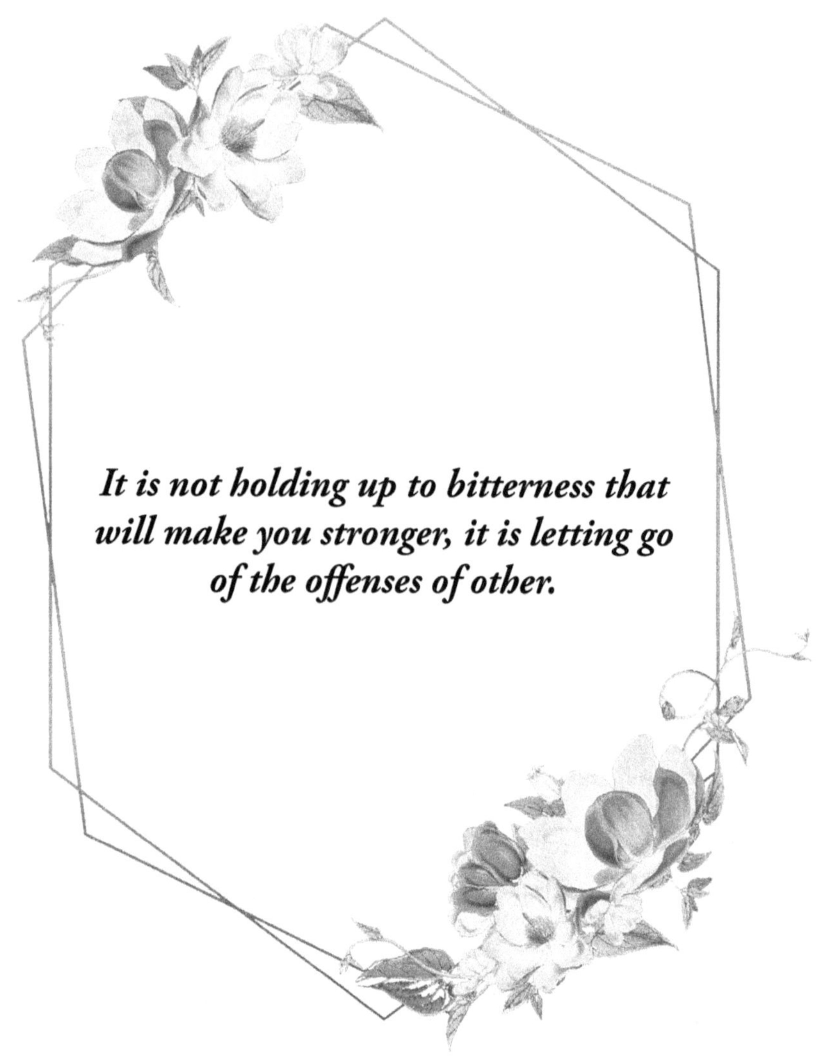

It is not holding up to bitterness that will make you stronger, it is letting go of the offenses of other.

CHAPTER 3 :
IS UNFORGIVENESS PERMISSIBLE?

You have no excuse for not forgiving

Certain people state some conditions under which they can forgive offenders. Some say, "If he comes to me to apologize, then I can forgive him." But for a mature believer, forgiveness should not be conditional, but rather be proactive. It involves both attitudes and actions. No wonder Jesus Christ said, If your brother sins against you, go and tell him his fault between you and him alone. If he hears you, you have gained your brother (Matthew 18:15). You need to learn how to go to your brother in love to reconcile with him even when he is the one at fault. Besides, there are times when some of the people that hurt you did not do that intentionally or do not even know that they have hurt you. In this type of situation, for example, you need not to burn your heart with bitterness and heaviness.

Many times, God never waits for us to come to Him before He makes a move that will foster His forgiveness for us. Right from Genesis, God has been in the business of seeking for man by Himself in order to forgive man and restore him to a perfect relationship with Himself.

***Some think that it is right to revenge
after one has forgiven once or twice.***

For example, after Adam and Eve fell into the trap of Satan in the Garden of Eden, they tried to run away from God. But God went in their pursuit, saying, Adam, where are you? God went after Cain to lighten the heavy burden of guilt that the sin of bloodshed had brought upon him. In the accounts of the Old Testament, God always sent His prophets to correct the Israelites whenever they drifted away from His will. He always restored them back to Himself when they heeded the messages of the prophets. God went after King David by sending Prophet Nathaniel to rebuke and to correct him when he killed Uriah and took Bathsheba, Uriah's wife (2 Samuel 12). Little wonder the Scripture says, While we were still sinners, Christ died for us (Romans 5:8).

At the point of salvation, when any sinner hears the gospel being preached, it is the Holy Spirit that convicts him of sin and opens his eyes to see and accept the "free gift" of God, that is, "eternal life" in Christ Jesus (John 16:8; Romans 6:23). And even after our conversion, the same Holy Spirit resides in us to prick our hearts to seek God's forgiveness when we miss the mark. This is God at work in us both to will and to act according to His good purpose (Philippians 2:13; Ephesians 1:4; 2 Timothy 1:14).

By the way, what is forgiveness? Forgiveness seems to take a form of a compound concept with two words " fore & give." Hence, forgiveness is fore-giving. Meaning that, it is given beforehand; it is given before it is asked for. Ideally, there are two major principles that make life worth living. These are "Giving and Forgiving.' The Scripture makes it clear that, he that sows (gives) generously will also reap (receive) generously (2 Corinthians 9:6). Hence, you have to be generous when it comes to the issue of forgiveness.

So you do not wait for someone to come to you and ask for it before you give it out, because, he may never come and you too must never die in that state of unforgiveness. Jesus Christ said, "And whenever you stand praying, if you have anything against anyone, forgive him, that your Father in heaven may also forgive you your trespasses. But if you do not forgive, neither will your Father in heaven forgive your trespasses" (Mark 11:25-26). If God were to be waiting for you and me to come and ask for forgiveness from Him without sending His only begotten Son to die for us and His Holy Spirit to convict us of guilt in regard to sin and righteousness and judgment, then none of us would ever be saved. This means we would be eternally doomed.

Some are of the opinion that we can forgive people for some certain offences, but there are some offences that one may not likely forgive the offenders. Whereas some think that it is right to revenge after one has forgiven once or twice. But let us go to the Scriptures to get a deeper knowledge of what it teaches concerning the necessary condition(s) when unforgiveness is permitted.

Then Peter came to Him and said, "Lord, how often shall my brother sin against me, and I forgive him? Up to seven times?" Jesus said to him, "I do not say to you, up to seven times, but up to seventy times seven." (Matthew 18:21–22 KJV)

Actually, for someone to have offended you this number of times (490), that person must be a devil incarnate. And you also must have been demon-possessed to have been able to count and accurately keep such records. Let us look at another passage on this before we draw our conclusion on condition(s) under which we cannot forgive.

If your brother sins, rebuke him, and if he repents, forgive him. If he sins against you seven times in a day, and seven times comes back to you and says, I repent, forgive him. (Luke 17:3–4)

But from this passage in Luke 17, what if he does not come back to say, "I repent"? The answer to this is not far-fetched. In Matthew 5:23–24, 18:15–17, we are told to go to him and show him his offence. And if peradventure he fails to acknowledge his wrongdoing, we are not told to hold the sin against him, but rather to view him as an unbeliever. What do you do to unbelievers whose spiritual eyes Satan has blindfolded? Of course, we intercede for them on a daily basis that they might come to the saving knowledge of Christ Jesus. We are neither to curse them nor pray for fire to come down from heaven to consume them. Sometimes, we are tempted to believe that, if people have done us wrong and talked ill about us, then it is right for us to be hard-hearted about it and get even by talking ill about them. But the Bible does not in any way support this. However, you may agree with me that no one will ever offend you for such a number, seventy times seven. What Christ was simply teaching is that there is no condition under which you must not forgive your brother. Besides, sincere forgiveness isn't colored with expectations that the other person apologizes or change. Don't worry whether or not they finally understand you. Love them and release them. Life feeds back truth to people in its own way and time—just like it does for you and me.[4]

> **Sometimes, we are tempted to believe that, if people have done us wrong and talked ill about us, then it is right for us to be hard-hearted about it and get even by talking ill about them too.**

God's grace is available to forgive

Lizzy (not her real name) is today by God's divine mercy a world renowned preacher. But during an open interview on CNN 2005 by Larry King, she opened up the ugly archive of her past. Lizzy said,

> *I had lots of hurt and lots of pain, lots of wounds, bruises, and broken heartedness in my life. I was abused sexually by my father, abused mentally, and emotionally … I told my mother once when I was about 9 years old. And I remember her examining me with a friend, and then going in and accusing my dad, and he just lied about it and said I was lying. And so, I guess, what woman wouldn't want to believe her husband? She didn't want her marriage to end. And so, when I realized that, you know, she didn't really know how to help me, wasn't going to help me, the more I realized nobody was going to help me. Somewhere along the line, I just decided, I'm going to survive this. I'm going to learn enough that I can support myself, and when I'm 18 years old, I'm moving out … which is exactly what I did.*

> *However, I thought when I walked away from the problem that I no longer had the problem, but I didn't realize … but I still had the problem in me. I still had the effects and the results of the abuse in me. And so that*

---

4 Sara Paddison, *"Forgiveness Quotes" http://www.tentmaker.org accessed March, 2010.*

was the part of me that had to be healed and the part of me that had to be dealt with, because I had fear. I was manipulative. I was controlling. I was obnoxious. I was frightened. I had all these different things inside. And, you know, that's why it's so important to have a relationship with God, because He's the only one that can get down inside of you and heal what needs to be healed inside.

. . .and obviously, you know, because of the way I'd been hurt—although I'd worked through the forgiveness thing and didn't have any hatred, I did come to realize, through that, that I did have some resentment. You know, I didn't want to have to take care of them (my parents), because they never took care of me. I didn't want to have to, you know, do that. But God really dealt with me, showed me a lot of things in the Scriptures about it. Their health wasn't real good, and so it was a kind of hard thing for me to do, but after God dealing with me for a while … we (my husband David and I) brought them to St. Louis, bought them a house and bought them a car and put them in it, and just showing them that unconditional love over a period of time really softened his heart. And, actually, they're both in assisted- living care now, and they live about four minutes from our house. I've seen my dad probably four times in the last week.

My dad never really apologized, and never admitted he did anything until three-and-a-half years ago (when he accepted Christ).

According to the CNN interviewer,

Lizzy's father did later provide a statement through his attorney addressing the abuse allegations. And that statement reads as follows: "I have committed acts in my past that I deeply regret and I'm not proud of. I currently have a wonderful and proper relationship with my daughter, Lizzy, of which I am very proud.

Lizzy further expressed that, "God permits things in our lives sometimes for reasons that we do not understand yet because of the spiritual level that we're on. We can't have any understanding of it, because we're not at a place of spiritual growth yet where we understand the deeper things of

God. But when you get through things and you get on the other side of them and you look back with hindsight, you realize that the person you are today is a result of all of these things that God didn't make disappear, that he made you go through.[5]

Three categories of people you need to forgive

Someone has rightly said that there are three sets of people you need to forgive on daily basis. Commenting on Matthew 18: 22, the writer said,

> *Truth is that offences must surely come and people around your life and ministry will regularly hurt you! The bitter truth is that not everyone will ask you for forgiveness. But to make sure your life's race is not hindered; you must forgive people regularly, even in advance, by building a pain absolving immune system of life that will make you un-reactive to the offences of people when they come.*

Not everyone will ask you for forgiveness. You must forgive people regularly, and even in advance.

A Hawaiian proverb says: "You will have to forgive three sets of people:

1. You must forgive yourself, for you will never be perfect.
2. You have to forgive your enemies, for the fire of your anger will (or may) only turn to consume you and your family.
3. Most difficult of all—you have to forgive your friends, because they are close enough to hurt you by accident."[6]

The writer added that, "indeed, when you think of the people you need to forgive; often they are the same people you love most." Henry Ward Beecher affirmed that we need to "keep a fair-sized cemetery in your backyard, in which to bury the faults of your friends."[7]This is why you must make forgiveness an unbroken rule of your life! Hence, sometime in

---

5 *Larry King: CNN Interview on May 19, 2005. For further reading, see Joyce Meyer, Do Yourself a Favor; Forgive (New York: Faith Words, 2012), 52–3.*
6 *In ODM Daily Devotional Guide, 2011, pg 24.*
7 *Henry W. Beecher, "Forgiveness Quotes" htt://www.tentmaker.org. accessed March, 2010.*

life, it is not holding on to bitterness that makes you stronger, it is letting go of offences of others. So, learn how to let go!

"And be kind to one another, tenderhearted, forgiving one another, just as God in Christ forgives you" (Eph.4:32).

Action

1. I tear all the records of the offenses that I have been keeping for days/ weeks/ years.

2. I shall keep no offense records in my heart, in my phone and in my diaries.

3. I refuse to allow thoughts of revenge to saturate my life again in Jesus' name.

4. I receive the grace not to react to my offenders as their deeds deserve.

CHAPTER FOUR

*THE DANGERS OF
UNFORGIVENESS*

He who cannot forgive breaks the
bridge over he himself must pass

CHAPTER 4:
THE DANGERS OF UNFORGIVENESS

Frankly speaking, there is nothing good that can ever come out of unforgiveness. But on the contrary, the dangers of unforgiveness cut across both physical and spiritual realms. Recently, I had an opportunity of praying with some group of people who are trusting God for healing. A young lady was there with a severe asthmatic cough, and another woman who had been trusting God for the fruit of the womb. After a short message on forgiveness, the two of them wept aloud. To the glory of God, the asthmatic cough vanished instantly. Surprisingly again, the other woman became pregnant two months later. As a matter of fact, both your physical and spiritual health are at stake when you harbor unforgiveness in your heart.

Do not pray or fast when you are not forgiving others, or else, your prayers and fasting will amount to a waste of time and energy.

i. You will neither receive nor enjoy God's forgiveness

But if you do not forgive men their sins, your Father will not forgive your sins (Matthew 6:15). What does it mean when you have not received the forgiveness of God? It simply means that you will never have a part with him when you die. Let us know quite well like George Herbert says,

"He who cannot forgive breaks the bridge over which he himself must pass."[8] It is easy to ask God for forgiveness but difficult to grant it to others. Whenever we ask God to forgive us our sin, we should firstly ask ourselves, Have we forgiven the people who have wronged us?[8]

ii. It opens doors for the avengers (Matthew 18:21–35)

From the above passage which contains what Christ Jesus the master teaches about forgiveness, we can deduce the following lessons:

∗ We owe God a debt beyond what we can ever pay even if eternity were to be given to us with which to pay. Yet He forgives us and clears our debts. We are no longer debtors, because His dear Son paid all our debt. If He has forgiven us this much, why should you find it difficult to forgive a brother who owes you just a penny? This will inevitably allow Satan, your accuser, to have a legal ground upon which he can peg his rope and drag you to hell where you will be forced to pay your debt for eternity. And this shows that you have not been born again right from the onset. Please think about this!

∗ Your freedom, peace, prosperity, and the likes can be withdrawn when you fail to forgive others.

∗ Note! It is not God that withdraws His protection or attacks you with sicknesses. Unforgiveness naturally opens the door for all these negative forces to come in. This is because unforgiveness opens a channel for the devil to successfully attack you. It creates a legal

---

8 George Herbert, "Forgiveness Quotes" online: http://www.tentmaker.org, accessed March, 2010.

ground with which the devil can stand and justifiably attack you. Don't give the devil a foothold through unforgiveness.

According to medical findings, sicknesses such as hypertension, paralysis, stroke and the likes are also companions of unforgiveness.

iii. It hinders answers to prayers

Have faith in God," Jesus answered. I tell you the truth, if anyone says to this mountain, "Go, throw yourself into the sea," and does not doubt in his heart but believes that what he says will happen, it will be done for him. Therefore I tell you, whatever you ask for in prayer, believe that you have received it, and it will be yours. And when you stand praying, if you hold anything against anyone, forgive him, so that your Father in heaven may forgive you your sins. (Mark 11:22ff).

From this teaching of Christ on faith, prayer and forgiveness, we can see that

- There is a strong connection between faith, prayer, and forgiveness.
- Unforgiveness clogs the faith-channel and keeps you powerless against the challenges of your life.
- Releasing those who have offended us is fundamental to receiving from God.
- You cannot have your prayers answered while you hold grudges in your heart.
- When your prayer is not answered, check your heart and let the Holy Spirit reveal to you whether or not you are holding grudges against somebody—your husband, wife, dad, mom, son, daughter, brother, sister, aunt, uncle, in-laws, friends, teacher, boss, pastor, and the likes.

Do not pray or fast when you are not forgiving others, or else, your prayers and fasting will amount to a waste of time and energy. In the Lord's prayer as seen in Matthew 6:12, 14, Jesus Christ made it clear that with the measure of forgiveness we measure to others, God uses the same scale or measurement to measure it back to us. "Forgive us as we forgive those who trespass against us." The fact that you need God every day is the reason you cannot afford to live in unforgiveness. In his emphasis on the need for believers to forgive their offenders, Pastor E. A. Adeboye affirmed that

> *Christ Jesus (according to Matthew 6: 12), did not say, "Help us to forgive". if you want to forgive, it is in your power. The grace is available. The issue is whether you are willing or not. Contrary to the prayer of some, you do not require any further assistance from God to forgive. He has already put what you need to do so in place. If you fail to forgive others, your sins will be recorded and held against you, starting from that moment you failed to forgive.[9]*

You need to unlock the channel of faith by forgiving, and you will soon see things you've been praying for come to pass. "True faith changes the heart. Real prayer dismantles pride and vengeance, filling the holes with love. Real faith seeks peace. For churches to have prayer power, harmony and forgiveness must be evident in the body of believers. Let go of hurts, abandon grudges, and forgive others."[10] The petition for forgiveness is one of the most important petitions in the Lord's Prayer because it is the only petition that Jesus repeated at the end of His prayer. Have you noticed that? Out of the six petitions in this prayer, Jesus emphasized one especially at the end. He said, "If you forgive men their trespasses your Heavenly Father will also forgive you. But if you do not forgive men their trespasses your Heavenly Father will also not forgive you" (Matthew 6:14, 15). Many Christians do not enjoy full and free fellowship with God because they have not taken this petition seriously.

The fact that somebody does not hold the same opinion with you on a matter does not make him your enemy.

iv.   It will make your offerings unacceptable to God

Broken relationships can hinder our relationship with God. If we have problem or grievance with anyone, we need to resolve the issue as soon

---

9 Pastor E. A. Adeboye, Open Heaven Devotional, 2011
10 NLT Life Application Study Bible, Comments on Mark 11: 25

as possible. "Therefore, if you are offering your gift at the altar and there remember your brother has something against you; leave your gift there in front of the altar. First go and be reconciled to your brother; then come and offer your gift" (Matthew 5:23–24).

When your brother is having a grudge against you especially because of what you have done (or said) to hurt his image or reputation (intentionally or unintentionally), the Bible commands that you first go to him for reconciliation before dropping your offering in the offering bag or plate in the church. If this is so, how much more when a man who is full of bitterness and unforgiveness toward others comes to God with his offerings? Without any doubt, our attitudes toward others reflect our relationship with God. Hence, we are hypocrites if we claim to love God while we harbor hatred in our hearts toward others (1 John 4:20).

v.   Unforgiveness is an obstacle to "Blessings"

Unforgiveness can make all of God's provisions for you to be blocked out of your life, just as we have seen in Matthew 18. It is a blessing's blocker. Hence, to forgive is to set a prisoner free and later to discover that the prisoner was you.

vi.   Unforgiveness is a door opener for sicknesses and diseases

In my little streams of experience, when a typical African man is on a sick bed, the suspected causes for his sickness include a spell, a curse, wizard or witchcraft, ancestral spirit, punishment from god(s) as a result of violation, attack from demonic enemy and the likes. In the same way, when a man from the Western sphere is battling with sickness, he consults medical experts for medical diagnosis. But little did people know that, unforgiving spirit and bitterness of heart are another serious cause of many diseases which defies medical instruments of diagnosis. According to medical findings, sicknesses such as hypertension, paralysis, stroke, and the likes are also companions of unforgiveness. These have sent many to their early graves, while others are bed- ridden for life. Herndon expresses that forgiveness releases one "from prolonged anger, rage, and stress that has been linked to problems, such as cardiovascular diseases, high blood pressure, hypertension, cancer, and other psychosomatic illness.[11]

When we don't forgive others, it can affect our bodies too. Disobedience to God's laws often brings physical suffering. If you bear a grudge against someone in your heart or if you're jealous of someone, and thus violate God's law of love, it can finally begin to affect your body. There are Christians today suffering from arthritis, migraine, rheumatism and asthma etc., who can't be healed - just because they have a grudge against someone. They may take any number of pills but they're not going to be healed until they learn to forgive. The cause of such diseases is not organic. It's not in their body. It is in their souls.

> *If you are sick and in need of divine healing, there are three or four indispensable ingredients or steps you need to take. First, you need to genuinely repent from your sins (Acts 3:19). Second, you need to forgive yourself and as well forgive others whom you harbor grudges against in your heart (Mark 11:23– 25). Third, you need to believe and have faith in the healing power of God (John 11:40; Acts 3:16; James 5:14–17). And lastly, living a life of love with everyone—loving others as yourself (1Corinthians 13:1f; Galatians 5:6).*

vii.   It makes you lose your liberty

It creates room for panic and fear, making you un-composed and nervous at the sight of your offender, who may not be aware of your anger and is going about freely. So, you are the one in bondage.

> *"Not to forgive is to be imprisoned by the past, by old grievances that do not permit life to proceed with new business. Not to forgive is to yield oneself to another's control ... to be locked into a sequence of act and response, of outrage and revenge, tit for tat, escalating always. The present is endlessly overwhelmed and devoured by the past. Forgiveness frees the forgiver. It extracts the forgiver from someone else's nightmare."[12]*

---

11 Harndon in "Forgiveness can be Good for your Health"
12 Lance Morrow, Online: http//www. Tentmaker.org. accessed March, 2010.

viii. It turns you into a murderer

It makes you a silent killer as you silently keep on wishing evil for your offender. And this can lead to physical killing. The Scripture clearly states that he that hates his brother is a murderer, and you know that no murderer has eternal life in him (1 John 3:15).

ix.   It makes you moody and unhappy

It gives you continuous sadness most especially when good things keep on happening to the one you refuse to forgive. Since you cannot stop God from having mercy on whom He will have mercy upon. How do you normally feel when somebody you hate or refuse to forgive is progressing and you are retrogressing? Think about this: that you hate somebody does not stop God from blessing him.

x.   An unforgiving man is in the danger of Hell

I have heard several people who refuse to forgive their brothers say, "We shall settle the matter when we get to heaven." Unfortunately, heaven is not a place for conflict resolution. Unresolved cases on earth are referred to hell. Therefore, all resolution and reconciliation with God and men must be done here and now on the planet earth. Failure to do so becomes too late when you breathe your last breath. Hence, that a man is still being dominated by unforgiving spirit means that he is yet to submit totally to Christ. Simply put, you have not allowed the atoning death of Christ Jesus, and the 'Blood' He shed on the Cross of Calvary to pay your debt and cleanse you from your sins. And this may make you find yourself locked out of the gate to Paradise (God's Kingdom) if you die in that state or the eminent last trumpet should sound and believers in Christ Jesus are rapture. Remember Jesus word again; But if you do not forgive others their sins, your father will not forgive your sins. One of the features of hell is that there is no mercy there. And in the measure in which you lack mercy in your heart towards others, in that measure you have got a little bit of hell right inside your heart. If you are unwilling to forgive someone, you've got a little bit of hell inside you. You may be considered very pious by others, because of all your religious activity. But you've got this little bit of hell right inside you all the time. And you can't go to heaven in that condition - because you can't take hell into heaven. You've got to get rid of it before you leave this earth. That's why the Lord taught us to pray, "Forgive us in exactly the same way that we have forgiven others."

Unforgiveness does a greater damage to the vessel in which it is stored, than on the object on which it is poured.

The Danger of Unforgiveness in the Church

If you forgive anyone, I also forgive him. And what I have forgiven—if there was anything to forgive—I have forgiven in the sight of Christ for your sake, in order that Satan might not outwit us. For we are not unaware of his schemes. (2 Corinthians 2: 10–11)

We must know that unforgiveness in the Church is to the devil's advantage. It gives him a foothold or an open door to attack the Church with all forms of divisions, hatred, conflicts, factions, confusion, suspicion, and the likes. During the course of my study in the seminary, during the long holiday, I was sent to a mission field where I was to work with an elder who was presiding over a local church as the pastor. He told me of the 'go areas' and the 'no-go areas' of the members' houses, because he suspected they were evil people. The places he did not want me to visit were the places of the members who had at one time or the other disagreed with him on certain issues. And since then he had seen them as stark enemies who were possessed with demons. During visitation time, and as a new student pastor, I believed it was part of my obligations to visit and to pray with every member of the Church. Hence, I decided to stay neutral. To my amazement too, one woman out of this set of people in the category of the no-go area told me myriad of stories about my boss, and how she had investigated and confirmed that my senior partner was diabolical.

But frankly speaking, I was able to see clearly that both of them were Christians, but because of the unresolved issues between them, Satan made use of that opportunity to turn them against each other.

Therefore, it is important to know that the fact that somebody does not hold the same opinion with you on a matter does not make him your enemy.

If I may ask this question, how can God's presence dwell in such a gathering where both the 'pastor-in-charge' and some selected members are not living in love and unity? Surely, God does not dwell in a place where there is disorderliness (1 Corinthians 14:33). To God's glory, this elder and the other members were able to unit together in love before I left the church.

Similarly, I have seen members changing from one Church to another, from Evangelicals to Pentecostals (and vice versa) just because they hold to the claim that a pastor, an elder/deacon, or fellow member in their former churches offended them and they went away without resolving the issues. More so, they keep on castigating their former Church anywhere they go. There are also many who just become founders and general overseers (G.O.) over night, all because of conflicts, divisions, and unforgiveness. The honest question is, Do you think that your worship to God will be acceptable to Him when you are loaded with grudges in your heart against fellow believer(s)?

Apostle James asks, 'What causes fights and quarrels among you? Don't they come from your desires that battle within you?' (James 4:1). So, the devil, the enemy of the Church of Christ, quickly penetrates the Church any time the loophole of unforgiveness is opened to him.

What you stand to lose is greater when you refuse to forgive, and it shows that you are yet to yield the control of your life to Christ who alone can give you His power to conquer flesh. For instance, you lose relationship and friendship, you lose your sound health, and you lose your joy and happiness, and will eventually lose heaven if you die in that state of holding grudges against anyone. No wonder Lawana Blackwell affirmed, 'The hatred you are carrying is a live coal in your heart, far more damaging to yourself than to others.'[13]Meaning that unforgiveness does

---

13 *Lawana Blackwell, Online: http//www.abundance-and-happiness.com/ forgiveness-quotes.html. accessed February 2010.*

a greater damage to the vessel in which it is stored, than on the object on which it is poured.

In the same way, unforgiveness has done a lot of damages to nations and governments of the world as we would later see the root cause of World War I for instance. People who assumed leadership positions with their minds set on revenge quickly miss their goals and fall. They easily lose integrity and focus as they embark on retaliation mission either on the previous administration or the group of people and community that fail to support them during the election process. I have seen many political leaders coming to detrimental ends just because they embarked on revenge mission as soon as they get hold of leadership positions.

Your time is too valuable, your destiny is so great, your assignment is very important than to get baited into battles that don't matter.

Heaven is not a place for conflict resolution.
Unresolved cases on earth are referred to Hell. All resolution and reconciliation with God and men must be done here and now on the planet earth.

Get out of that bondage

Hatred and anger can hold you captive and make you a slave. According to medical researchers, verbal expressions of animosity toward others call forth certain hormones from the pituitary, adrenal, thyroid, and other glands, an excess of which can cause disease in any part of the body. Someone rightly says, 'The minute you begin hating someone, you become his slave. Hatred holds you captive and robs you of peace of mind, and your time is spent recounting unpleasant situations. Your enemy consumes your every waking moment and hatred holds your mind hostage.' When you are tormented by the demons of hatred, jealousy, and envy, your only desire is for revenge. It isn't worth it; let it go! Release the hatred, bitterness, and resentment, and the healing powers within you will begin to function.[14]

---

14 *Free Sermon outlines and Bible Studies Online: http://www.pe2000.com/anger.*

Booker T. Washington, a black American who became famous in spite of prejudices against his color and who was insulted on numerous occasions, wrote, 'I will not let any man reduce my soul to the level of hatred. 'The famous physiologist Dr. John Hunter knew what anger could do to his heart when he said, 'The first scoundrel that gets me angry will kill me.' And this sounds prophetically, as he later died of anger. At a medical meeting, a co-worker made assertions that incensed Hunter. As he stood up and bitterly attacked the speaker, his anger caused such a contraction of the blood vessels in his heart that he fell dead! Know for sure that powerful negative emotions can make one sick and even cause death![15]

After an angry exchange, you can be affected for hours or even days as you endlessly go over the event in your mind, churning up the anger feelings and adding to them. And during this period, your mood is being ruled by the memory of the person you are angry with. You are a victim of the event. When you allow someone else's behavior to make you angry, you are indeed the victim. They are likely to go off and forget about it. You are being controlled by them without their even knowing about it— as you fume and fret and relive the event for days or months afterwards.[16] An anonymous writer once defined anger as "the punishment we give to ourselves for somebody's mistake." Beware, anger, hatred, malice, bitterness of heart, jealousy, and unforgiveness are all cancerous or killer habits. Avoid any of these in your life at all cost!

---

15 *Ibid*
16 *Ibid*

PRAYER

1. Father, I thank you that in spite of all my short comings you still forgive me.

2. Please God, help me to stop sinning.

3. God, I refuse to be intimidated by recurrent accusations of my past sins as there is no longer any condemnation against me from you. Christ forgave the paralyzed man lowered on a mat through the roof

4. Thank you father for removing the burden of guilt and granting me peace.

THE BENEFITS OF FORGIVENESS

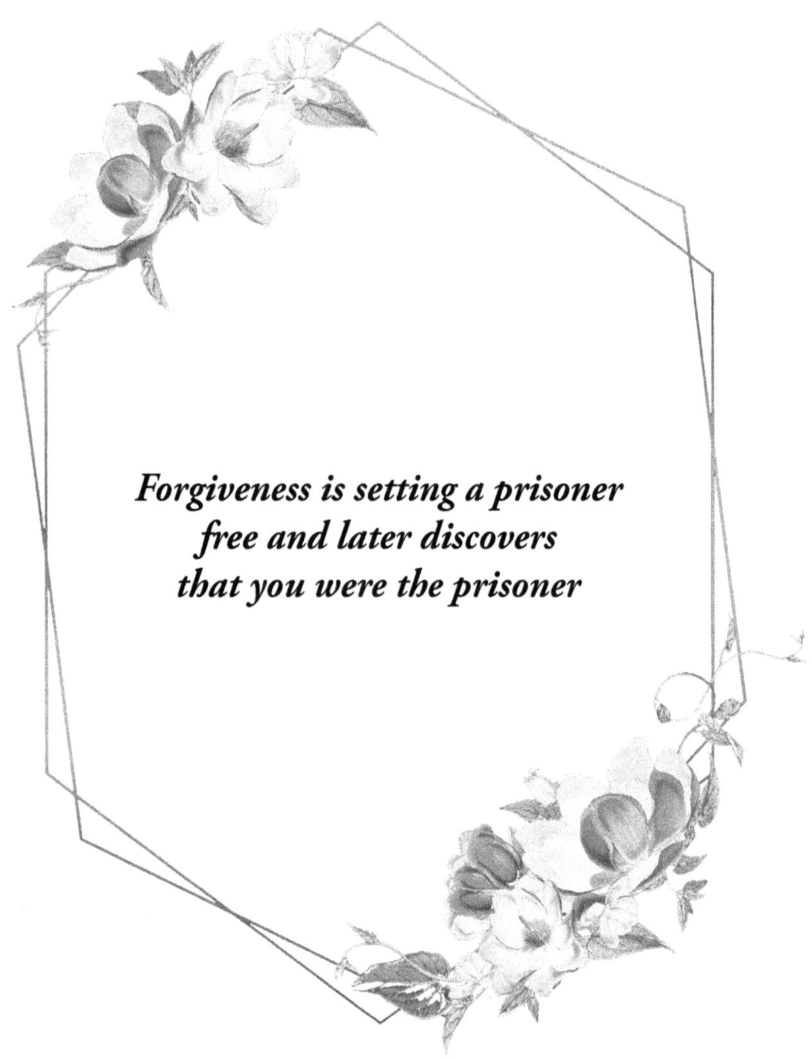
Forgiveness is setting a prisoner
free and later discovers
that you were the prisoner

CHAPTER 5 :
THE BENEFITS OF
FORGIVENESS

The best revenge is forgiveness. Unforgiveness is costlier than forgiveness. When you forgive, you are the one who benefits. Not to forgive places you at a serious disadvantage. You have nothing to lose when you forgive, but rather, you gain all things. And as a child of God, you should act like your heavenly Father who never recalls your offences.

1. You will be forgiven by God

"For if you forgive men when they sin against you, your heavenly Father will also forgive you" (Matthew 6:14).

2. Forgiveness closes the door against the devil's attack

Because unforgiveness opens the way for bitterness and malice, both of which are Satan's keys to entering a person's life (Ephesians 4: 26–27 GNB). Therefore, forgiveness closes the door to the devil's attack and activities in your life.

3. It causes the power of God in you to flow unhindered.

Every prophet of God in the Old Testament had his own strength and weakness. None could boast of sinless perfection. For instance, Prophet Elisha, by my own personal observation (which is opened to constructive criticism), was a harsh, easily provoked and a no-

nonsense prophet. He was always quickly embittered and irascible with trivial matters. In his fiery anger, he cursed the little children (and several others) who provoked him, and instantly, forty-two of them were killed by bears (2 Kings 2:23–25). These children might have become great people in Israel, I suppose. Shortly after this, in 2 Kings 3:14–16, the prophet needed to employ a harpist to play before the Hand (Spirit) of God could come upon him to prophecy. Because the Holy Spirit did not dwell in man then, "The Spirit came and went." However, when you are always irascible in the spirit, your spirit cannot always easily connect to the Spirit of God. When you harbor bitterness, hatred, and unforgiveness, the power and the anointing of God upon your life will not flow freely to impact others. Your anointing can be corrupted by the spirit of anger. You can still remember, Elisha out of anger and unforgiveness cursed his successor, Gehazi, when the other desecrated the office of prophethood by out of greediness stealthily requested for the same gifts earlier on rejected by his master. Elisha ended up without a successor for his ministry (2 Kings 5:25–27, 13:14).

4. Forgiveness will keep you in good health

Truly, one of the reasons some people are sick and miss out on God's blessings as earlier mentioned is because they refuse to forgive. There are scores of testimonies and miracles I have at the tip of my fingers that several people received when they forgave their offenders. I have heard of sudden disappearance of goiter when a woman forgave the person she needed to forgive. I have witnessed several long-time barrenness cases terminated when couples learned how to forgive one another. Tumors of various kinds have been healed without surgical operations when the victims surrendered their lives to Christ and forgave their debtors. Victims of high blood pressure and other related body and life-threatening diseases easily receive their healings and sound health back when they forgive. A woman received her joy and freedom back with tears rushing down her cheeks after she forgave a senior colleague in the office who debarred her of promotion over twenty-five years ago when this senior colleague hid one of the documents vital to her promotion. So, for over twenty-five years, she was carrying a pregnancy of hatred and enmity. Her experience reveals the high cost of living in unforgiveness because you lose many things when you refuse to forgive. You lose fellowship with God, you lose your relationship with men, and your wealth and your health are at stake when you cannot forgive. Truly speaking, you cannot enjoy your wealth and health if your life is ramped up in the cage of unforgiveness.

5. You will be like your Father in heaven

You have heard that it was said, 'Love your neighbor and hate your enemy. But I tell you: Love your enemies and pray for those who persecute you, that you may be sons of your Father in heaven. He causes his sun to rise on the evil and the good, and sends rain on the righteous and the unrighteous. If you love those who love you, what reward will you get? Are not even the tax collectors doing that? And if you greet only your brothers, what are you doing more than others? Do not even pagans do that? Be perfect, therefore, as your heavenly Father is perfect. (Matthew 5:43–48)

Forgiveness is one of the communicable attributes of your Heavenly Father. Hence, you must resemble Him.

6. Divine instrument for brokenness

There are times when God uses an avenue of forgiveness to break us down and empty us of the flesh. Without deep humility, true forgiveness is impossible, and will never happen since forgiveness involves giving up your right. Forgiveness is accepting God's sovereign use of people and situations to strip you of self-importance, and humiliate yourself love.[17]

7. Forgiveness is like employing God to act in your stead

Beloved, do not avenge yourselves, but rather give place to wrath; for it is written, "Vengeances is mine, I will repay," says the Lord (Romans 12:19 NKJV).

Never make up your mind to embark on revenge mission because the problem with revenge is that it never gets what it wants; it either mete out judgment below expectation or above it; it never evens the score, fairness never comes. The chain reaction set off by every act of vengeance always takes its course. It ties both the injured and the injurer to an escalator of pain.

---

17 *Martha Kilpatrick, Online: http//www.tentmaker.org. accessed March, 2010.*

Forgiveness in marriage

My wife and I are still young in marriage, but someone recently asked me for the secrets of living happily with one's spouse. My answer to this question is not farfetched as I replied that "forgiveness is topmost on the list of these secrets. We forgive each other always and without any reservation. We never sleep over any unresolved issue." As a matter of fact, a happy marriage is the union of two good forgivers. The sweetness of your home and marriage depends greatly on how proactive you are in forgiving your spouse. Husband and wife are prone to remind each other of their past mistakes every time something goes wrong. There is no way they can develop a good relationship if they keep doing that. Because, constantly reminding each other of past mistakes and failures will ruin their prayer's life. It will make their faith inoperative. Marlene Dietrich rightly put it when she said, "Once a woman has forgiven her man, she must not reheat his sins for breakfast."[18] Husband and wife need to forgive as God forgives. They should be able to say to each other, Honey, I was wrong, you are right, forgive me! Many Christians do not enjoy the new-covenant power because of unforgiveness. Some remain powerless because they are unwilling to go and ask for forgiveness from people they need to. We all have a flesh and we are living among others who have a flesh. And so we are constantly liable to injure one another knowingly and unknowingly. The only place where we'll never get hurt by anyone is in heaven. And so we need to forgive one another as long as we live on this earth. To err is human, to forgive is divine.

Actually, the vision for this book began over ten years ago, with forgiveness between husbands and wives forming one of the primary concerns. A very nice young lady I used to know suddenly developed hypertension owing to her alleged refusal to forgive her husband who committed adultery and gave birth to a child out of wedlock. She affirmed her unfaultable faithfulness to her husband prior and after their marriage and would never believe that her husband could betray her trust. Despite several attempts made by friends and other members of the families to beg her to forgive him, she was implacable. This is a very grievous sin quite right, but forgiveness is still the way out even when your spouse betrays you. There are couples who have killed God-given sexual instinct in their marital relationships. Even though they live together under the same roof, yet for months or years they have deprived each other of sexual union because of unforgiveness. In some other families, like the costly

---

18 *Marlene Dietrich, Online: http://www.brainyquote.com/topic forgiveness3. html. accessed April 27, 2011.*

mistake Isaac and Rebecca made, they are operating a two-party system of stack enmity. The father is in one party with a child or two, and the mother is in the other party with the other children as she teaches them against their father. This type of lifestyle has broken many homes today.

A happy marriage is the union of two good forgivers. The sweetness of your home and marriage depends greatly on how proactive you are in forgiving your spouse.

Recently, a friend told me a story he witnessed on how a wife filed for divorce just because the husband was not helping enough to walk her dog around on daily basis as she claimed. I wonder how many couples have allowed their pets to stand in between their marriages to the extent of divorcing one another because of pets.

There are couples who are just living together like roommates in the high schools. Though they are not divorced physically, but spiritually, emotionally, and economic-wise, they have divorced. Some have killed the God-giving sexual intent, which should exist between married couples because of unresolved pile up grudges that have built up mountains of unforgiveness in their homes. A man in his early fifties was once boasting before me on his ability to restrain from sex with his wife when he said, "For good seven years now, I have not had sex with her though we live under the same roof. I will not have sex with her until she knows and accepts me as the head of this family." Not long after he told me this that I received news of how he was caught having affair with another man's wife. The damage of unforgiveness to marriage has no limit.

Recently, in my Sunday class here in the States, a man raised a prayer request for his first wife who was sick in the hospital. He added, "Even though she left me, I still love her with the love of Christ, I wish her good, I want her healed, and I won't entertain any grudge in my heart toward her." I was indeed touched by this honest confession. Try to put yourself in the same shoe and ask this honest question, What would you do if the one you invest your love upon decides to leave you for another man or woman?

PRAYER

1. As I have forgiven my offenders, I receive my peace, joy and happiness back in full in the name of Jesus.
2. I pray against the spirit of hatred and divorce families caused by unforgiveness in Jesus' name.

EXAMPLES OF PEOPLE THAT FAILED TO FORGIVE

Forgiveness is the attribute of the
strong, not the weak

CHAPTER 6 :
EXAMPLES OF PEOPLE
THAT FAILED TO FORGIVE

In this chapter, we shall briefly examine the lives of few individuals and groups of people in the past that lived out lives of unforgiveness and the consequences.

Cain failed to forgive Abel his brother

> *Now Cain said to his brother Abel, "Let's go out to the field." And while they were in the field, Cain attacked his brother Abel and killed him. Then the LORD said to Cain, "Where is your brother Abel?" "I don't know," he replied. Am I my brother's keeper? The LORD said, "What have you done? Listen! Your brother's blood cries out to me from the ground. Now you are under a curse and driven from the ground, which opened its mouth to receive your brother's blood from your hand."* (Genesis 4:8–11 NIV)

Abel was the first innocent man that died in the pool of his own blood from the hand of a revengeful, wicked, and devilish blood- brother of his. Bitterness and unforgiveness turned Cain to be the first murderer the Bible recorded. Check your heart now, are you holding something against your brother? Please do let go so that you too can receive your freedom.

Lamech the first polygamist was an evil genius

Lamech said to his wives, "Adah and Zillah, listen to me; wives of Lamech, hear my words. I have killed a man for wounding me, a young man for injuring me. If Cain is avenged seven times, then Lamech seventy- seven times." (Genesis 4:23–24)

Lamech, as we note, was the first polygamist who took two wives, Adah and Zillah. This attempt to improve on God's design for marriage bears sorrow and frustration for many who followed in his footsteps: Jacob, David, and Solomon are obvious examples.[19] But more brutal than this was that, in his revenge mission, he killed a young man and without any sense of remorsefulness. Although Lamech earns just a few brief verses in the Scriptures, those words say much about the rapid advance of sins in the days after Adam and Eve. And interestingly, Lamech was a descendant of Cain. Hence, it is not an exaggeration to say of him: like grandfather, like grandson. He became a murderer as he could not forgive the young man.

The Edomites and the Israelites

There are times when parents fail to establish cordial relationships among their children before they die. This singular act has a power to create a partial or permanent enmity among the children they left behind. Today, there are numerous siblings, families, and relations that are living in a great world of hostility just because parents failed to create peace before they passed away. Going by an inductive analysis of the Scriptures, we have a score of cases. Isaac and Rebecca gave birth to twin brothers— Esau and Jacob. The two brothers had a serious conflict over their pursuit of destinies. This clash culminated in unresolved issues and bitterness of heart. Several years after the death of the two brothers, their children and their great grandchildren continued in this attitude of enmity. The descendants of Esau, who had become a great nation called the Edomites, became cruel and hostile to the Israelites their brothers. Let us see the story below as a case study.

---

19 People Parallel Devotional (Nigeria, Lagos: Unusual Publishers, 2011), pg. 7.

Moses sent messengers from Kadesh to the king of Edom, saying: "This is what your brother Israel says: You know about all the hardships that have come upon us.

Our forefathers went down into Egypt, and we lived there many years. The Egyptians mistreated us and our fathers, but when we cried out to the LORD, he heard our cry and sent an angel and brought us out of Egypt. Now we are here at Kadesh, a town on the edge of your territory.

Please let us pass through your country. We will not go through any field or vineyard, or drink water from any well. We will travel along the king's highway and not turn to the right or to the left until we have passed through your territory."

But Edom answered: "You may not pass through here; if you try, we will march out and attack you with the sword." The Israelites replied: "We will go along the main road, and if we or our livestock drink any of your water, we will pay for it. We only want to pass through on foot—nothing else." Again they answered: "You may not pass through." Then Edom came out against them with a large and powerful army. Since Edom refused to let them go through their territory, Israel turned away from them. (Numbers 20:14–21)

In verse 14 of the passage above, Moses sent messengers to the descendants of Esau with a mind of brotherhood saying, "This is what your brother Israel says: You know about all the hardships that have come upon us." One may quickly assume that, if an enemy out there is pursuing a man, his own blood brother's tent that is nearby may be a safe place of refuge for him. But as far as the Edomites were concerned, the reverse was the case. Hundreds of years later, they even joined forces with other hostile enemies (like the Philistines) to see to the downfall of their brothers (the Israelites) just because of unforgiveness. We see this glaringly in 2 Chronicles 28:17–18:

The Edomites had again come and attacked Judah and carried away prisoners, while the Philistines had raided towns in the foothills and the Negev of Judah.

God, through Prophet Amos, in Amos 1:11–12, clearly highlighted the offences of the Edomites. They are summarized follows:

* He disregarded the bond of brotherhood.

* He pursued his brother with the sword.

* He failed to treat his brother with compassion and acceptance.

* His anger raged continually (for centuries) against his brother.

* His fury flamed unchecked against his own blood-brother.

* He allied with other foreign enemies to attack his brother.

God, in turn, said that He would send consuming fire that would destroy the two major cities (Teman and Bozrah) of Edom. It is unfortunate that many who are suffering from body-consuming diseases like cancer, hypertension, kidney, and liver deformities and the likes may be as a result of the fire that their unforgiveness kindled. These two cities of Edom were the main sources of the Edomites' economic and financial stability. But now, God promised to cut off their hope of existence. And today, it is highly pathetic to know that Edom as a nation had long been wiped out from the Map of the World due to the sin of unforgiveness of their ancestors. You do not need to wait till unforgiveness cut off your hope of living.

There are families today that are still perpetrating the bitterness of their ancestors just because of the "evil" stories their fathers told them. In some families, children, grandchildren, and great grandchildren are stark enemies to one another just because their fathers died without settling trivial matters which have now breed permanent hatred for their lineage.

The unfaithful or ungrateful servant

Jesus Christ our Lord and Savior Himself told His disciples the parable of the unmerciful servant when they became very inquisitive about this subject of discussion. Hence, Jesus Christ wants everyone to know the disastrous end of anyone who fails to forgive his brother from the bottom of his heart.

> *Then Peter came to him and asked, "Sir, how often should I forgive a brother who sins against me? Seven times?" "No!" Jesus replied, "seventy times seven!" The Kingdom of Heaven can be compared to a king who decided to bring his accounts up to date. In the process, one of his debtors was brought in who owed him $10 million! $10 million, literally, "10,000 talents." Approximately £3 million. He couldn't pay, so the king ordered him sold for the debt, also his wife and children and everything he had. But the man fell down before the king, his face in the dust, and said, "Oh, sir, be patient with me and I will pay it all." Then the king was filled with pity for him and released him and forgave his debt. But when the man left the king, he went to a man who owed him*

> *$2,000, approximately £700, and grabbed him by the throat and demanded instant payment. The man fell down before him and begged him to give him a little time. "Be patient and I will pay it," he pled. But his creditor wouldn't wait. He had the man arrested and jailed until the debt would be paid in full. Then the man's friends went to the king and told him what had happened. And the king called before him the man he had forgiven and said, "You evil-hearted wretch! Here I forgave you all that tremendous debt, just because you asked me to—shouldn't you have mercy on others, just as I had mercy on you?" Then the angry king sent the man to the torture chamber until he had paid every last penny due. So shall my heavenly Father do to you if you refuse to truly forgive your brothers. (Matthew 18: 21–35 TLB)*

Let us further look at the gravity of this man's offence in today's language. He owed his master a sum of money (according to the Living Bible) that was worth 10 million dollars ($10,000,000). And even if he himself was sold in the market, the selling price would not have been enough to pay his debt. But he pleaded with his master, and the master looked on him with compassion and cancelled his debt. But immediately after he left his master, this man met a man who owed him two thousand dollars ($2,000) only. The one that owed two thousand dollars ($2,000) pleaded as well, saying, "Please be patient with me, and I will pay you back." But despite the prior mercy that this man had received, he failed to have mercy on his debtor that owed him a smaller amount. So, with a callous heart, he went off and had the man thrown into prison until he could pay the debt. The master who heard what this ungrateful servant of his whom he had forgiven did, in anger, he turned him over to the jailers to be tortured, until he should pay back all the sum of money he owed.

Jesus Christ had gone to the Cross of Calvary to pay our debt with His own precious blood and His atoning death, of which even if given "eternity," we can never finish paying it. This same Christ Jesus, who knows every hidden intention of man, said, This is how my heavenly Father will treat each of you unless you forgive your brother from your heart. Think about this!

In a nutshell, this story tells us how much we owe God an "unpayable debt," and yet, when we come to Him through Christ Jesus, He forgives us. If we have been so much forgiven, why won't we forgive those who owe us just a token? Hence, we cannot be a beneficiary of God's forgiveness when we fail to forgive others. This story helps me to forgive if I take time to remember all the mistakes and errors I have made and needed not only God's forgiveness, but people's as well.

Note again in this parable, the torturers are evil spirits who are permitted to harass us until we learn to be merciful to others. Jesus used this parable to illustrate how great the debt is that God has forgiven us, and how unmerciful and evil it is for us not to forgive someone who has hurt us.

Has someone done you some harm? Maybe someone has spread false stories about you. Maybe your neighbor, or your wife, or your father or your mother-in-law etc, has done you some harm. Maybe they have ruined your life in some way. Maybe the doctor who operated on you made a mistake that has caused you untold suffering. But the Lord says that all those sins put together are so tiny compared to the debt you had to God and which God forgave you. So there is absolutely no reason why you should not be able to forgive all those people freely from your heart. The important part of Matthew 18:35 is "from your heart". If you are not willing to forgive your fellow-man from your heart, don't waste your time coming to God and saying, "Forgive us our trespasses," for God won't listen to your prayer. If there is one single soul in the whole world whom you haven't forgiven, you cannot be forgiven yourself; and this this scriptures affirm that 'no unforgiven soul can ever enter God's presence.' This is far more serious than we realize. "Blessed are the merciful for they shall receive mercy" (Matthew 5:7). The more merciful you are to others, the more merciful God will be to you in the day of judgment. But "judgment will be merciless to one who has shown no mercy" (James 2:13). God will treat you exactly as you treat others. For BY YOUR STANDARD OF MEASURE IT WILL BE MEASURED TO YOU IN RETURN" (Luke 6:38).

Herodias and John the Baptist

When a man is full of bitterness in his heart toward his fellow brother, he can go on extra miles to revenge at all cost. Herodias could have allowed her daughter to ask for better thing. Precious opportunities to make it to the top and become somebody important in life can be wasted on revenge mission. Such is the case of Herodias toward John the Baptist, a holy Prophet of God in Mark 6:14–29.

Herodias could not forgive John the Baptist for exposing her sin of immorality. In spite of the imprisonment of John for the accusation, she would still after three years requested for his head and John was beheaded. Are you too still waiting for an opportune time to retaliate? Unforgiveness is a terrible sin. It can cause irreparable loss to a nation, a church, or a family. The Scripture does not give us the later end of Herodias, but her concubine, King Herod, who was the instrument of revenge, indeed became the diet of worms and died immediately. Hence she lost her dignity.

Adolf Hitler lacked forgiving spirit

It is good to take a glimpse into the historical antecedents. Hitler's father was the illegitimate child of a cook named (Maria Anna) Schickelgruber. This cook, the grandmother of Adolf Hitler, was cooking for a Jewish family named Frankenburger, when she became pregnant. Frankenburger paid Schickelgruber a maternity allowance from the time of the child's birth up to his fourteenth (14th) year. Adolf was born on 20th April 1889 at Braunau, by Alois and Clara. Alois was very hostile, hot tempered, and strict. But on the contrary, Clara, Adolf's mother, was completely the opposite. She was gentle, meek, loving, and caring so much that Adolf used to carry her photo with him wherever he went.[20]

Adolf was a weak student in the school. He was lazy and did not perform well at school work. Nevertheless, he liked History and Arts works. Alois, Hitler's father, died when Hitler was 13, and so there was no strong influence to keep him at school when he was older. After doing very badly in his examinations, Hitler left school at the age of 15 without any qualification. Consequently, when he started his political career, he certainly did not want people to know that he was a poor achiever in school.[21]

Hitler had never given up his dream of being an artist. After leaving school, he left for Vienna to pursue his dream. However, his life was shattered when, at age 18, his mother died of cancer. In Vienna, the Academy of Art rejected his application as "he had no school leaving certificate." His drawings which he presented as evidence of his ability were rejected. The examining board did not just want a "landscape artist." Without work and without any means to support himself, Hitler, short of money, lived in a doss house with tramps. He spent his time painting post cards which he sold; he also did the job of clearing pathway of snow. It was at this stage in his life, about 1908, that he developed a hatred for the Jews. He thought it was a Jewish professor that had rejected his artwork. He became convinced that a Jewish doctor was responsible for his mother's death. He cleared the snow bound paths of beautiful town houses in Vienna where people lived, and he became convinced that only Jews lived in those homes. By 1910, his mind had become warped and his hatred of the Jews—known as anti- Semitism—had become set.[22]

---

20 *Online: Enquires@historylearningsite.co.uk accessed June, 2010*
21 *Ibid*
22 *Ibid*

Adolf Hitler on a revenge mission

When Hitler came to power legally on January 3, 1933, as the head of a coalition government, his first objective was to consolidate power and to eliminate political opposition. In a nutshell, and to avoid the tearful and pathetic story of mass killing of the Jews, the Holocaust was the genocide of approximately six million European Jews during World War II, a systematic State-sponsored extermination by the Nazi Germany. However, he ended up committing suicide on April 30, 1945.[23] This is how terrible an unforgiving person can go.

Some Church members find it difficult sometimes to forgive their pastor who, being led by the Spirit of God, preaches about sins that affect them, believing that he was using the pulpit to attack them. Some continue to nurse grudges, hatred, and bitterness against their pastor. On the contrary, anytime a sermon touches your life, you only need to think and repent because it simply means that God loves you and that is why He is instructing you. But some go as far as reducing the amount they give as offering so that the pastor's remuneration will be affected. Some go as far as making destructive criticism, backbiting, blackmailing, and even engaging the servant of God in both spiritual and physical battles, and even killing him as the case of Herodias aforementioned. But you cannot fight against a servant of God and expect God to hold His peace. You are in a way fighting against God and not man. Remember that God Himself said, "Touch not my anointed and do my prophets no harm" (Psalm 105:15).

Few years ago in a particular community of Africa, it was reported that a church member had a clash with his pastor over some issues in the church. He felt offended and wanted to revenge or harm the minister of God. As a result, he brought poisoned tubers of yam to church as first-fruits. Eventually, the two children of the pastor died after eating the yam. This is to let you know how horrible it is when a man is possessed with the spirit of unforgiveness. The man never went scot free. The pastor

---

23 *Michael Berenbaum, 'Holocaust,' Britannica Electronic CD.*

was later transferred to another church childless. A while later, the man found himself in jail for two years for another offence and in turn died of an incurable protracted illness. How I wish he was privileged to ask for God's forgiveness before his demise!

PRAYER

1. I refuse to pass negative stories to my children which can make them grow nursing hatred toward others in my family lineage or anywhere.

2. All root of bitterness in my life caused by unforgiveness, be uprooted in the name of Jesus.

3. All generational hatred in my lineage breeding unforgiveness, come to a halt and be uprooted as from today as I forgive my offenders in Jesus' name.

4. Father, please destroy every pending doom on my lineage due to generational unforgiveness.

5. God, create in me a new tender heart that forgives easily in Jesus' name.

76

EXAMPLES OF PEOPLE THAT FORGAVE

Without forgiveness, there is no
profitable future

CHAPTER 7 :
EXAMPLES OF PEOPLE THAT FORGAVE

It is highly pathetic today that several believers in Christ Jesus quickly result in saying, "I am not Jesus" when it comes to matters of sins and forgiveness.

This is simply because they are not ready to follow biblical injunctions and want to do things in their own ways. Many take law into their hands in order to carry out revenge. But glory be to God that, there are several ordinary men like us in the Scriptures who demonstrated perfect forgiveness. They left for us examples to follow. Nevertheless, if it were only Jesus Christ that ever lived a life of total forgiveness, we still do not have any excuse not to forgive. As His followers, it is expected of us to follow in His footsteps.

Joseph forgave his wicked brothers

Being the favorite son of his father, Jacob, and because of the dreams he had relayed to his brothers, Joseph swas hated with passion by them. His brothers threw him into a pit to die, but later sold him to some Ishmaelite slave traders who in turn sold him into Egypt. He would eventually be jailed for an offence he didn't commit (Genesis 37:25–29). He experienced different trauma in thirteen years. If blood brothers could be so cruel, how much more can anyone else do? However, God exonerated him and brought his dreams to extraordinary reality. Joseph forgave his brothers even when they didn't recognize him. He forgave them before they showed remorse or requested for it. Likewise, God expects you to always forgive no matter how grievous the offence might be.

> *His brothers then came and threw themselves down before him. We are your slaves, they said. But Joseph said to them, "Don't be afraid. Am I in the place of God? You intended it to harm me, but God intended it for good to accomplish what is now being done, the saving of many lives. So then, don't be afraid. I will provide food for you and your children. And he reassured them and spoke kindly to them." (Genesis 50:18–20)*

There is one more thing to learn from Joseph in dealing with beloved ones who hurt us. God gave Joseph two sons. He named them Manasseh, which means "God has made me forget," and Ephraim, which means "God made me fruitful in the land of my afflictions" (Genesis 41:51). Hence, we need to rely on God's given strength and grace in order to forgive and forget people's offences. Joseph was not Christ, he was an ordinary man like us. Besides, there was not any written Scripture for him to read then. Yet, in spite of the opposition and agony he went through in the hands of his brothers, he forgave them. Sad to say, many so-called Christians today have taken vows never to forgive relations who at one point or another had offended them. But we can learn from the story of Joseph and his brothers that when you forgive, you in no way change the past. But you sure do change the future. Without forgiveness, there is no profitable future.

Job forgave his unreliable friends

In times of trial and hardship, however, one should expect soft and healing words from true friends. But the reverse was the case when Job was passing through a harsh time of test of faith. All Job's friends, Eliphaz, Bildad, and Zophar, with no exemption, turned against him. One could discern from their comments that they had all the while doubted the integrity of their friend Job, and when calamity struck, they quickly made true their premonitions in concluding that he was a secret sinner whom nemesis caught up with. They in essence stabbed Job in the back with their words. Instead of cursing these friends of his, whom he would have at one time or the other helped greatly (due to his vast wealth), he chose to forgive them of their false accusations. God restored his health and gave him fortunes in double portions (Job 42:10).

Kindly ask yourself at this point that, "Am I ready to forgive my friends in spite of the weight of their offences against me?"

David never gloated over the death of Saul

King Saul was David's boss, with all the treacherous deeds and wickedness of Saul to David, he never allowed bitterness in his heart toward Saul. David was chased out of his father's land by Saul and his vast army. This was the same nation where David had displayed his loyalty and patriotic charisma by killing the giant Goliath who threatened them for forty days. Stories abound of many people who would not forgive their nations and would never do anything for the development of their land as a result of the trauma and agony they had experienced in the past in the hands of an individual or group of individuals. A young man visited his country after a long stay abroad. On arrival, he was duped by some gangsters. On the third day, he journeyed back and vowed never to forgive his nation for this singular act. But David would not have done this if he were to be alive today. Several times, David narrowly escaped death and was treated like an outcast by people he delivered from the fiery swords of the Philistines. Yet with all these, in the land of the hostile enemies where David was banished to, he heard about the death of King Saul. Instead of rejoicing and gloating over this news, with a tender heart of love, he wept aloud. He summoned all the cities in Israel including all the army to many days of mourning for King Saul's death (2 Samuel 1:1–27). What would you have done if you were David upon hearing the news that the one who was relentlessly seeking after your life is dead?

The Father of the Prodigal Son (Luke 15:11–32)

Jesus told a story of a father and his rebellious son commonly known as the "prodigal son." But unfortunately, many who have read this story several times only concentrate on the nasty behavior of this son, but never see the great message of "love and forgiveness" that Christ was passing across. Let us analyze the mischievous attitudes of this son clearly.

Normally, parents' possessions are inherited by their children after their death. But this son went straight to his father and forcefully made a demand for his own share of the father's property even when the father was still active and alive. He was too audacious to have wanted to inherit his father's property while the father was still alive. If African elders were to interpret this act, this boy would have been said to have already killed his father and this was a big "taboo," an abomination. Secondly, he went away to a foreign land where he squandered his share of this property with harlots and other vagabonds. But in the long run, all his wealth was gone, and he had nothing left, not even any of the friends who had enjoyed his money with him.

When all hope of living was gone, and with his condition getting worse to the point of even eating with pigs, he decided to return home to face his fate, but never with an expectation of receiving any warm welcome.

> *But while he was still a long way off, his father saw him and was filled with compassion for him; he ran to his son, threw his arms around him, and kissed him. (Luke 15:20)*

The father, out of the heart of forgiveness, lavished "an undeserved love" on this prodigal son.

But today, there are many fathers who have made up their minds not to forgive their erring children. Some have gone to the extent of disowning their children because of the so-called "unpardonable sins" of blackmailing family's name. If truly you are a child of God, you should have the same heart He has for sinners. God never disowns His own children, even when they err, He run after them, chastises them, and restores them to Himself with His everlasting love (Psalm 27:10; Isaiah 64:8; John 20:17; Hebrew 12:7).

Stephen forgave his murderers (persecutors)

Jesus Christ was not the only one that said, Father forgive them for they know not what they do, when He was being tortured to the point of death without committing any sin. If not, many would have said "only Jesus could have said that." Here was Stephen, one of the early Church believers, at the point of death in the hands of his persecutors because of his faith in Christ, and following his master's example, he joyfully exclaimed, "Lord, do not hold this sin against them" (Acts 7:54–60).

Philemon forgave Onesimus

It is highly interesting to know that the message of the whole Book of Philemon centers on forgiveness.

> *Onesimus, a slave of Philemon, had stolen from his master and ran away to Rome. There he came in contact with Paul [who was under house arrest, Acts 28:16–30] and with the claims of Jesus Christ. After his conversion, Onesimus faced yet another confrontation, this time with his estranged master Philemon. Paul sends him back with this letter in hand, urging Philemon to extend forgiveness to Onesimus. Onesimus had left him as his bondservant. Now he was returning as his brother in the Lord. Therefore, Paul exhorts, "Receive him as you would receive me." (v. 17)*[24]

Does Christian brotherly love really work, even in situations of extraordinary tension and difficulty? Will it work, for example, between a prominent slave owner and one of his runaway slaves? Paul had no doubt! He wrote a "postcard" to Philemon, his beloved brother and fellow worker, on behalf of Onesimus—a deserter, thief, and formerly worthless slave, but now Philemon's brother in Christ. With much tact and tenderness, Paul asked Philemon to receive Onesimus back with the

---

24 *Bruce Wilkinson and Kenneth Boa: "Talk Through the Bible Electronic CD"*

same gentleness with which he would have received Paul himself. Any debt Onesimus owed, Paul promised to pay him back. Although Paul placed Onesimus' debt on his account, he reminded Philemon of the greater spiritual debt which Philemon himself owed as a convert to Christ (vv. 17–19). Knowing Philemon, Paul was confident that brotherly love and forgiveness would prevail.

Philemon developed the transition from bondage to brotherhood that was brought about by Christian love and forgiveness. Just as Philemon was shown mercy through the grace of Christ, so he must graciously forgive his repentant runaway servant who had returned a brother in Christ. Paul wrote this letter as his personal appeal that Philemon should receive Onesimus even as he would receive him (Paul). This letter was also addressed to other Christians in Philemon's circle, because Paul wanted it to have an impact on the entire Church of Christ.[25]

The forgiveness that the believer finds in Christ is beautifully portrayed by the analogy in Philemon. Onesimus, guilty of a great offense (vv. 11, 18), was motivated by Paul's love to intercede on his behalf (vv. 10–17). Paul laid aside his rights (v. 8) and became Onesimus' substitute by assuming his debt (vv. 18–19). By Philemon's gracious act, Onesimus was restored and placed in a new relationship (vv. 15–16). In this analogy, we are as Onesimus. Paul's advocacy before Philemon is similar to Christ's work of mediation before the Father. Onesimus was condemned by law but saved by grace.[26]

Apostle Paul on forgiveness

The Church of Corinth was established by Apostle Paul during one of his missionary journeys. But after Paul had left the Church for Ephesus, several issues came up that were highly disgusting and annoying. Some other teachers of the gospel (which he called another gospel) came "preaching themselves" to the members. They presented themselves as more important than Paul whom God had used to establish the Church. You will remember Paul saying to the Corinthians that, Even though you

---

25 *Ibid*
26 *Ibid*

have ten thousands of guardians in Christ, you do not have many fathers. For in Christ Jesus I became your father through the gospel (1 Corinthians 4:15). Some of these preachers divided the Church into several factions, so much that some claimed they belonged to Paul, some to Peter, some to Apollo, some to Christ, and some to other teachers (1 Corinthians 3). How will you feel as a pastor if the credit of your successful labor in a particular station is given to somebody else, or another person appears from nowhere to claim the credit for himself without any reference to your previous effort?

Another bogging incident was the case of incest in this same Church where Paul had labored vigorously. It was highly disgusting and disappointing. But, in spite of all of these (and others not mentioned here), Paul still says,

> *If you forgive anyone, I also forgive him. And what I have forgiven—if there was anything to forgive—I have forgiven in the sight of Christ for your sake. (2 Corinthians 2:10)*

Jesus Christ laid down examples for us

Jesus did not only teach frequently about forgiveness, He also demonstrated His own willingness to forgive. Here are several examples that should encourage us to recognize His willingness to forgive us also:

* Christ forgave the paralyzed man lowered on a mat through the roof (Luke 5:17-26).

* He forgave the woman caught in the act of adultery (John 8:3–11).

* He forgave the woman who anointed His feet with perfume (Luke 7:44–50).

* Peter denied knowing Jesus Christ, yet He forgave him(John18:15–18, 25–27; 21:15–19).

* The criminal on the Cross received Christ's forgiveness (Luke

23:39–43).

* He also forgave those who crucified Him (Luke 23:34).[27]

This is just to mention but a few. And more importantly, John the Baptist when he saw Jesus far off exclaimed, Behold! The Lamb of God, who takes away the sin of the world! (John 1:29). And for the purpose of forgiveness, Christ came to shed His Blood for mankind, because, without the shedding of blood, there is no remission of sins (Matthew 26:28; Hebrew 9:22).

Children forgave the Murderer of their Father

Robert Godwin Sr., a father and a grandfather was senselessly murdered over the Easter weekend after a deranged man, who would later broadcast his actions to the internet, announced he was looking to randomly kill someone. Three of his children gave an interview to CNN on the night of April 17, 17 and they left Anderson Cooper (and quite frankly, anyone watching) in awe at their faith and perspective as they deal with this horrible tragedy. One of the children of the murdered Robert Godwin explained to Cooper what their dad taught them about faith:

The thing I would take away most from my father is he taught us about God, how to fear God, how to love God and how to forgive. Each one of us forgive the killer, the murderer, we want to wrap our arms around him.[28]

This is a mind-blowing testimony. As earlier mentioned, you may not be able to change the past, but with forgiveness, you can actually make the future better.

Deby forgave her father.

The story below is from a dear friend of our family. Permit me to call her Deby (not her real name though but for security purpose).

---

27 New Living Translation (NLT) Life Application Study Bible's Text Note on Matthew 18.
28 http://www.faithwire.com/2017/04/18/children-of-man-murdered-on-facebook-live-give-stunning-testimony-during-anderson-cooper-interview/

I grew up in California and from the age of five without my father in the home. I did not spend very much time with him throughout the years. When his life was going well I would see him more frequently but when he was struggling I would not hear from him for months. As I grew older I began to see the pattern of promises made and promises broken. The alcoholism and the self-deception caused him to believe that he was doing the best he could and that he was a good father. I began to resent the lies, missed birthdays and the promises made—promises broken cycle. When his parents lost their home due to ruined finances and my beloved grandpa was forced to move in to public housing, I blamed their financial distress on my dad's continual legal problems from DUI arrests. I moved across the country when I was 19 and became engaged to be married. After the death of my grandpa, my dad and his mother moved away and I had no information of where they had gone. After nearly a year, we were finally able to get an address for both of them and mail them invitations to the wedding that was to take place in my hometown. My dad called me at my mother's house the day we arrived, one week before the wedding. He pretended to be surprised to reach me. I told him about the wedding, he said he had not received the invitation and would not be able to travel from where he was living. After our wedding, I spoke to my grandmother and what she told me revealed a different. My dad had lied to me, because, he did received the invitation. That was the final blow to our relationship and I walked away determined never to speak to him again.

I came to know Jesus when I was 17 years old and after my marriage, my husband and I attended church, we began growing in our knowledge of God and his word. One Sunday about two years later, I heard a sermon about forgiveness. It seemed as if the pastor was preaching only to me, and the message went straight to my heart. I knew I had to obey the Lord and forgive my dad. I prayed for the strength and then resolve to forgive. I prayed that my forgiveness would be genuine, that the Lord would enable me to really, truly forgive and not look back. I wrote a letter to him explaining that I forgave him whether he wanted it, needed it or even cared. I explained that I had been forgiven much (by Christ), I am also forgiving him from the depth of my heart, and that the past would never be spoken of between us again. I included the photo of our first child who was just six months old. I didn't hear from him though, but every six months, I sent a note with new photos of his two grand-children to him. The children were two and four years old when I received a phone call from my dad and we got a new start. We travelled home that summer to visit my family. While we were there we met him, his wife and her two sons at a park. He met his grandchildren for the first time. Nothing was materially different about my father but I was different and that was all that mattered, I had forgiven him and we would allow the past to stay in the past. Four years later on Christmas night my dad called. He usually called when he had been drinking and was emotional. He told me how much he loved me and my family. They were having to move out of their house by the end of the week but he didn't know where they would be so he couldn't give me an address. Seven months passed and I had not heard from him and had no way of reaching him. While visiting my family that summer, my uncle gave me a phone number for my dad. He had given it to him when they ran into each other in a store. This was the first time they had seen each other for many years. The phone number belonged to a friend of my father that I recognized as someone from my childhood. I waited until I returned home from California to call the number, when I did, I was not prepared for what I would hear. I told the friend who I was and why I was calling. He told me he hadn't seen my dad in a month or more but if he did he would give him my number. I asked him how my dad was; after hesitating and saying my dad wouldn't want him to tell me, he revealed that my father was homeless. I gave the man my home and cell phone numbers and told him if he saw my dad, he should tell him to call me any time of the day or night. After recovering from the shock of that revelation, we began to pray that we would be able to find him. But how do you find a homeless man when you live across the country? Every day I prayed that he would call and that if we never found him, that the Lord would enable me to bear it. Only one week later, I received a call and it was him! After arranging countless details and getting him in to a hotel for a few days, we bought a plane ticket to bring him to the city where I live. Only 10 days after his first call to me, our Sunday School class had completely furnished a one-bedroom apartment only two blocks from my house. Within two weeks of his arrival, he was hired at our church to be on the building crew. He was a painter by trade. He began going to church with us and building friendships in the church.

The following year, while attending an out of town event with a friend, he began asking about salvation. The friend pulled off the highway and led him in prayer of repentance and to faith in Christ! He was baptized on Father's Day. Every Sunday we sit next to each other for worship and he occasionally plays drums in the worship band. We celebrate birthdays and holidays together. We talk about the Lord and what we are learning about him. I marvel at the miracle that has come from that moment of obedience to God's word about forgiveness. Only the Lord can restore the years the locusts have eaten and he deserves all the glory.

I want you to know that Deby was able to forgive her Dad through the help of the Spirit of God. You too can forgive anyone— your Dad, Mom, aunty, brother, sister any relation or friend who has hurt you in the past or now.

Congressman forgives teenager who threatened to kill him

"I will kill Carlos Curbelo." This was posted to Twitter on October 24. Curbelo, a Republican congressman in Florida, responded: Political intoxication is making some Americans more prone to both verbal and physical violence. It's a serious crisis and we all have to do our part to put an end to it. Not sure what's more disturbing; the fact that someone tweeted this or that 4 accounts liked it."

The next day, FBI and local police arrested nineteen-year-old Pierre Alejandro Verges-Castro of Homestead, Florida, for making the death threat on his Twitter account. Curbelo's office thanked the police and said the congressman would continue with his schedule as planned. But that's not the end of the story. Last Thursday, more than a week after the arrest, Curbelo held a news conference with the teenager who threatened to kill him.

Curbelo told reporters: "Today I want everyone to know that I forgave him. As for Pierre, I wish him the best. He made a mistake and his life shouldn't be ruined because of it." Verges-Castro stood silently next to the congressman, who explained that the state attorney still had an open case against the teenager and that Verges- Castro would not be speaking because of that. The next day, Curbelo told CNN's Cuomo Prime Time that he had called authorities to ask if the teenager was truly dangerous or "just some kid who said something I'm sure he really regrets right now." Police told him it was the latter.

So Curbelo asked for a meeting with Verges-Castro. He learned that the teenager was a "really, really good kid" who played the piano and guitar and was going to school to earn an associate degree. "He explained to me that he had some issues in his personal life that he thinks pushed him to do something like this, and he also talked about the toxicity of our politics and how nasty and negative everything is." Curbelo told Cuomo, "I hope this young man can also share his story and we can all learn from it, and it can help put us down a better path–because I'm really worried about things in our country these days." The number of threats made against members of Congress grew from 902 in 2016 to more than two thousand last year. That's forty a week. Carlos Curbelo made headlines, not because he was threatened, but because he forgave the person who threatened him. [29]

---

29 *Dr Jim Denison is the Founder of Denison Forum where he posts Daily Articles. This information is from the daily email I received form Denison Forum on November 5, 2018.*

PRAYER

1. I have been given grace to overcome all sins (Romans 6:14; Titus 2:11). By this same grace, I forgive all.
2. Like Joseph, Stephen and Christ Jesus; I forgive and let go of all my offenders in Jesus' name.

STEPS TOWARDS FORGIVENESS

If you keep hanging on to the past, you will be handicapped all the rest of your life in living for God.

CHAPTER 8 :
STEPS TOWARDS FORGIVENESS

An unexpected hurt or offence from people normally brings pains and wounds. In most cases, forgiveness passes through stages before a complete healing is attained.

A. Stages

I quite agree that, at times, forgiveness is not an easy task. It is highly spiritual. This is why it is only the spiritually mature ones who rely absolutely on the grace of God who can forgive. Forgiveness is the attribute of the strong. A mature Christian has the capacity to absorb the offences and weaknesses of others, not just demand they perform up to the code of ideals.[30]

There are times when demonic spirits may be influencing a man and making it difficult for him to forgive. It will take an experienced and Spirit-filled counselor to be able to discern these types of demonic cases. The stages of healing from the wound caused by people's offenses include the following:

---

30 Stephen Crosby, Online: htt//www.tentmaker.org. accessed July, 2010.

1. Shock: There is always an expression of shock when somebody you least expect says or does something to hurt you.

2. Open wound: No doubt, a wounded heart always follows this sudden shock.

3. Pains: This open wound is followed by different kinds of painful thoughts.

4. Controllable or uncontrollable anger: Make sure you are not consumed by your own anger when you are offended. Dr. John Hunter, the famous English Surgeon and anatomist, maintained that anger has the power to destroy the person who harbors it. While he was presenting a paper on this subject at an academic seminar, he became involved in an argument and his anger became so strong that he had a heart attack and died on the spot.[31] Control your anger at all cost when someone offends you.

5. Contemplated actions: Several thoughts on what to do either to revenge or to let go will normally come to your mind.

B. Things that will help you forgive easily

Before you conclude that someone has indeed offended you, there are certain issues you must address. The following questions are very important. Did I conclude that someone has offended me because

* he refused to do or act in the way I want?

* he always opposed my opinion or offered contrary opinion to mine?

* he does not allow me to control him?

These questions and other related egocentric issues must be out of way

---

31 David Yonggi Cho, *Salvation, Health & Prosperity (Yoido Full Gospel Church, 1967),* pg. 111–3.

before you can establish offense against you. When you see who quickly pick offense at the slightest matter, it is always as a result of innate pride and ego. The best way to go along with people is to give them the right to be what they are, which is different from you or different from what you want them to be.

Have a large mind to accommodate would-be offenders.

The few hints below can be helpful if they are duly followed, to develop and foster a heart of forgiveness.

1. Scriptural injunctions: Apply what the Bible teaches on forgiveness (Ephesians 4:26)
2. Look at the Cross where the sting and poison of all pains had been siphoned (Galatians 6:14).
3. Avoid "nose-pokers"

There are some rumor mongers and busy bodies in the society. Their work is to poke-nose into matters they are not invited to. These are the people I call 'nose- pokers.' They are directly or indirectly part of the agents of Satan with whom he carries out his operation in the world. These types of people never want joyful and happy relation- ship to exist between two friends, a set of people or community at large. They delight in seeing conflicts and divisions escalate. Hence, these people may come to you in the disguise of love, telling you all kinds of negative things concerning the one that has hurt you. All they are out to do is never to heal your wounded heart, but to poison your mind the more. They make it difficult for you to forgive your offender. Hear what the wise King Solomon said, Where there is no wood, the fire goes out; And where there is no talebearer, strife ceases (Proverbs 26:20). Please avoid these kinds of people at all cost.

4. The reality of practical love; Let Christ's love in you be seen at work.

5. Call on God's divine grace: Forgiveness is a highly spiritual phenomenon, and the divine grace of God is highly needed. It is not

by man's strength or power.

For the grace of God that brings salvation has appeared to all men, teaching us that, denying ungodliness and worldly lusts, we should live soberly, righteously, and godly in the present age, looking for the blessed hope and glorious appearing of our great God and Savior Jesus Christ, who gave Himself for us, that He might redeem us from every lawless deed and purify for Himself His own special people, zealous for good works. (Titus 2:11–14)

C. Conflict of memory

Remembrance and forgetting after one might have forgiven an offender are sometimes an ongoing battle in one's mind. Some are of the opinion that if truly you have forgiven, it is wrong to remember the incident again. On the contrary, you may remember occasionally because the make-up of the human brain has a place where information is stored. But the difference is, even though you remember, it is no longer with a revengeful heart or pain. Neither will you attach any guilt to the offence. And sooner or later, the memory fades away from your sub-conscious mind. You will know that forgiveness has begun when you recall those who hurt you and feel the power to wish them well. This is because; genuine forgiveness warms the heart and cools the sting. Moreover, as God's child, you can learn to forgive just as your heavenly Father does, as I have earlier mentioned. How? When He forgives, He forgets. God said, "I, even I, am He who blots out your transgressions for My own sake; And I will not remember your sins" (Isaiah 43:25).

Any time the devil brings pictures reminding you of what someone else did to you, just laugh at the devil and say, "Mr. Devil! That happened all right, but that is just a picture of what happened because I have forgiven that person. As far as I am concerned, that doesn't exist anymore."

So if God can forget about your mistakes and your past, you need to forget about them too! Then you need to forgive and forget about other people's past mistakes. On this, I agree with Kenneth Hagin when he says, "If you really love people and forgive them, you will not keep reminding them of their past mistakes, sins, and failures. You will not keep reminding them about the way they hurt you, let you down, or offended you."[32]

Sometimes ago in a certain country, a leader of the land was offended by a citizen who later pleaded for his forgiveness. But this leader was quoted saying, "Even if I forgive you, I will never, never forget." By this, everyone knew that he was speaking from a bitter and revengeful heart. Few years later, this same leader re- contested as one of the presidential candidates of the country, but one of the issues raised against him was that; "he lacked forgiveness," and so must not be voted for. And truly, he lost the election. I quite agree with Henry W. Beecher who said, "I can forgive, but I cannot forget, is only another way of saying, I will not forgive. Forgiveness ought to be like a cancelled note—torn in two, and burned up, so that it never can be shown against one."[33]

The devil may bring a picture to your mind of something that happened between you and another person. But you do not have to entertain the devil's thoughts. Any time the devil brings such pictures reminding you of what someone else did to you, just laugh at the devil and say, "Mr. Devil! that happened all right. But that is just a picture of what happened because I have forgiven that person. As far as I am concerned, that doesn't exist anymore."

Similarly, do you know that, sometimes, you can forgive others and yet not forgive yourself? So many people battle with self- condemnation just because the devil keeps showing them the ugly pictures of their past sins. Know this for sure that, if you look too much to the back, you will soon be heading that way. If you keep hanging on to the past, you will be handicapped all the rest of your life in living for God. You won't be able to be a successful Christian if you're always looking backward. Sometimes, maybe you look at yourself and say something like, "I am such a failure! I've made such a mess of my life and such a fool of myself!"

---

32 Kenneth E. Hagin, Love: The Way to Victory (USA: Kenneth Hagin Ministry, Inc.), 117.
33 Henry W. Beecher, Online: http//www.tentmaker.org. accessed July 2010.

But the truth is, we have all sinned and missed it from time to time. You have to forgive yourself so that you can go on and succeed in God. You won't be able to succeed in anything if you allow your past to be weighing you down. And as long as you allow the devil to keep reminding you of past sins and failures, he will take advantage of you. Hence, constant dwelling on the past will keep your faith inoperative.

D. Complete healing

A times, forgiveness may not NECESSARILY mean that we should be best of friends forever! It does not sometimes mean that it is a must for us to pick up from where we left if circumstances do not warrant. We thinks that as Christians, after we have forgiven, we need to have a relationship as we had before! Hence, we try to force it and sometimes end up in another pseudo or unhealthy relationship! If it doesn't work out exactly as it used to be, we thought forgiveness has not taken place! Forgiveness may not exactly follow this pattern! However, forgiveness does mean that out of the depth of my heart, I don't have anything against you anymore. I can , and am ready to fellowship with you anytime the opportunity to do so comes up.

This healing process, sometimes, may be gradual, and the deeper you are in Christ and with His love shed upon your heart, the quicker you will get to a state of complete healing. Though you may remember the offence, it will have no effect on you again.

Healing therapy

• Expect hurts from people or loved ones; because to err is human and to forgive is divine. Do not be caught unawares.
• Develop a shock absorber or immunity for hurt by the grace of God.
• Beware of nose-pokers who only come to increase your pains.
• Have a large mind to accommodate would-be offenders.
• Be deeper in love (Romans 5:5; Ephesians 3:17f). "Love covers a multitude of sins" (1 Pet.4:8).
• Apply the Word of God, which is the manual of life.
• Be filled with the Holy Spirit always.

• Always think about your "Big Debt" that Christ cancelled with His precious Blood.

• Meditate on Scriptures instead of thinking on the issues. Ephesians 4:26 says, "In your anger, do not sin. Do not let the sun go down while you're still angry."

Things counselors need to know during counseling sessions

There are things counselors need to know when counseling people who find it difficult to forgive. These include the following:

• Start with a prayer.

• Give your counselee full attention and time to tell his/her story in totality without interruption.

• Be careful or sensitive to know when he is shying away from the truth that will expose his own fault.

• Do not stop your counselee from crying.

• Watch out at times for some unusual manifestations.

• Minister salvation in Christ Jesus.

• Use the Word of God all the time.

• Sympathize, but don't be carried away, and don't compromise the truth.

• Do not try to judge or condemn your counselee.

• Correct and rebuke him where and when necessary.

• Do not force him to forgive, but let it come out of a sincere heart.

• Know when it is necessary (if need be) to bring in the offender to dialogue with the offended.

• Always listen to the voice of the Holy Spirit.

• Don't be discouraged when you are not seeing instant positive change. Leave that for the Holy Spirit and keep on praying for God to perfect His work.

Evidences of unforgiving spirit

Abrupt interaction: his is an act of brushing someone off or cut at shoulder. Developing an avoidance behavior is still evidence that your forgiveness is not down-to-earth. You need not keep at an arm's length if you have forgiven. If you do, then you are still carrying a pain that you think might be puncture again. Several people at this point do say, I have forgiven him, but only that I do not want him to cause me an irreparable harm again. This is quite understood if the offender has not repented nor show any form of remorse.

Dirty look: this has to do with ignoring someone stylistically or sobbing him off. If you have really forgiven, avoid a dirty look attitude.

Critical spirit: if a man has repented truly, and forgiveness has taken place in your heart, you need not to develop a critical spirit against the fellow again.

Intentional coldness (or silence treatment) at the presence or sight of the fellow— silence treatment. Several couples are good using silence treatment whenever there is discord at home. It is still one of the ways to show that you have not genuinely let go issues.

Complaining and grumbling: if you keep on grinding and grumbling over past issues, then forgiveness has not taken place in your heart.

Action & Prayer

1. I disassociate myself from tail bearers, back-biters and whore mongers that keep feeding me with negative information to poison my heart the more against my offenders.

2. Anyone sent to me across my path as stumbling block from satanic world shall miss target in the name of Jesus.

3. Perhaps it is me that needed to be forgiven, I empty myself of all pride and ego. I shall go ahead to seek for my sister/ brother forgiveness.

4. Lord, please heal every wound I sustained due to offenses from others to me.

5. I release everyone from any curse I pronounce on him/ her due to every offence against me.

6. O God, give me a large heart to accommodate every form of offence in Jesus' name.

CHAPTER NINE
LOVE FORGIVES

To forgive is the highest, most
beautiful form of LOVE

CHAPTER 9 :
LOVE FORGIVES

One characteristic of the God-kind of love is that it forgives. God Himself is love and this same love that God is has been shed abroad in our hearts by the Holy Spirit (Romans 5:5KJV). We know that we have passed from death unto life, because we love the brothers. Anyone who does not love remains in death (1 John 3:14; 4:8).

The Scripture above reveals the "love test." We know we have passed from death to life because we love the brethren. As a Christian, you must make the categorical choice to work in love always and forgive others, whatever wrong they might have done against you. Decide that there will never be anybody anywhere that you will begrudge, dislike, or be bitter against by the grace of God. Definitely, there is no love without forgiveness, and there is no forgiveness without love.

It does not matter the extent of hatred and animosity you experience from those around you, you have the obligation as a Christian to love and not hate; hence, you must learn to forgive those who hurt or do you wrong. Consider the Lord Jesus as He was being nailed to the Cross amidst torture and curses. Yet, He looked up to heaven and said, "Father, forgive them; for they know not what they do" (Luke 23:34). That is love! He could have destroyed them all in a moment; but his love overlooked their ignorance and forgave their wrong doings.

Love forgives easily. Do you remember the story of Stephen? The Jews stirred up false charges against him for preaching Jesus and they ordered his execution. The Bible says ". . .as the murderous stones came hurting at him, Stephen … fell to his knees, shouting, 'Lord, don't charge them with this sin!' and with that he died" (Acts 7:59–60 TLB). That is love! Even at the point of death, he did not ask God to revenge for him or punish his accusers; he prayed that God should forgive them.

Can you look into your life and confidently say that you hold nothing against anyone? Can you love the most difficult person even under the most difficult circumstances? It is time to make that choice today, because by God's grace you can! The Bible says, "The love of God is shed abroad in your heart by the Holy Ghost" (Romans 5:5). A heart filled with anger has no room for love, and one forgives to the degree that one loves.

It is time to forgive those who have wronged you and choose to love them. Remember, every man is worth the blood of Jesus Christ. So make up your mind to walk in love today. Moreover, forgiveness should not just be your occasional act; it should be your permanent attitude. Forgiveness is the final form of love, and it is like faith that one keeps reviving on daily basis.

***There is no love without forgiveness, and
there is no forgiveness without love.***

APOSTLE JOHN ON LOVE

Apostle John is popularly called the apostle of love. You will remember that most of his writings center on love, the horizontal and vertical dimensions of love. Let us do a brief inductive study of his writings on love and try to see the indispensable role that love plays in forgiveness.

Love is laying down your life for others

The pivotal verse that holds the whole Scriptures together is John 3:16, which says, For God so loved the world that he gave his one and only Son, that whoever believes in him shall not perish but have eternal life. John seems to draw a complementary parallelism to this verse when in

1 John 3:16 he says, This is how we know what love is: Jesus Christ laid down his life for us. And we ought to lay down our lives for our brothers. So, John 3:16 and 1 John 3:16 go hand in hand. Therefore, you cannot keep on living in hatred with the one you are called to lay down your life for.

Love is a gospel message preached from the beginning

Dear friends, I am not writing you a new command but an old one, which you have had since the beginning. This command is the message you have heard. . . (1 John 2:7–9). This is the message you heard from the beginning: we should love one another (1 John 3:11). When John wrote in this way, he was referring to the gospel message of love in the Old Testament and the teaching of Christ Jesus on love respectively. For example, the law says, "Love the LORD your God with all your heart and with all your soul and with all your strength" (Deuteronomy 6: 5); "Do not seek revenge or bear a grudge against one of your people, but love your neighbor as yourself. I am the LORD" (Leviticus 19:18). Jesus Christ in the same vein quoted this in His teachings when He was confronted with a question about the Law. "Teacher, which is the greatest commandment in the Law? Jesus replied: 'Love the Lord your God with all your heart and with all your soul and with all your mind. This is the first and greatest commandment. And the second is like it: Love your neighbor as yourself.' All the Law and the Prophets hang on these two commandments." (Matthew 22:37–40). Jesus further summarized the whole Old Testament Law under one heading which is Love: "A new command I give you: Love one another. As I have loved you, so you must love one another. By this all men will know that you are my disciples, if you love one another" (John 13:34–35). No wonder Paul also said that love is the fulfillment of the Law (Romans 13:10).

Zac Poonen once wrote, 'Forgive US means, Father, I won't be satisfied if you just forgive me my sins. There are other brothers and sisters around me. I want you to forgive them their sins too.

Hence, according to Apostle John, the whole message of the entire Bible centers on LOVE. The following can be deduced from John's message on love:

* He that hates his brothers is living in total darkness, 1 John 2:9–11.

* He that does not love his brother belongs to the evil one, 1 John 3:10–13.

* He that loves has crossed from death to life, 1 John 3: 14a.

* He that hates is living in death, 1 John 3: 14b.

* He that hates his brother is a murderer, 1 John 3:15.

* Anyone that loves is born of God and knows God, 1 John 4:7.

* Anyone that fails to love does not know God, 1 John 4:8.

* God demonstrates His love to us, 1 John 4:9–12.

* God Himself is love personified, 1 John 4:16.

* There is no fear in love. But perfect love drives out fear, 1 John 4:18.

* A liar claims to love God; but hates his brother, 1 John 4:19–21.

* Obedience to God is the proof of our genuine love to Him, 1 John 5:1–3.

APOSTLE PAUL'S TEACHINGS ON LOVE

Loving others is a continuous debt that must be paid

Let no debt remain outstanding, except the continuing debt to love one another, for he who loves his fellowman has fulfilled the law. The commandments, "Do not commit adultery," "Do not murder,"

"Do not steal," "Do not covet," and whatever other commandment there may be, are summed up in this one rule: "Love your neighbor as yourself" (Romans 13:8–9). Hence, love is a debt that cannot be paid completely. So we must continue to love.

***Can you love the most difficult person even under t
he most difficult circumstances?
Yes! this is what we are called to do as Christians.***

Love is the fulfillment of the Law

You cannot love and at the same time hate. The two cannot co-exist in one person. And you cannot love somebody like yourself and at the same time be hurting him. When you steal, rob, take a bribe, fight, curse, and engage other devilish behaviors, it is a clear indication that the love of Christ is far from you. This is why Paul the Apostle clearly says, therefore love is the fulfillment of the law (Romans 13:10).

Love does not harm his neighbor

Sometimes, it surprises me when some set of people claim that the more they kill people who are not members of their own religion, the more their "god" will reward them. But our God, in the Holy Bible, says, "Love does no harm to its neighbor" (Romans 13:10).

Love says no to vengeance

Do not take revenge, my friends, but leave room for God's wrath, for it is written: It is mine to avenge; I will repay, says the Lord. On the contrary: If your enemy is hungry, feed him; if he is thirsty, give him something to drink. In doing this, you will heap burning coals on his head. Do not be overcome by evil, but overcome evil with good (Romans 12:19–20).

In this age of lawsuit and incessant demands for legal rights, Paul's command sounds almost impossible. When someone hurts you deeply, instead of giving him what he deserves, Paul said to befriend him. Why did Paul tell us to forgive our enemies? Forgiveness can break a cycle of retaliation and lead to mutual reconciliation. It can make the enemy feel ashamed and change his or her ways. Even if the enemy never repents, forgiving him or her will free you of a heavy load of bitterness.[34]Truly speaking, the glory of Christianity is to conquer by forgiveness (Luke 23:34; Acts 7:60).

At this point, permit me to say that you have to be aware of satanic bait. According Strong's Concordance, the Greek word σκάνδαλον (skandalon) really means the trigger of a trap (or a stick for bait of a trap), the means of stumbling block, an offense, a cause for error, generally a snare. It is described as putting a negative cause-and- effect relationship into motion. It is the stick in the trap that springs and closes the trap when the animal touches it. In the same way, the offence of others toward you is a trap and bait to make you fall into sin—the sin of unforgiveness. This is one of the devil's great tactics.

According to Dr. Chris, unforgiveness can provoke bitterness which can provoke closed heaven! You must take heed to yourself that you do not grow bitter against God or man. Truth is that, offences must surely come (Luke 17:1). People must betray you! Yes, your most trusted soul could betray you the most! Those you have helped in the past could betray you! Indeed, someone could have hurt or betray you recently, but you must determine that you will never live your life with wound in your heart. When Satan wants to hinder your prayers and delay your miracle, he will send people to deliberately hurt you in order to make you become embittered. Never make up your mind to embark on revenge mission because the problem with revenge is that it never gets what it wants; it never evens the score, fairness never comes. The chain reaction set off by every act of vengeance always takes its course. It ties both the injured and the injurer to an escalator of pain. . .[35]

Loving others with genuine love is the litmus test of our son-ship as believers. It is impossible for you to love God and at same time hate your pastor, deacon, elder or chorister.

---

34 *NLT Life Application Study Bible, Comments on Romans 12:19–21.*
35 *Dr. Chris, Our Daily Manna: A Devotional Booklet for Champions, December 28, 2011*

Love keeps no record of wrong doings

Love is patient. Love is kind. It does not envy; it does not boast; it is not proud. It is not rude. It is not self-seeking. It is not easily angered, and it keeps no record of wrongs. Love does not delight in evil but rejoices with the truth. It always protects, always trusts, always hopes, and always perseveres. Love never fails. (1 Corinthians 13:1–8)

If love does not keep record of wrongs, then why do you keep one? I went to the house of a Christian couple sometime in the past to settle a conflict between them. As soon as I entered, the husband said, "Pastor, you are welcome! But before you say anything, give me just one minute." He rushed into the bedroom and came out with a notebook which he handed over to me to open and read. I opened the first page and saw a caption that read, twenty-six (26) sins my wife committed. We have several people like that in Christendom that keep records of their brothers' sins.

Love is a fruit of the regenerated human spirit

The picture of the heart and the condition of an unregenerate person are well explained in the Scriptures.

The acts of the sinful nature are obvious: sexual immorality, impurity and debauchery; idolatry and witchcraft; hatred, discord, jealousy, fits of rage, selfish ambition, dissensions, factions and envy; drunkenness, orgies, and the like. I warn you, as I did before, that those who live like this will not inherit the kingdom of God (Galatians 5:19–21). Do you not know that the wicked will not inherit the kingdom of God? Do not be deceived. Neither the sexually immoral nor idolaters nor adulterers nor male prostitutes nor homosexual offenders nor thieves nor the greedy nor drunkards nor slanderers nor swindlers will inherit the kingdom of God (1 Corinthians 6:9– 10). But the cowardly, the unbelieving, the vile, the murderers, the sexually immoral, those who practice magic arts, the idolaters and all liars—their place will be in the fiery lake of burning sulfur. This is the second death. (Revelation 21:8)

But the fruit of the Spirit is love, joy, peace, patience, kindness, goodness, faithfulness, gentleness and self-control. Against such things there is no law (Galatians 5:22–23).

The unregenerate heart cannot know the beauty of agape love and genuine forgiveness. If Christ the living Son of God is really the One that is enthroned and ruling in your heart, then His love must be shed upon your heart. Loving others with genuine love is the litmus test of our sonship as believers. For example, how can you love God and also hate your pastor, or deacon or deaconess, or elder, or choir member, or your unit leader, and so on?

A true believer cannot love God and at the same time hate men. Claiming to love God either through your religious commitment in the Church and at the same time hating her member(s), or anyone at all is an indication of unregenerate heart. Christ's love is shed abroad in a regenerate heart, and it cannot harbor the darkness of hatred toward others. Check your life, have you really been born again?

Moreover, hatred does the work of stealing, killing, and destroying anything it touches. It takes on the characteristics of Satan and is pleased over the misery of its victims. The most devastating part of hatred, however, is its self-destructiveness; for when a man harbors hatred in his heart, he becomes negative. Thus he himself becomes the first victim of his own hatred.

To forgive is the highest, most beautiful form of love.

Love has endless dimensions

I pray that out of his glorious riches He may strengthen you with power through his Spirit in your inner being, so that Christ may dwell in your hearts through faith. And I pray that you, being rooted and established in love, may have power, together with all the saints, to grasp how wide and long and high and deep is the love of Christ, and to know this love that surpasses knowledge—that you may be filled to the measure of all the fullness of God. (Ephesians 3:16–19)

From the passage quoted above, we can understand the love of God through Jesus Christ:

The "width" (how wide) of Christ's love means that there is no tribe, tongue, language, or race that this love does not embrace. No racial or tribal discriminations.

The "length" (how long) of Christ's love means that His love began from eternity past and into eternity to come, having no beginning and no end. More so that love began with God who is an "eternal, uncreated being."

The "height" (how high) of Christ's love means that this love reaches to the heaven of heavens.

The "depth" (how deep) of Christ's love means that this love is unfathomable.

A heart filled with anger has no room for love.

Faith works by love

Truly speaking, love, forgiveness, and faith are inseparable triplet that every believer in Christ Jesus must possess. For in Christ Jesus neither circumcision nor uncircumcision has any value. The only thing that counts is faith expressing itself through love (Galatians 5:6). Similarly, never forget the three powerful resources you always have available to you: love, faith (prayer), and forgiveness.

Love makes forgiveness possible

The love of God has been shed upon your hearts by the Holy Spirit. This means that God even furnishes the love for you and me to forgive with. But too many believers make the mistake of going by their head-knowledge instead of staking their life at the Word of God. Are you not glad God said I will not remember your iniquities (Isaiah 43:25; Psalm 103:3)? Another Scripture says, He will cast all our sins into the depths of the sea (Micah 7:19; Hebrew 8:12; 10:17). Is that not wonderful? If we have repented and asked for God's forgiveness, God does not remember that you and I ever did anything wrong. You may still want to ask, "How can God do that?" Because the Bible says that love covers or blot out a multitude of sins (1 Peter 4:8).

So divine love does not only forgive, it forgets. That is the way God wants us to forgive too. And we can forgive and forget because God has already implanted His love in our hearts. Therefore, there is no excuse for failure in our ability to forgive. According to Robert Muller, "To forgive is the highest, most beautiful form of love. In return, you will receive untold peace and happiness."[36] Hence, if we love someone the way Christ loves us, we will be willing to forgive. If we have experienced God's grace, we will want to pass it on to others. And remember, grace is undeserved favor. Hence, there is no love without forgiveness, and there is no forgiveness without love.

A Jewish Nurse treated killer with grace

Ari Mahler also made headlines over the weekend, not because he is one of 2.9 million registered nurses in the US, but because of the way he treated one patient. Mahler was on duty at Allegheny General Hospital when Robert Bowers allegedly went on a shooting rampage that left eleven people (Jews) dead. When Bowers was brought to his hospital, the Jewish nurse treated him with grace.

"I didn't say a word to him about my religion," Ari wrote on Facebook last Saturday. "I chose not to say anything to him the entire time. I wanted him to feel compassion. I chose to show him empathy. I felt that the best way to honor his victims was for a Jew to prove him wrong." Mahler said that his father is a rabbi and that he experienced "a lot" of anti-Semitism as a kid. He explained his motives for treating Bowers as he did: "Love. That's why I did it. Love as an action is more powerful than words, and love in the face of evil gives others hope. It demonstrates humanity. It reaffirms why we're all here." Let your light shine before others.[37]

---

36 *Robert Muller, Online: http//www.inspirationalspark.com/forgiveness-quotes. html. accessed July 2010.*
37 *Dr Jim Denison Daily Articles, November 5, 2018.*

In his emphasis on the need for believers to forgive their offenders, Pastor Enoch A. Adeboye has a bit different opinion. Adeboye affirmed that

> *Christ Jesus (according to Matthew 6:12), did not say, "Help us to forgive." If you want to forgive, it is in your power. The grace is available. The issue is whether you are willing or not. Contrary to the prayer of some, you do not require any further assistance from God to forgive. He has already put what you need to do so in place. If you fail to forgive others, your sins will be recorded and held against you, starting from that moment you failed to forgive.*[38]

Nevertheless, the fact that you need God every day is the reason you cannot afford to live in unforgiveness.

---

[38] *Pastor E. A. Adeboye, Open Heaven: A Daily Devotional Guide, December 26, 2011*

PRAYER

1. I begin to operate in the spirit of genuine agape loves from now onward in Jesus' name.

2. Offenses of others shall not be bait of destruction for me in Jesus' name.

3. Oh LORD, let your love dominate me to forgive others in Jesus' name.

4. The Scripture says loves covers a multitude of sins. I therefore clothe myself in love against all form of revenge in Jesus' name.

5. I conquer every satanic battle against me as I forgive my offenders in Jesus' name.

CHAPTER TEN
PRAYING FOR OR AGAINST YOUR ENEMIES

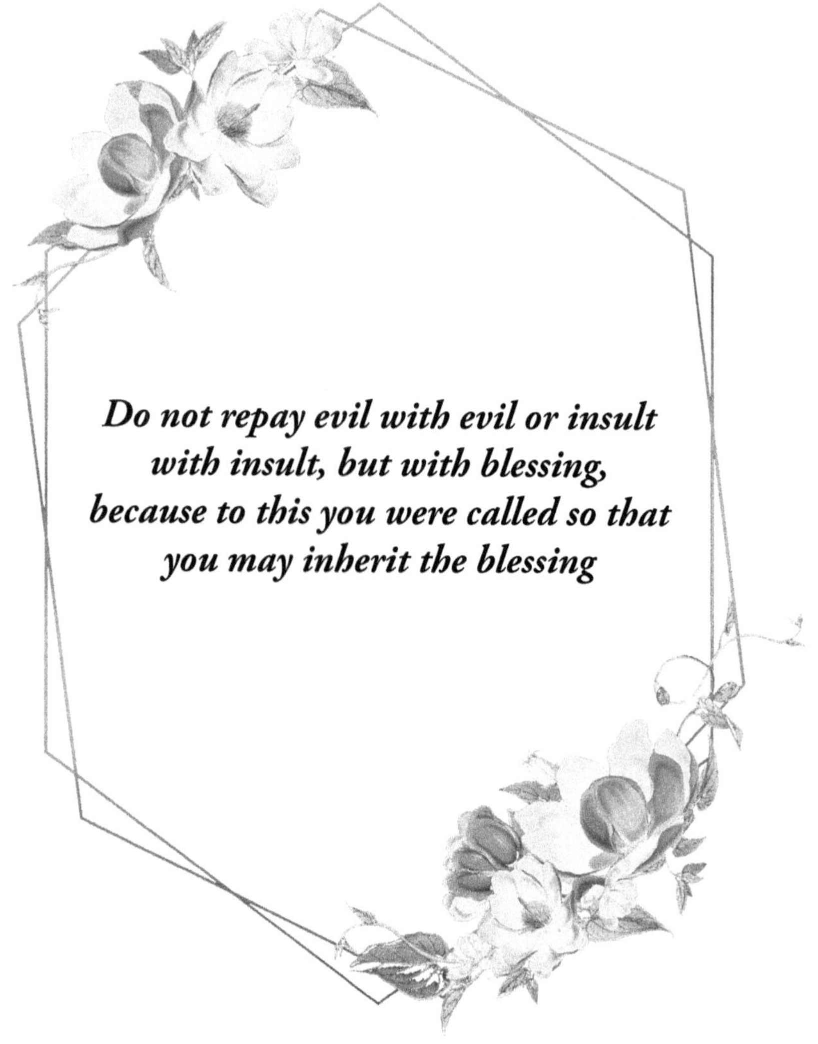

Do not repay evil with evil or insult
with insult, but with blessing,
because to this you were called so that
you may inherit the blessing

CHAPTER 10 : PRAYING FOR OR AGAINST YOUR ENEMIES

You have heard that it was said, "Love your neighbor and hate your enemy." But I tell you: Love your enemies and pray for those who persecute you, that you may be sons of your Father in heaven. He causes his sun to rise on the evil and the good, and sends rain on the righteous and the unrighteous. If you love those who love you, what reward will you get? Are not even the tax collectors doing that? And if you greet only your brothers, what are you doing more than others? Do not even pagans do that? Be perfect, therefore, as your heavenly Father is perfect. (Matthew 5:43–48)

Satan's deceptive strategy among the believers

One of the greatest successes of Satan is to make man believe that his enemy is his fellow brother(s). Some set of people see another set as their enemies. Believers in one Church see other believers in the same or another Church as their enemies. This is why in Africa today, many never believe in natural death. They always suspect that someone is responsible for the death, sickness, failures, and other calamities that happen to man. Another deceptive way of Satan's schemes is to be there and make you believe he is not there. Recently, a seminary student here in the United States told me that one of his professors said there is no demon. The professor added that it is because of lack of civilization and low literacy level in Africa and other third world nations that they believe in the existence of demons. This professor is missing out this truth of God's Word:

> *For our struggle is not against flesh and blood, but against the rulers, against the authorities, against the powers of this dark world and against the spiritual forces of evil in the heavenly realms. (Ephesians 6:12)*

The passage above is not limited to any geographical location. It is universal. However, the reality of satanic and demonic activities in the Western world is not farfetched. The devil and his demons are at work in Africa in the practices like idolatry, fetish, spell, witchcraft, and the likes. But in the Western world, the devil changes his approach and methodology. For instance, the current moves of gay marriage, lesbianism, homosexuality, Satanism, high rate of divorce, drug addictions, removal of Christian and biblical values from the government and public places, attempt to remove Christ from Christmas, legalization of abortion (of which over 60 million unborn babies were killed recently) and the similar practices are all expressions of satanic and demonic activities.

Let us use this medium to "dig down" into Satan's deception, because it is high time we know our real enemies and how to wage war against them. Your real enemy is not your fellow brother that has flesh and blood in him. Satan and his demons are our real enemies and are everywhere as we have seen in Ephesians 6:10–12.

Demons cannot rest without being in the possession of somebody through whom they can find expression.

Knowing your real enemies

When the Bible talks about rulers, authorities, powers, and principalities of this dark world, and the spiritual forces of evil in the heavenly realms, it is actually talking about the devil and the company of his demons at various cosmic regions of the universe. Let me at this juncture borrow from the works of T. L. Osborn on demons and Satan, and relate it to the subject under discussion.

Demons are actual personalities, which are wicked, hateful and destructive. Demon-spirits are personalities, just like human- spirits, but they have no bodies in which to dwell. We are spirits with bodies. Our spirits are from God; demon-spirits belong to Satan, to whom they sold themselves when they rebelled against God in the beginning, consequently causing man to fall in the Garden of Eden.[39]

Difference between the body and the spirit

A clear understanding of the difference between spirit and body will help you to understand the work of demons better.

I have a body, but I am a spirit. I (my spirit) dwell in my body. I express myself (my spirit) within the faculties of my body. Someone else can see my body, but he cannot see me because the real "me" is a spirit living inside this body of mine. My body is simply the house I (my spirit) live in. Someday, my body will die and return to the dust, but I (my spirit) shall never die. I shall return to God from whom I came.

I (my spirit) am a personality. I express myself through my body. If you would take away my body, I (my spirit) could not express myself. Cut off my tongue, and my spirit will not talk. Destroy my ears and I will not hear. Put out my eyes and I will not see. Even though my eyes are blind, my ears are deaf, and my tongue is cut off, still my spirit is there, but it cannot see, hear, or speak. It is difficult to express myself, thus making me handicapped.

Then proceed to cut off my legs and arms, and destroy my sense of smell and vocal cords and still you have not destroyed my spirit, but my spirit can no longer express itself. My spirit still has a body, but its faculties of expression have been destroyed. Now you can understand what I mean when I talk about the difference between the spirit and the body, or the difference between me and my body.[40]

---

39 T. L. Osborn, *Healing the Sick (Tulsa, Okla: Osafo Publication), 115.*
40   *Ibid*

The mode of operation of demons

Demons are evil spirits without bodies with which to express themselves. They long to find expression in the world, but cannot do so until they are in possession of some body. Now you can understand why the evil spirit which was cast out of a demon-possessed man had no rest and could not be satisfied, because he was a spirit of Satan sent forth to destroy and kill. When he could not find expression in a body, he was tormented until he, with the aid of seven other spirits more wicked than himself, was able to re-enter the man and again find expression for his hatred and destruction (Matthew12:43).

Remember, I said a demon is a personality—a spirit, just like you and me. And as you yearn to do good, to speak kind words, to hear music, to see the flowers, to express yourself in every conversation, and to respond to every impulse with some expression, even so demon-spirits yearn to express themselves. But since they have no bodies of their own, they must wander through the land (Matthew 12:43) seeking somebody whom they can inhabit and find expression to carry out their mission of evil. Demons delight to use human lips to do their dirty works. Their choice power to defile, to destroy, or to lead astray is through the use of human instrumentality.

God must use human instruments, anointed by the Holy Spirit, to bless, to inspire, to encourage, and to lift up those who need His divine help. The Holy Scripture was written by Holy MEN of God who were moved by the Spirit of God. The message of "Good News" must be spread and reported by human lips. God uses human instruments to minister to the human family; likewise, Satan uses human instruments (along with evil spirits) to destroy the human family.[41]

It is a pity that man would yield himself to the devil as a medium through which his fellow human would be destroyed. How often Satan uses some vile men or women to defile innocent boys and girls, then send such boys and girls out as his agents into public schools and colleges to

---

41 Ibid, 116.

defile the minds of others who are innocent.

Your real enemy you need to wrestle with is not your fellow brother. But the one (without blood and flesh—the devil and his demons), who peradventure hides himself within that man or woman and works in deception, he is your real enemy.

Understanding who Satan is

Satan is the "being" who is ruling the earth (the god of this world) today, who sits as the prince of nations. He is the author of all human miseries and sorrows, of diseases and pains, yes, of death itself. He is the king and ruler of all demon-spirits.

He rules the dark hosts of hell. His chief desire and design is to destroy human life and the fellowship between God and man. We can best understand who Satan is by his names given in the Bible.

In Matthew 13:19, 38, he is called the "wicked one." In verse 39, he is called the "enemy," and the "devil." Devil means "accuser" (who accuses believers day and night), "defamer," or "slanderer." In Revelation 12:10, he is called the "adversary," compared to a "roaring lion," seeking whom he may devour (1 Pet.5:8). In Revelation 20:2, he is described by a group of names almost too hideous to contemplate: "the dragon, that old serpent, which is the Devil, and Satan." In John 8:44, he is called by Jesus a "murderer," a "liar," and "the father of all lies." In Matthew 4:3, he is called the "tempter." In Matthew 12:24, the "prince of the demons." In Ephesians 2:2, the "prince of the power of the air." In John 14:30, the "prince of this world." In 2 Corinthians 11:3, he is known as the "corrupter of the minds."[42]

These names and many more show us the terrible nature of Satan and of his army of demon-spirits. Satan rules these demonic spirits (beings) as they work day and night at their wicked plots to destroy and mar the wonders and beauty of God's creation. No wonder the Bible says, He

---

42   *Ibid, 117.*

who sins is of the devil, for the devil has sinned from the beginning. For this purpose the Son of God was manifested, that He might destroy the works of the devil (1 John 3:8).

Man—the prized possession of demons

Since a human body has the broadest means of expression, having been the only one made in the likeness of God, demons seek as their highest prize to enter human beings. In the body of a man or woman, demons have the broadest scope of manifestation and expression. But when they cannot find this most prized position of dwelling, then a body of less expression will do. But one thing is certain: they cannot rest without being in possession of somebody through whom they can find expression.

Perhaps now you can understand better why, when Jesus went to cast out the legion of demons from the maniac, the demons begged, saying, "Let us go into the swine then." And upon being cast out of the man, they entered the whole herd of swine and they all ran into the water and were drowned.

Since demon-spirits are actual personalities, they manifest their own personalities in the persons whom they possess. There are various classes or types of demon- spirits just as there are different types of people. The Bible records many different types of demon-spirits at work. The tragedy of ignorance in Christendom is that many have not been taught what the Bible clearly sets forth about the work of demons. Some people who understand the existence of demons have been influenced to fear them, all because of a lack of understanding of their legal defeat by the Cross of Christ Jesus.[43]

The reason I have gone this far is to let you understand that your real enemy whom you need to wrestle with is not your fellow brother. But the one (without blood and flesh), who peradventure hides himself within that man or woman and works in deception, is the arch enemy—devil (and his demons). Satan is the one opposing you, but in deception, he

---

43 T.L. Osborn, 118.

turns off your eyes from himself and makes you believe that your fellow human being is your enemy. A demon needs a house or medium that will host him before he can attack you. This is why the Bible says,

> *Finally, my brethren, be strong in the Lord and in the power of His might. Put on the whole armor of God that you may be able to stand against the wiles of the devil. For we do not wrestle against flesh and blood, but against principalities, against powers, against the rulers of the darkness of this age, against spiritual hosts of wickedness in the heavenly places. (Ephesians 6:10–12)*

It does not matter "the prophet," "deliverance minister," or "Man of God" who has told you that your mother is the one behind your misfortunes, as the case is in most places in Africa. Please turn off your eyes from your mummy, and fight your real enemies—Satan and his cohorts. They are the real enemies behind the scene. I have heard series of stories where people stabbed or shot relations to death just because some fake prophets or herbalists told them that those relations were the ones they needed to eliminate if they wanted to make progress in life. However, despite killing the said relations, their calamities keep on increasing.

Jesus in His earthly ministry needed not to remove his collar and suit with profuse sweat before he sent them (the demons) out of any one they possessed. He cast out the evil spirits with a word.

How Jesus handled cases of demon possessions

Let us learn this little lesson from Jesus Christ. A man was possessed with legion of demon and was disturbing the peace of a whole community. I thought Jesus would call fire from heaven to destroy him since a verse in the Old Testament says, you shall not permit a sorceress to live (Exodus 22:18), but Jesus cast out the demons in him, and the man became useful to the society.

> *And when He got into the boat, he who had been demon- possessed begged Him that he might be with Him. However, Jesus did not permit him, but said to him, "Go home to your friends, and tell them what great*

things the Lord has done for you, and how He has had compassion on you." (Mark 5:18–19)

Jesus immediately sent him forth to go and herald the gospel of God's compassion to the world of lost sinners.

Mary Magdalene was a woman possessed with seven evil spirits, but when she met the Savior, the Savior turned her to a lady evangelist. "Now when He rose early on the first day of the week, He appeared first to Mary Magdalene, out of whom He had cast seven demons" (Mark 16:9 and Luke 8:1f). When evil spirits are cast out, the people they possessed turn out to be instruments in God's hand. There are scores of similar stories in the Bible.

Jesus in His earthly ministry cast out these unclean demonic spirits with word of authority. He needed not to remove his collar

And when He had called His twelve disciples to Him, He gave them power over unclean spirits, to cast them out, and to heal all kinds of sickness and all kinds of diseases ... And these signs will follow those who believe: In My name they will cast out demons; they will speak with new tongues; they will take up serpents; and if they drink anything deadly, it will by no means hurt them; they will lay hands on the sick, and they will recover. (Matthew 10:1; Mark 16:17–18)

In the Old Testament period, the Law says, you shall not permit a sorceress to live (Exodus 22:18). But I think the gospel truth that Christ is passing to us here is that, cast that evil spirit out of a sorcerer, and when the spirit is gone, the real man can turn out to be instrument in God's hand. In my short time in ministry, I have come across many people with demonic spirits whom God set free after they received the gospel message and today they are waxing stronger in Christ.

Bless those who curse you

Bless those who persecute you; bless and do not curse. Rejoice with those who rejoice; mourn with those who mourn. Live in harmony with

one another. Do not be proud, but be willing to associate with people of low position. Do not be conceited. Do not repay anyone evil for evil. Be careful to do what is right in the eyes of everybody. If it is possible, as far as it depends on you, live at peace with everyone. (Romans12:14–18)

Let us try to examine these two verses of the Holy Bible. According to Jesus' teaching:

But I tell you: Love your enemies and pray for those who persecute you, that you may be sons of your Father in heaven (Matthew 5:44-45).

According to Apostle Paul

Bless those who persecute you; bless and do not curse. (Romans12:14)

Let us go into the Scriptures together to dig out relevant issues on this. God told his covenant son Abraham:

I will make you into a great nation and I will bless you; I will make your name great, and you will be a blessing. I will bless those who bless you, and whoever curses you I will curse; and all peoples on earth will be blessed through you (Genesis 12:2–3).

In the same way, being born again makes you a seed of Abraham, so you are a blessed child, not a cursed child.

Christ redeemed us from the curse of the law by becoming a curse for us, for it is written: "Cursed is everyone who is hung on a tree. He redeemed us in order that the blessing given to Abraham might come to the Gentiles through Christ Jesus, so that by faith we might receive the promise of the Spirit (Galatians 3:13–14). If you belong to Christ, then you are Abraham's seed and heirs according to the promise. (Galatians 3:29)

Many people do not know the riches of the glory and blessing they have in Christ. There are so many ministers of God that claim to be specialists in removing curses from people's lives. We have seen various revival handbills, posters, and advertisements telling people to come to the great men of God that would help them remove the curses of life over them.

But the truth that sets free is that, at the point of conversion, you have entered a new family where curses can no longer operate when you make use of the new power at work in you. The Bible says,

> *Christ redeemed us from the curse (Galatians 3:13); Do not repay evil with evil or insult with insult, but with blessing, because to this you were called so that you may inherit a blessing (1 Peter 3:9); "Praise be to the God and Father of our Lord Jesus Christ, who has blessed us in the heavenly realms with every spiritual blessing in Christ. (Ephesians 1:3)*

You are no longer a candidate for a curse. According to the Scriptures:

> *God is not a man, that he should lie, nor a son of man, that he should change his mind. Does he speak and then not act? Does he promise and not fulfill? I have received a command to bless; he has blessed, and I cannot change it. No misfortune is seen in Jacob, no misery observed in Israel. The LORD their God is with them; the shout of the King is among them. God brought them out of Egypt; they have the strength of a wild ox. There is no sorcery against Jacob, no divination against Israel. It will now be said of Jacob and of Israel, "See what God has done!"*

> *The people rise like a lioness; they rouse themselves like a lion that does not rest till he devours his prey and drinks the blood of his victims. Then Balak said to Balaam, "Neither curse them at all nor bless them at all! Balaam answered, "Did I not tell you I must do whatever the LORD says?" (Number 23: 19–26)*

Any time Prophet Balaam wanted to curse these blessed people of God, God turned his tongue to bless them. This means that as a child of God; "you are 'un-curse-able', and you deserve no curse." Those who curse you are only cursing themselves, so anyone who is cursing you is only wasting his time, because an undeserved curse never comes to rest (Proverbs 26:2 NIV). Every tongue that is set to curse you shall be condemned. Prophet Isaiah attests to this when he says,

No weapon formed against you shall prosper, and every tongue which rises against you in judgment you shall condemn. This is the heritage of the servants of the LORD, and their righteousness is from me, says the LORD. (Isaiah 54:17 KJV)

Know for sure that the children of God have a curse-repellant nature as part of their new nature in Christ Jesus. Even the Goliath of old cursed David the anointed son of God in the names of his gods and goddesses (1 Samuel 17:43), but it was to no avail. And unfortunately, for him, he could not live to tell the story, because God indeed gave his flesh to the birds of the air for a feast (1 Samuel 17:45–54).

Hence, engaging in curses with those who curse you is like revenging for yourself. It is a serious declination to the arm of the flesh. And when you are not walking in the Spirit, you become vulnerable (Romans 8:1–15). At this juncture, if the one that is cursing you is operating with a higher authority than you, you can be rest assured that his curses will affect you. But when you remain in the Spirit, you remain seated with Christ. And at this realm, you are operating at the highest level that is far above powers and principalities (Ephesians 2:6–7).

Sometimes ago in a particular village, a very wayward young lady was raining dangerous and heavy curses on a child of God whom God has been using to evangelize the land just because of a little matter for which he was even innocent. But he kept quiet without uttering a word. Surprisingly, everything she uttered in her word against this child of God happened to her exactly in less than seven months. Her mother, who was in her middle age, died of a terrible sickness that came from nowhere. Her uncle who was living in the same house died as well. Other terrible misfortunes attacked the entire house. But the young man continued to wax stronger and stronger. Those relations of hers who were affected were all there when she was raining the curses that night but failed to stop her. Please, do not stay in an atmosphere where people are throwing bombs of curses. It is demonic.

Now I understand why the Bible says, "Pray for those who curse you." It is very possible that if this child of God had prayed, the curses might have been neutralized and the lives of these victims spared. If truly you are God's servant, it may never go well in life with anyone that curses you (Genesis12:1–4). I think this is why the Bible commands you to pray for the person that curses you as if interceding for a soul of an unbeliever. To the body of believers, Jesus said,

> *If you forgive the sins of any, they are forgiven them; if you retain the sins of any, they are retained. (John 20:23)*

Apostle Paul understood this truth when he said to the Corinthian church,

> *If you forgive anyone, I also forgive him. And what I have forgiven—if there was anything to forgive—I have forgiven in the sight of Christ for your sake, lest Satan should take advantage of us; for we are not ignorant of his devices." (2 Corinthians 2:10–11)*

Paul equally added,

> *We work hard with our own hands. When we are cursed, we bless; when we are persecuted, we endure it; when we are slandered, we answer kindly. Up to this moment we have become the scum of the earth, the refuse of the world. (1 Corinthians 4:12–13)*

I, however, don't doubt what Dr. Albert Yeyeodu once said that "curse (or curses) rests upon a disobedient child of God. It is important to know that disobedience invites a curse, whereas, obedience invites blessing. This explains the sort of confusion the church in Nigeria is experiencing today."[44] Similarly, Pastor Enoch

A. Adeboye maintained, "The rate at which ministers of God are having AIDS/ HIV today is highly frightening. AIDS is a curse for disobedience."[45] A true child of God should live in obedience to the Word of God.

---

44 *Dr. Albert Yeyeodu, A lecturer at Physic Department of LAUTECH, Ogbomosho-Nigeria, 2010.*
45 *Pastor E. A. Adeboye*

At the point of conversion, you have entered a new family where curses can no longer operate as you make use of the new power at work in you.

Ignorance on rampage in Christendom

It is quite unfortunate today that so many people travel far and near to mountains of prayers to pray or to see "prophets" so that God will help kill their fellow beings that they see as their enemies. What a big ignorance! Little do they know that God has and will never enter into the business of an assassin or hired killer. And besides, He has no delight in the death of sinners, but for them to come to the saving knowledge of His dear Son, Jesus Christ.

A friend of mine was invited by a friend to his Church during his Church's special prayer meeting that was coupled with fasting. At the middle of the prayer, "the man of God" said, "It is now time for the business of the day." At this juncture, everybody began to open his or her pocket and bag to bring out either picture or a piece of cloth. Little did he know that "the man of God" (MOG) had told the people on the first day of the prayer to come with any item or material belonging to anyone they know is their enemy, who is hindering their progress in life. The pews were filled to the brim as people queued before this man of God who brought out a bottle of oil and was anointing those materials and shouting 'holy ghost fire; consume them; Die! Die! Die!' By this act, he convinced them that those enemies would die between seven to fourteen days. The person my friend followed to that Church brought out the picture that carried his own father's face. He also joined in calling "holy ghost fire" to consume his father since many prophets and prophetesses had convinced him that his own father was the one behind his misfortune. What a big deception! I usually call these types of prophets "modernized spiritualists, herbalists, or religious hired assassins."

However, the answer to this big ignorance and deception is not farfetched. In Africa, the general view is that, all evil happenings and misfortunes are always attributed to the handiworks of enemies or evil spirits. And in African Traditional Religion (ATR) or according to Africa-Worldview, it is a normal thing for people to run to herbalists (spiritualists) who will help to appeal to the spirits or help in killing one's enemies through charms, incantation, or invocation of evil powers. Consequently, when people turn Christians, they still carry this mentality along, and this is why they always run to such prophets or "men of God" who will help them to pray for the death of their so-called human enemies. And may I say that, if peradventure you are able to kill somebody by this kind of prayer, "you are the killer," not God.

Glory be to God that he is not a son of man, and so does not answer this kind of prayers, or else we would have finished killing one another, because you yourself may be an enemy to another person who is also praying against you to die.

* The one you call your enemy may be the one Jesus Christ calls His friend.

* The one you are cursing may be the one the Lord is busy blessing.

* The one you are calling fire upon may be the one He is interceding for.

* God does not want anyone to perish (Matthew18:14).

This is ignorance on rampage, because no amount of prayer can kill the devil and demons. They are spirit beings and cannot die. They will be judged and condemned at last and be banished to their eternal destination in hell (Revelation 20). But believers in Christ Jesus have the power to cast out, rebuke, and command them.

In the same vein, this kind of prayer reminds us of the error of Christ's Apostles about how to handle your enemy.

Now it came to pass, when the time had come for Him to be received up, that He steadfastly set His face to go to Jerusalem, and sent messengers before His face. And as they went, they entered a village of the Samaritans, to prepare for Him. But they did not receive Him, because His face was set for the journey to Jerusalem. And when His disciples James and John saw this, they said, "Lord, do You want us to command fire to come down from heaven and consume them, just as Elijah did?" But He turned and rebuked them, and said, You do not know what manner of spirit you are of. For the Son of Man did not come to destroy men's lives but to save them. And they went to another village. (Luke 9:51–56)

James and John wanted Christ to call down fire to consume the people that rejected him. But Christ Jesus simply answered, "He is not a killer but the Savior; For the Son of Man did not come to destroy men's lives but to save them. And they went to another village." If it were today's men of God, they would have quickly commanded "holy ghost fire" to consume these Samaritans. Similarly, Apostle Peter also drew a sword and cut off the ear of one of those that came to arrest Jesus, but He rebuked Peter for this (Matthew 26:51–54).

Other reasons why we must love our enemies

In real life, these categories of people are commonly tagged as enemies:

• Anyone that hates you.
• He that does not love your progress in life.

• He that is always looking for your downfall.
• Anyone that is always wishing you evil.
• Anyone that is always opposing your side of view.

According to Roland S. Babatunde, the following are some of the reasons why we must love our enemies:

✳ God loves those ones you call your enemies, 1 Timothy 2:3–5.

✳ We are in the light and are the light of the world, Matthew 5:14–15.

✳ A sinner's soul or salvation is precious to God's heart, Ezekiel 18:23.

✳ A sinner can later repent of his evil way and turn to God, Ezekiel

33:19; 20:13.

✶ Failure to revenge will cause you to see God's miracles, Psalm 37:9; Job 42:10.

✶ Failure to revenge brings glory to God, Matthew 5:16.

✶ God commands us not to revenge, Matthew 5:44; Luke 6:27–28.

✶ To revenge is an evil thing. It is like taking law into one's hand, Luke 6.

✶ A revengeful heart gives the devil or the enemy a legal ground against you, Romans 12:21.

✶ Only God knows the measure of penalty to pay to an offender. We don't know and cannot measure it.

✶ Revenge is of God, not man, Deuteronomy 32: 35; Romans 12:19.

✶ You will experience a peace of mind when you do not revenge, Rom.12:18.[46]

As young minister of God, irrespective of oppositions and hurts from any church member, I have learned never to treat anyone as enemy.

The wise King Solomon said,

> *If you are sensible you will control your temper. When someone offends you, it is great virtues to (forgive him) ignore it (Proverbs 19:11 GNB). He also added, "Do not take it on yourself to repay a wrong. Wait for the LORD to handle the matter." (Proverbs 20:22 GNB/NLT)*

Many believers fear the devil more than God. They believe in what the enemy can do instead of trusting God's covenant of protection.

---

46 *Rowland S. Babatunde, A Lecture Note (2nd ECWA Amilegbe, Ilorin 2010).*

How then do I pray for an enemy who is after my life?

You may want to ask how then do I pray for my enemy who is evidently after my downfall and my death? But the real question is, How should I be afraid of an enemy whose none of his weapons fashioned against me can ever harm me? I am dwelling under a divine Shadow, where the divine presence abides. The true gospel message here is that, the body of Christ must be delivered from all forms of teachings and prayers that will continually put them under the bondage of fear of enemies, either Satan, demons, or other fellow human beings. Many believers fear the devil more than God. They believe in what the enemy can do instead of trusting God's covenant of protection and all His promises that are yes and amen in Christ Jesus (2 Corinthians 1:20). But as God's children, we must know that it is God alone that has the final say over our lives. It is needless to fear enemy. Hence, the truth that must be taught to every believer is that, everyone must desist from whatsoever secret sin he/she is indulging in, that is making the enemy gain upper hand in his/her life.

Back to Christ's Word in Matthew 5:43–48:

> *You have heard that it was said, "You shall love your neighbor and hate your enemy. But I say to you, love your enemies, bless those who curse you, do good to those who hate you, and pray for those who spitefully use you and persecute you, that you may be sons of your Father in heaven; for He makes His sun rise on the evil and on the good, and sends rain on the just and on the unjust . . .*

From the passage above, this is the new order our Lord Jesus Christ gave his Church. This new order is superior to that which was in the Law of Moses. No wonder, even at the point of death on the Cross, He cried; "Father forgive them. . ." And this is why when you do the thorough exegesis of the New Testament from Matthew to Revelation, you cannot see anywhere that prayers for the death of one's enemy are being offered. The only place where we have a related prayer (which was even far from it) being offered was when Alexander the coppersmith blocked all the opportunity Paul would have used to witness for Christ, and Paul said,

Alexander the coppersmith did me much harm. May the Lord repay him according to his works. (2 Timothy 4:14)

* We have the power to stop, control, and bind the activities of Satan and his demons in a particular place, region, or life, but we cannot kill them by saying die! die! die! They are spirit beings and would not die (Mark 5:10–13; Ephesians 6:10–12)! The Apostle James put it right when he said, Submit yourselves, then, to God. Resist the devil, and he will flee from you (James 4:7).

* We can pray like David who said, "O LORD, turn Ahithophel's counsel into foolishness" (2 Samuel 15:30–31).

* Lord, send confusion into the camp of the enemies (Exodus 23:27; Psalm 40:14; Jeremiah 20:11).

* The LORD will frustrate or thwart the plans of the wicked so that their hand will not be able to perform their enterprises (Job 5:12).

* The Lord will render the enemy powerless.

* My God will deliver me/us (Daniel 3:17, Esther 4:14).

* Psalms 23, 27, and 91 are good defensive weapons for every believer.

* Use the name of Jesus Christ to order powers andprincipalities to bow (Philippians 2:9–11).

* If God is for us, who can be against us (Romans 8:31).

The list actually has no end.
But focusing your prayers on a particular individual so that the fellow will die or get injured is contrary to the type of prayer Christ taught us in His Word.

Faith confessions

* No weapon fashioned against me shall be able to do me any harm (Isaiah 54:17).

∗ Greater is He that is in me than he that is in the world (1 John 4:4).

∗ I shall not die, but shall live to proclaim the goodness of God in the land of the living (Psalm 118:17).

∗ I am more than a conqueror through Christ (Romans 8:37).

∗ God is with His disciples (us) till the end of the age (Matthew 28:18–20).

∗ I am immortal until my purpose on earth is fulfilled (Acts 13:36; 2 Timothy 4:7).

You can go on and on to search for more of these in the Scriptures. We should be more conscious of these scriptural truths than exhibiting fear of enemies. There is incomparable power of deliverance in God's Word.

Improper biblical interpretation causes many ministers of God today to go into Old Testament passages to back themselves up when praying for injury to and the death of enemies. But Jesus in His ministry while on earth would often say, "It was said by the prophets of old that … But I tell you" (Matthew 5: 21, 27, 31, 33, 38, 43). Nevertheless, you must know that the Scripture can never, and will never contradict itself. Jesus Christ has come to give us the new order, with its root affirmed in the Old Testament.

Cursing or praying against your enemies is a matter of faith and obedience. A child of God must be His child enough to believe that God is able to do according to His stated words. As a child, each believer has a choice to make. The choice is either to be obedient to God in this matter or not. Let me, however, commend faith and obedience to you. And the Lord shall grant you victory. It works. The Bible affirms it, if a man's ways please God, He makes his enemy to be at peace with him (Proverbs 16:7).

PRAYER

1. Help me LORD to see and to fight the real enemy at the spiritual realm than my fellow human beings.

2. I pray against the demon (spirit) of unforgiveness that is on the rampage in the churches of Christ and among the people of God all over the world in the name of Jesus.

3. All Satanic forces clutching my heart against forgiveness, take your leave in the name of Jesus.

4. I receive the divine grace to always bless those who curse me and pray for those who offend me in the name of Jesus.

WHEN GOD AVENGES FOR HIS CHILDREN

Revenge is of God, not man.

CHAPTER 11 :
WHEN GOD AVENGES FOR HIS CHILDREN

Do not take revenge, my friends, but leave room for God's wrath, for it is written: "It is mine to avenge; I will repay, says the Lord. On the contrary: If your enemy is hungry, feed him; if he is thirsty, give him something to drink. In doing this, you will heap burning coals on his head. Do not be overcome by evil, but overcome evil with good. (Romans 12:19–21)

The Psalmist gives us a clue that when the revenge's cup of God is full, He revenges a sin in seven folds.

And return to our neighbors sevenfold into their bosom their reproach with which they have reproached you, O Lord (Psalm 79:12).

It is a terrible thing for God to rise on His throne for a revenge mission on behalf of His oppressed children on any matter. Many times we have lost our battles because we fought for ourselves. God defends only those who refuse to take law into their hand to defend themselves. Scores of people in the Bible, if they were to be alive, will have a dreadful story to tell as God rose to the cause of His servants.

Do not engage God in battle by conspiring against the leaders he puts in place, because, the consequences can be disastrous.

Korah, Dathan, and Abiram

Korah, Dathan, and Abiram gathered about 250 Israelite men, well-known community leaders who had been appointed members of the council to conspire against the administration of Moses and Aaron.

> *When Moses heard this, he fell facedown. Then he said to Korah and all his followers: In the morning the LORD will show who belongs to him and who is holy, and he will have that person come near him. The man he chooses he will cause to come near him. . . When Korah had gathered all his followers in opposition to them at the entrance to the Tent of Meeting, the glory of the LORD appeared to the entire assembly. . . Then the LORD said to Moses, "Say to the assembly, 'Move away from the tents of Korah, Dathan, and Abiram. . .'" Then Moses said, "This is how you will know that the LORD has sent me to do all these things and that it was not my idea: If these men die a natural death and experience only what usually happens to men, then the LORD has not sent me. But if the LORD brings about something totally new, and the earth opens its mouth and swallows them, with everything that belongs to them, and they go down alive into the grave, then you will know that these men have treated the LORD with contempt." As soon as he finished saying all this, the ground under them split apart and the earth opened its mouth and swallowed them, with their households and all Korah's men and all their possessions. They went down alive into the grave, with everything they owned; the earth closed over them, and they perished and were gone from the community. At their cries, all the Israelites around them fled, shouting, "The earth is going to swallow us too!" And fire came out from the LORD and consumed the 250 men who were offering the incense. (Numbers 16:1–35)*

You cannot rebel against God's instituted authorities or leadership and go unscathed, because it is God Himself that you are rebelling against, and more so that the sin of rebellion is like sin of witchcraft. . . (1 Samuel 15:23). Do not engage God in battle by conspiring against the leaders he puts in place, because the consequences can be disastrous.

Five kings and their armies against Joshua

Five kings of the Amorites, the king of Jerusalem, the king of Hebron, the king of Jarmuth, the king of Lachish, and the king of Eglon, gathered together and went up, they and all their armies camped to make war with Joshua. If you have a battalion of vibrant soldiers with you but have God against you, you are in trouble. It is like the usual saying: One with God is one with the majority. Such was the case of these five kings with their vast army who ganged up against Joshua the servant of the LORD God of hosts.

And the LORD said to Joshua, "Do not fear them, for I have delivered them into your hand; not a man of them shall stand before you." Joshua therefore came upon them suddenly, having marched all night from Gilgal. So the LORD routed them before Israel, killed them with a great slaughter at Gibeon, chased them along the road that goes to Beth Horon, and struck them down as far as Azekah and Makkedah. And it happened, as they fled before Israel and were on the descent of Beth Horon, that the LORD cast down large hailstones from heaven on them as far as Azekah, and they died. There were more who died from the hailstones than the children of Israel killed with the sword. Then Joshua spoke to the LORD in the day when the LORD delivered up the Amorites before the children of Israel, and he said in the sight of Israel: "Sun, stand still over Gibeon; And Moon, in the Valley of Aijalon." So the sun stood still, and the moon stopped, till the people had revenged upon their enemies And there has been no day like that, before it or after it that the LORD heeded the voice of a man; for the LORD fought for Israel. Then Joshua returned, and all Israel with him, to the camp at Gilgal No one moved his tongue against any of the children of Israel. Then Joshua said, "Open the mouth of the cave, and bring out those five kings to me from the cave." And they did so, and brought out those five kings to him from the cave ... And afterward, Joshua struck them and killed them, and hanged them on five trees; and they were hanging on the trees until evening. So it was at the time of the going down of the sun that Joshua commanded, and they took them down from the trees, cast them into the cave where they had been hidden, and laid large stones against the cave's mouth, which remain until this very day. (Joshua 10:5–27)

When God is fighting against the enemies of His children, all the creatures and the forces of nature can be at work against such enemies. So it was with these five kings and their armies, just as the Red Sea was against the Egyptians and swallowed them while the Israelites· walked safely across the dry land on the sea safely. The sun and the order of earth rotation were against them and cooperated for the destruction of these wicked enemies. Here again we see the first "atomic bomb" of hailstones killing the enemies of God en masse. Therefore, if you do not want the forces of nature to be against you, stop oppressing the people of God.

God fought the vast armies that came against Jehoshaphat

After this, the Moabites and Ammonites with some of the Meunites came to make war on Jehoshaphat. Some men came and told Jehoshaphat, "A vast army is coming against you from Edom, from the other side of the Sea. It is already in Hazazon Tamar" (that is, En Gedi). Alarmed, Jehoshaphat resolved to inquire of the LORD, and he proclaimed a fast for all Judah.

. . . Then Jehoshaphat stood up in the assembly of Judah and Jerusalem at the temple of the LORD in the front of the new courtyard and said: "O LORD, God of our fathers … For we have no power to face this vast army that is attacking us. We do not know what to do, but our eyes are upon you." All the men of Judah, with their wives and children and little ones, stood there before the LORD. Then the Spirit of the LORD came upon Jahaziel son of Zechariah, the son of Benaiah, the son of Jeiel, the son of Mattaniah, a Levite and descendant of Asaph, as he stood in the assembly. He said, "Listen, King Jehoshaphat and all who live in Judah and Jerusalem! This is what the LORD says to you: 'Do not be afraid or discouraged because of this vast army. For the battle is not yours, but God's . . .'" Jehoshaphat bowed with his face to the ground, and all the people of Judah and Jerusalem fell down in worship before the LORD.

Then some Levites from the Kohathites and Korahites stood up and praised the LORD, the God of Israel, with very loud voice.   As they began to sing and praise, the LORD set ambushes against the men of Ammon and Moab and Mount Seir who were invading Judah, and they were defeated There was so much plunder that it took three days to collect it. On the fourth day, they assembled in the Valley of Beracah, where they praised the LORD. This is why it is called the Valley of Beracah to this day. Then, led by Jehoshaphat, all the men of Judah and Jerusalem returned joyfully to Jerusalem, for the LORD had given them cause to rejoice over their enemies. They entered Jerusalem and went to the temple of the LORD with harps and lutes and trumpets. The fear of God came upon all the kingdoms of the countries when they heard how the LORD had fought against the enemies of Israel. And the kingdom of Jehoshaphat was at peace, for his God had given him rest on every side. (2 Chronicles 20:1–28)

Do you know that when God is in the battle with His children to fight enemies, ordinary broomstick can be a sufficient weapon to defeat soldiers with swords, bows, and arrows? Here, it was the weapon of praise that routed the enemies, and the place was named "the Valley of Praise." Can anyone engage in a battle with the Lord and win? So it is when one is fighting with God's child, because the battle is of the Lord.

God avenged for Hezekiah over Sennacherib

Sennacherib was a very wicked, oppressive, and tyrannical king of Assyria, but he met his waterloo when he gathered his valiant army together to attack King Hezekiah. God on His throne intervened divinely to deliver Hezekiah and all the Israelites in a miraculous way.

After all that Hezekiah had so faithfully done, Sennacherib king of Assyria came and invaded Judah. He laid siege to the fortified cities, thinking to conquer them for himself. When Hezekiah saw that Sennacherib had come and that he intended to make war on Jerusalem, he consulted with his officials and military staff about blocking off the water from the springs outside the city, and they helped him.

. . He appointed military officers over the people and assembled them before him in the square at the city gate and encouraged them with

these words: "Be strong and courageous. Do not be afraid or discouraged because of the king of Assyria and the vast army with him, for there is a greater power with us than with him. With him is only the arm of flesh, but with us is the LORD our God to help us and to fight our battles." And the people gained confidence from what Hezekiah the king of Judah said. . . Later, when Sennacherib king of Assyria and all his forces were laying siege to Lachish, he sent his officers to Jerusalem with this message for Hezekiah king of Judah and for all the people of Judah who were there: "This is what Sennacherib king of Assyria says: On what are you basing your confidence, that you remain in Jerusalem under siege? When Hezekiah says, "The LORD our God will save us from the hand of the king of Assyria," he is misleading you, to let you die of hunger and thirst. . . Sennacherib's officers spoke further against the LORD God and against his servant Hezekiah. . . King Hezekiah and the prophet Isaiah son of Amoz cried out in prayer to heaven about this. And the LORD sent an angel, who annihilated all the fighting men and the leaders and officers in the camp of the Assyrian king. So he withdrew to his own land in disgrace. And when he went into the temple of his god, some of his sons cut him down with the sword. So the LORD saved Hezekiah and the people of Jerusalem from the hand of Sennacherib king of Assyria and from the hand of all others. He took care of them on every side. (2 Chronicles 32:1–22)

Any time God's children are faced with overwhelming challenges, they should always take their matters to God with cries for help and deliverance. And God will never hear their voices without coming to deliver them from their afflictions. In Exodus 2:23–25, 3:7–10, for example, the cry of the people of Israel went up to God when the evil-genius king Pharaoh exclaimed: Who is that God (Yahweh) that will deliver you from my hand? You could still remember that Pharaoh and his soldiers were all at last drowned in the Red Sea when God intervened to liberate His people from this oppressor (Exodus 14:1f).

A serious warning!

It is a sin to intentionally go and hurt your neighbor and then stand on the ground that he must forgive you because the Bible teaches forgiveness.

Do not be a stumbling block across your brother's path, because the same Bible condemns being a stumbling block. As a similitude, please be very careful in hurting the children of God, and most especially God's ministers. It can be a terrible thing to fall into the fury of God's vengeance. When a poor man or a less privileged man says, "May God judge between you and me," it is a dangerous prayer as well. It means he has been oppressed and stressed beyond limit. Meekness never means stupidity.

That you are oppressing an innocent child of God without seeing any immediate repercussion does not mean you will forever go scot free.

Neither does humility court humiliation. But unfortunately, there are several unbelievers who take advantage of the meekness and humility of the children of God to oppress, cheat, and humiliate them as well. I do believe that it would be a hundred times safer for the oppressor if the oppressed man avenged for himself rather than God.

I wonder how terrible it is going to be when a matter on earth causes God to rise on His throne to send forth his divine hand upon mortal men in an unquenchable anger. God can never rise on His throne without His enemies being scattered (Number 10:35; Psalm 68:1–2). There is nothing God cannot use to fight against the enemies of His dear children. There are places in the scriptures where he used thunder, snow, flies, wind, boil, darkness, frogs, blood, death, famine, drought, locust, hail, sicknesses and diseases, and the likes to fight. Moreover, Moses and the Psalmist made known to us how terrible and awesome is the appearance of God whenever He rises on His throne.

> *Then it came to pass on the third day, in the morning, that there were thunderings and lightnings, and a thick cloud on the mountain; and the sound of the trumpet was very loud, so that all the people who were in the camp trembled. And Moses brought the people out of the camp to meet with God, and they stood at the foot of the mountain. Now Mount Sinai was completely in smoke, because the LORD descended upon it in fire. Its smoke ascended like the smoke of a furnace, and the whole mountain quaked greatly. And when the blast of the trumpet sounded long and became louder and louder. . . (Exodus 19:16–19)*

When the people saw the thunder and lightning and heard the trumpet and saw the mountain in smoke, they trembled with fear. They stayed at a distance and said to Moses, "Speak to us yourself and we will listen. But do not have God speak to us or we will die." (Exodus 20:18–19)

The voice of the LORD is over the waters; The God of glory thunders; The LORD is over many waters. The voice of the LORD is powerful; The voice of the LORD is full of majesty. The voice of the LORD breaks the cedars, Yes, the LORD splinters the cedars of Lebanon. He makes them also skip like a calf, Lebanon and Sirion like a young wild ox. The voice of the LORD divides the flames of fire. The voice of the LORD shakes the wilderness; The LORD shakes the Wilderness of Kadesh. The voice of the LORD makes the deer give birth, And strips the forests bare; And in His temple everyone says, "Glory! The LORD sat enthroned at the Flood, And the LORD sits as King forever. (Psalm 29:3–10 NKJV)

You can just imagine how disastrous it is going to be when God in the above appearance unleashes His anger on a man because the man is tormenting His servants, sons, daughters, or His Church. When anyone is maltreating a child of God (or His Church), the person is indirectly doing that to God. The old prophet Eli, through his words to his rebellion children, knew how terrific its end could be when man engages in battle with his "Maker" (1 Samuel 2:25). It is like kicking against thorns without wearing shoes. I have seen men's mouths swelled up or turned aside because they insulted God's servants. A complete family has been wiped out because they rebelled in the Church against a pastor. Sicknesses and diseases have claimed several lives as a result of the curses they brought upon themselves via pointing accusing fingers against men of God. I have also heard of the sudden ruin and the pitiable end of some men who went about destroying God's servants through newspaper or other media. Similarly, a complete town had gone into a state of oblivion when God rose to avenge his persecuted Churches.

Many nations of the world that hated Christ, rejected the gospel, and persecuted missionaries to death have not at one point in time known perfect peace. Many of them experience turbulent climatic upheavals. Strange fire is breaking out to consume the people. Animals and even trees with rivers are drying up in some places. Today, some places are experiencing disastrous flooding and some are in constant bloody wars all because God has risen from His throne to avenge the blood of his children that was shed unjustly.

When God's Word says, "Touch not my anointed and do my prophet no harm" (1 Chro. 16:22; Psalm 105:15), it includes destruction of his children through tongues (i.e., your mouths), pen (printing blackmailing papers), sword, and other means. Even the press men who are expert in publicizing the fall of the men of God aren't exempted. With all the cruelty and hostility of King Saul toward David, when Saul died, David warned that the news of his shameful death must not be spread abroad in order to cover Saul's shame.

Tell it not in Gath, proclaim it not in the streets of Ashkelon— Lest the daughters of the Philistines rejoice, lest the daughters of the uncircumcised triumph. (2 Samuel 1:20)

But on the contrary, today pressmen are very happy in making their fortunes through bastardizing the pages of the newspaper with fascinating captions of the Achilles' heels of men of God. However, it is quite understood when this is being done to fake men of God when they expose their deceptive practices to the society. But they still need to be very careful.

Again, you can still remember the history of King Pharaoh and his vast army by the Red Sea when God rose to defend the children of Israel (Exodus 14:31). In all their ways to the promise land, He allowed no one to oppress them; for their sake He rebuked kings (Psalm105:14). King Herod decayed and was eaten up by worms when he was still alive because God rose in defense of his Church (Acts 12:21–23). When you are fighting God's children, you automatically become the enemy of God, and He becomes your enemy as well. In talking about his children, God said, I will be enemy to your enemies, and will oppose he that opposes you (Exodus 23:22). Do not let God become your enemy because of the accusing finger you are pointing at His dear children. The Psalmist expresses the terror of God becoming one's enemy when he said, Fire goeth before Him, and burneth up his enemies round about (Psalm 97:3 KJV). Just as He is a compassionate God, so also He is a consuming fire (Hebrew 12:29). It is better to enjoy His compassion and never to have an experience of His consuming fire.

The Psalmist makes us known that God is on a daily revenge mission (with deadly weapons) for His children.

> *Arise, O LORD, in your anger; rise up against the rage of my enemies. Awake, my God; decree justice. God is a righteous judge, a God who expresses his wrath every day. If he does not relent, he will sharpen his sword; he will bend and string his bow. He has prepared his deadly weapons; he makes ready his flaming arrows. He who is pregnant with evil and conceives trouble gives birth to disillusionment. He who digs a hole and scoops it out falls into the pit he has made. The trouble he causes recoils on himself; his violence comes down on his own head. (Psalm 7:6,11–16)*

It is therefore very necessary for you to repent and turn away from oppressing God's people before He gets at you. That you are oppressing an innocent child of God without seeing any immediate repercussion does not mean you will forever go scot free. You will be paid back in your own coin one day if you fail to repent. Therefore, please stay off from harming God's children!

The problem with man

There are various reasons why people cannot wait for God, but rather take the law into their own hands to avenge themselves. For some, God is too slow in avenging the offenders. Even the souls of the saints who died as martyrs kept on crying for revenge over the inhabitants of the earth who killed them because of their faith in Christ Jesus.

When He opened the fifth seal, I saw under the altar the souls of those who had been slain for the word of God and for the testimony which they held. And they cried with a loud voice, saying, "How long, O Lord, holy and true, until You judge and avenge our blood on those who dwell on the earth?" Then a white robe was given to each of them; and it was said to them that they should rest a little while. . . (Revelation 6:9–11)

That you have a revengeful heart is enough for your own sins and imperfection to be punished.

To some, God is too compassionate and merciful. Even the prophet Jonah of old fell victim of this notion. That was why he was reluctant when God told him to go and preach to the people of Nineveh. Jonah indeed wanted God to unleash His anger on them because they had long been maltreating his people.

Then the word of God came to the king of Nineveh; and he arose from his throne and laid aside his robe, covered himself with sackcloth and sat in ashes.

And he caused it to be proclaimed and published throughout Nineveh by the decree of the king and his nobles, saying, Let neither man nor beast, herd nor flock, taste anything; do not let them eat, or drink water. But let man and beast be covered with sackcloth, and cry mightily to God; yes, let everyone turn from his evil way and from the violence that is in his hands. Who can tell if God will turn and relent, and turn away from His fierce anger, so that we may not perish? Then God saw their works, that they turned from their evil way; and God relented from the disaster that He had said He would bring upon them, and He did not do it. But it displeased Jonah exceedingly, and he became angry. So he prayed to the LORD, and said, "Ah, LORD, was not this what I said when I was still in my country? Therefore I fled previously to Tarshish; for I know that You are a gracious and merciful God, slow to anger and abundant in loving kindness, One who relents from doing harm.

Therefore now, O LORD, please take my life from me, for it is better for me to die than to live!"

. . .But the LORD said ... "And should I not pity Nineveh, that great city, in which are more than one hundred and twenty thousand persons who cannot discern between their right hand and their left—and much livestock? (Jonah 3:6–4:3, 10–11)

Prophet Jonah was the first messenger/evangelist (so to say) I have ever known who wanted his audience to perish. Jonah accused God of being too merciful and compassionate. In fact, he wanted to commit suicide because God had forgiven the people of Nineveh. The Book of Jonah clearly portrays the mercy of God in human affairs. Though Jewish nationalism blinded God's covenant people to an understanding of His concern for the Gentiles, the prophet learned that "salvation is of the Lord," and God's gracious offer extends to all who repent and turn to Him. Jonah did not want God to show mercy to the Ninevites, but he later learned how selfish and unmerciful his position was. There are too many pastors like Jonah today who call for God's fire from heaven to consume their enemies, whereas, while we were yet sinners, Christ died for us—He died for the ungodly.

The one that offended you and you think God must kill or punish may be the one He has chosen to be merciful to. Moreover, if God will mark iniquities, you will not go without having your own share of His wrath. That you have a revengeful heart is enough for your own sins and imperfection to be punished.

Many also think that God must always punish everyone that steps on their toes. But God is not you; He does not always pay us back according to our sins. More so, we do not know His time of revenge and the measurement of the befitting penalties. But you can be sure that no un-repented sinner will go unpunished. For example, God said to Abraham: But in the fourth generation they shall return here, for the iniquity of the Amorites is not yet complete (Genesis 15:16). And do you know that despite their idolatrous practices, the cup of God's wrath for them was not full until over four hundred years later when the land "vomited them out." God is indeed slow to anger and abounding in love. He never wants anybody to perish, but that all should come to repentance. So, you too should give people a chance to repent, instead of calling "holy ghost fire" to consume your fellow brother (s). Moreover, the one that hurts you today may tomorrow turn out to be your "helper."

The glorious victory over enemies

Permit me to share with you my own understanding of what a glorious victory over one's enemy really means.

Even though I walk through the valley of the shadow of death, I will fear no evil, for you are with me; your rod and your staff, they comfort me. You prepare a table before me in the presence of my enemies. You anoint my head with oil; my cup overflows. (Psalm 23:4–5)

He who dwells in the shelter of the Most High will rest in the shadow of the Almighty.

I will say of the LORD, He is my refuge and my fortress, my God, in whom I trust.

Surely he will save you from the fowler's snare and from the deadly pestilence.

He will cover you with his feathers, and under his wings you will find refuge; his faithfulness will be your shield and rampart. You will not fear the terror of night, nor the arrow that flies by day, nor the pestilence that stalks in the darkness, nor the plague that destroys at midday. A thousand may fall at your side, ten thousand at your right hand, but it will not come near you. You will only observe with your eyes and see the punishment of the wicked. If you make the Most High your dwelling—even the LORD, who is my refuge—then no harm will befall you, no disaster will come near your tent. For he will command his angels concerning you to guard you in all your ways; they will lift you up in their hands, so that you will not strike your foot against a stone. You will tread upon the lion and the cobra; you will trample the great lion and the serpent. "Because he loves me," says the LORD, "I will rescue him; I will protect him, for he acknowledges my name. He will call upon me, and I will answer him; I will be with him in trouble, I will deliver him and honor him. With long life will I satisfy him and show him my salvation. (Psalm 91)

God preparing a table before you while your enemy remains
powerless is the best.

So many people think that seeing their so-called enemies (their fellow men) dead is the greatest joy and achievement they could ever have. Then they exclaim, "I have seen the end of my enemy." But the most glorious victory in life is not for your enemy to die (if at all you have one) before you become successful. The greatest of it all is for you to progress without the enemy being able to stop you or do you any harm. God preparing a table before you while your enemy looks on powerlessness is the best. The enemy shall see the success of the righteous and their children's children. And even when they gnash their teeth, it will be to no avail.

> *Praise the LORD. Blessed is the man who fears the LORD, who finds great delight in his commands. His children will be mighty in the land; the generation of the upright will be blessed. Wealth and riches are in his house, and his righteousness endures forever. The wicked man will see and be vexed, he will gnash his teeth and waste away; the longings of the wicked will come to nothing. (Psalm 112)*

Frankly speaking, protection is not an absence of danger, but the presence of God in the face of danger. From the passages above, true victories over enemies include

• God preparing a table before you (abundant prosperity) as your enemy watches you and is powerless in harming you;
• walking fearlessly and majestically at the sight of your enemies;
• you and your children prosper as your enemies bow their heads in shame; and
• longevity of life and salvation of God for you.

Protection is not an absence of danger, but the presence of God in the face of danger.

PRAYER

1. The LORD is able to defend my case and protect me from all oppositions

2. Help me O Lord to love and fellowship genuinely and without deception with fellow brothers and sisters in Christ.

3. I pray earnestly for the salvation of my offenders and accusers in Jesus Name.

CHAPTER TWELVE
UNPARDONABLE SIN THE LIMIT OF GOD'S FORGIVENESS

As far as the east is from the west, so far has He removed our transgression from us.

CHAPTER 12 : UNPARDONABLE SIN —THE LIMIT OF GOD'S FORGIVENESS

Many people have anchored their misconceptions on the seemingly controversial passage of the Scriptures that talk about unpardonable sins. This forms the basis on which they hold one grudge or another against their offenders. Let us study this passage carefully and in its context as we try to do a little comparative analysis with other passages.

> *And so I tell you, every sin and blasphemy will be forgiven men, but the blasphemy against the Spirit will not be forgiven. Anyone who speaks a word against the Son of Man will be forgiven, but anyone who speaks against the Holy Spirit will not be forgiven, either in this age or in the age to come. (Matthew 12:31–32)*

In this passage, Christ Jesus made mention of the sin which cannot be forgiven. Does this mean that God has drawn an arbitrary line of sinfulness beyond which his grace of forgiveness will not reach? The act of the Pharisees which led Jesus to speak of the unpardonable sin was the attributing of a good deed performed by him through the Holy Spirit of God to Beelzebub (Matthew 12:27).

Throughout the Scriptures, we see God's benevolent act of forgiving sins that are very grievous. For example, Rahab was a professional harlot in Jericho, yet she was the only one (except her relations she pleaded for) who was shown mercy and spared from destruction. In fact, the genealogy of the Messiah is not complete if Rahab is not mentioned.

King David committed adultery with Uriah's wife, and at the same time wrote a death letter of that man (Uriah) and handed the letter to the same man to be delivered at his point of execution. Simply put, David snatched a man's wife, and then killed the man in order to cover up the sin that lay open before God. Yet when he turned to God with a genuine heart of repentance, he was forgiven and the LORD still called him "a man after His own heart." God went as far as making an everlasting covenant with him and his descendants.

Peter was a disciple who had worked, walked, and lived with Christ for three good years. But when trouble came, he denied knowing Christ three times. But when he came back with a remorseful heart of repentance, he was pardoned, and later became the "chief of the Apostles."

A criminal had a few hours left to end up his life in eternal damnation in hellfire. Yet when he turned to Christ on the Cross, he was forgiven, and the Lord said,

> *I tell you the truth, today you will be with me in paradise.*

The Apostle Paul, prior to his conversion, was highly injurious to the Church. He persecuted, imprisoned, and even consented to be part of those who murdered believers in Christ. But God's saving arm was stretched out to him in forgiveness, and Paul later became a mighty vessel in God's hand. We have earlier mentioned of a man and a woman who were possessed by legion of demons and seven evil spirits, respectively, yet God reached out to them and they were forgiven, saved, and later became useful for the Lord's works.

What then is unpardonable sin?

An unpardonable sin is for a man to die in his act of intentional sealing up of his mind against the truth of which the Holy Spirit convinced him. Hence, an unpardonable sin is a continued state of unbelief even when the Holy Spirit has opened your eyes to see and to know the truth. It is a blatant, intentional, and perpetual rejection of truth of the gospel.

For example, there are many people (of other religions) who really know that among the prophets, Christ Jesus stands out uniquely and has no equal, and that He is indeed the Savior of the world. Only Jesus Christ said,

He is the way, the truth, and the life. No one can get to God, the Father except through him. (John 14:6)

Yet, they still deliberately decide to seal up their minds from believing the truth. There are as well atheists who claim that God does not exist even though God's creatures alone have convinced and preached to humanity with undeniable facts that there is a higher being behind this universe. No wonder that Apostle Paul affirmed that

for in the gospel a righteousness from God is revealed, a righteousness that is by faith from first to last, just as it is written: "The righteous will live by faith. The wrath of God is being revealed from heaven against all the godlessness and wickedness of men who suppress the truth by their wickedness, since what may be known about God is plain to them, because God has made it plain to them. For since the creation of the world, God's invisible qualities—his eternal power and divine nature— have been clearly seen, being understood from what has been made, so that men are without excuse. For although they knew God, they neither glorified him as God nor gave thanks to him, but their thinking became futile and their foolish hearts were darkened. Although they claimed to be wise, they became fools . . .

Furthermore, since they did not think it worthwhile to retain the knowledge of God, he gave them over to a depraved mind, to do what ought not to be done.

They have become filled with every kind of wickedness, evil, greed, and depravity. They are full of envy, murder, strife, deceit, and malice. They are gossips, slanderers, God-haters, insolent, arrogant, and boastful; they invent ways of doing evil; they disobey their parents; they are senseless, faithless, heartless, and ruthless. Although they know God's righteous decree that those who do such things deserve death, they not only continue to do these very things but also approve of those who practice them. (Romans 1:17–22, 28–32)

On a daily basis, the Holy Spirit is still doing the work Christ said He will do when He comes. When he comes, he will convict the world of guilt in regard to sin and righteousness and judgment: in regard to sin, because men do not believe in me (John 16:8–9).

Thus, the downplay of God's benevolent arm of grace; the rejection of the Sonship, and the Lordship of Christ and his sacrificial death; and the rejection of the works and ministry of the Holy Spirit to bring about salvation, all lead to unpardonable sin. It is a sin of dying in the state of unbelief. Surely, this is why the Bible says,

. . .because those who are led by the Spirit of God are sons of God (Romans 8:14).

Therefore I tell you that no one who is speaking by the Spirit of God says, "Jesus be cursed," and no one can say, "Jesus is Lord," except by the Holy Spirit. (1 Corinthians 12:3)

Who is the liar? It is the man who denies that Jesus is the Christ. Such a man is the antichrist—he denies the Father and the Son. No one who denies the Son has the Father; whoever acknowledges the Son has the Father also. (1 John 2:22–23)

Jesus, while on earth, knew that in a short while, he would return to heaven and the Holy Spirit would come to earth and dwell to continue the work of men's salvation. The Truth, that is, the gospel, which Christ will no longer be here to convince the world of (since he was returning to the Father), the Holy Spirit will always be here on earth to do. This was why He told the Pharisees that if they blasphemed against Him and as well blasphemed against the Holy Spirit, who is the last but not the least Person in the "Trinity (the Godhead)" concerning the salvation of men, then there will be no remedy. This is because no one else (not even the angels) will come after the Holy Spirit to preach the truth to men again. Furthermore, in the salvation of mankind, "God the Father is the Chief Initiator and the Planner; God the Son is the Chief Executor; and God the Holy Spirit is the Chief Revealer." This is why it is safe for you to believe the gospel as the Holy Spirit convinces you when you hear it being preached.

Jesus answered, "I am the way and the truth and the life. No one comes to the Father except through me. Salvation is found in no one else, for there is no other name under heaven given to men by which we must be saved. (John 14:6; Acts 4:12)

For God so loved the world that he gave his one and only Son, that whoever believes in him shall not perish but have eternal life. Whoever believes in him is not condemned, but whoever does not believe stands condemned already because he has not believed in the name of God's one and only Son. Whoever believes in the Son has eternal life, but whoever rejects the Son will not see life, for God's wrath remains on him. (John 3:16, 18, and 36)

Become a child of God today

You can make the right decision now by giving your life to Jesus Christ. If you want to, make this prayer of confession:

"Lord Jesus Christ, I believe with all my heart that you are the Son of the living God. You came to this world to die and to redeem sinners like me with your precious blood. On the third day you rose from the grave and ascended to heaven. I surrender my life to you today. Cleanse me with your blood. Today, I become a child of God; I have eternal life through Christ Jesus. Amen."

Congratulations! I welcome you to the family of faith in Christ Jesus the Son of God. You are forever free from hell and from the condemnation of God. You are no longer a sinner. You become the righteousness of God. Kindly join a body of believers (church) to keep strong in faith.

Action

1. I shall not seal up my mind to the correction and rebuke of the spirit of God

2. Who are the people you need to forgive? Make a list of them and call them one-by-one for reconciliation

3. Be proactive in making reconciliation. Let go of pride, ego and self.

4. Refuse to take up you offenders. God is always there to defend and fight for you.

5. O Lord, no offence against me shall be unpardonable by me in the name of Jesus.

168

BEYOND FORGIVENESS

We have to carry the heart of God for the world of lost sinners.

CHAPTER 13 : BEYOND FORGIVENESS

It is so interesting that God does not want us to stop at forgiving people alone. God wants us to take steps further. Forgiveness itself is one of the difficult spiritual tasks except a man has been completely broken by the Holy Spirit of God. But these preceding steps after forgiveness are really herculean tasks. Nevertheless, the Word of God left us with no option.

Love your enemies

You have heard that it was said, "Love your neighbor and hate your enemy." But I tell you, love your enemies ... that you may be children of your Father in heaven. He causes his sun to rise on the evil and the good, and sends rain on the righteous and the unrighteous. If you love those who love you, what reward will you get? ... Be perfect, therefore, as your heavenly Father is perfect. (Matthew 5:43–48)

Much has been said about love already in the previous chapters. Love still remains as the strongest weapon of victory. We need to show the genuine love of Christ to a hostile enemy.

Pray for those who persecute you

But I tell you ... pray for those who persecute you (Matthew 5:43–44). It is really difficult to do. But you may want to ask, What kind of prayer should I pray for a wicked enemy? Pray that his heart may be opened to receive the gospel of Christ and become instrument in God's hand. This kind of prayer from the early Church was what led to the conversion of Saul to Paul. Again, you know already that if you die today, you are going to heaven. If a wicked enemy dies without Christ, he is going to hell. But God never has any delight for anyone to perish. We have to carry the heart of God for the world of lost sinners.

Bless those who curse you

Bless those who persecute you; bless and do not curse (Romans 12:14). To curse back on anyone who curses you is to decline to the same lower level in the spirit realm with your enemy. We have been given a sanctified tongue that utter out blessings and words of grace seasoned with salt.

What kind of prayer should I pray for a wicked enemy? Pray that his heart may be opened to receive the gospel of Christ and become instrument in God's Hand.

Let your conversation be always full of grace, seasoned with salt, so that you may know how to answer everyone (Colossians 4:6). With the tongue we praise our Lord and Father, and with it we curse human beings, who have been made in God's likeness. Out of the same mouth come praise and cursing. My brothers and sisters, this should not be. Can both fresh water and salt water flow from the same spring? My brothers and sisters can a fig tree bear olives, or a grapevine bear figs? Neither can a salt spring produce fresh water. (James 3:9–12)

Provide the needs of your offender

If your enemy is hungry, feed him; if he is thirsty, give him something to drink. In doing this, you will heap burning coals on his head (Romans 12:20).

God wants us to provide both the physical and the spiritual needs of our enemies. One of my professors here at The Southern Baptist Theological Seminary, Louisville, Kentucky, made us read some life-transforming books for the class "Cultural Anthropology." One of the books is titled Gentle Salvage Still Seeking the End of the Sword. A man led four other friends to a very hostile and unfriendly tribe to reach them with the gospel. Unfortunately, the mission of these five men was misunderstood by these tribal men. They came out with furious anger to attack these missionaries with spears. They sobbed and sobbed as they died in the pool of their blood. But few years later, the wife and son of this team leader went back to the same tribe and won them over with the love of Christ. The men of this tribe dropped their sword and embraced the Word of God.[47] There is power in forgiveness. Can you go back to the same place you have been hurt to show them kindness?

Take the blame

Surely he took up our pain and bore our suffering, yet we considered him punished by God, stricken by him, and afflicted. But he was pierced for our transgressions, he was crushed for our iniquities; the punishment that brought us peace was on him, and by his wounds we are healed.

We all, like sheep, have gone astray, each of us has turned to our own way; and the LORD has laid on him the iniquity of us all. (Isaiah 53:3–6)

All this is from God, who reconciled us to himself through Christ and gave us the ministry of reconciliation: that God was reconciling the world to himself in Christ, not counting men's sins against them. … God made him who had no sin to be sin for us, so that in him we might become the righteousness of God. (2 Corinthians 5:18–21)

This is what Jesus did for us. Jesus Christ took the blame for our sins. One of the ways to maintain peace between couples and our relationship with others is to always take the blame and let peace reign. To admit that you are at fault when indeed you are right and the other party is at fault may sound odd. But it is the way to spiritual brokenness. To take the

---

47 *Read more in Aenkaedi, Menkaye, Kemo, and Dywoe. Gentle Savage: Still Seeking the End of the Spear. Maitland, FL: Xulon Press, 2013.*

blame may mean to say sorry when you have not committed any crime. It may also mean to apologize when you have not sinned so that your brother may be able to see the light.

Hence, forgiveness has not taken place until you are ready to fellowship with your repented brother.

Fellowship with the one you have forgiven

Two rebels were crucified with him, one on his right and one on his left. Those who passed by hurled insults at him. . . In the same way the chief priests, the teachers of the law and the elders mocked him. . . In the same way the rebels who were crucified with him also heaped insults on him. (Matthew 27:38–44)

We read this same historical account in Luke as this:

Two other men, both criminals, were also led out with him to be executed. When they came to the place called the Skull, they crucified him there, along with the criminals—one on his right, the other on his left. Jesus said, "Father, forgive them, for they do not know what they are doing." And they divided up his clothes by casting lots. The people stood watching, and the rulers even sneered at him. . . The soldiers also came up and mocked him . . .There was a written notice above him, which read: this is the king of the jews. One of the criminals who hung there hurled insults at him: "Aren't you the Messiah? Save yourself and us!" But the other criminal rebuked him. "Don't you fear God," he said, "since you are under the same sentence? We are punished justly, for we are getting what our deeds deserve. But this man has done nothing wrong." Then he said, "Jesus, remember me when you come into your kingdom. Jesus answered him, "Truly I tell you, today you will be with me in paradise. (Luke 23:32–43)

Sandeep Poonen in his comments on these passages above maintained that the two criminals were both railing insults on Jesus Christ. But along the line, one of the criminals repented. Jesus then promised to have fellowship with this repented criminal later in Paradise—His Father's kingdom.[48] This is the same way Jesus forgave us, calls us His own, and fellowships with us. He assured us that God the Father loves exactly as He love Him— Christ (John 17). Hence, forgiveness has not taken place until you are ready to fellowship with your repented brother.

Dear reader, let me congratulate you for having the grace to read this book. If you are not a Christian, God must have been the One that has given you the privilege to read this book. In that case, I appeal to you today to confess your sins, commit your life to Him, and ask God to send the Holy Spirit into your heart. Do this and you by faith become a child of God.

In case you are already a believer in Christ, I congratulate you. Let me, however, implore you not to take the grace of God in vain by indulging yourself in sin. Search your heart and daily plead with God to cleanse you and keep you walking in the spirit. Also, if you are a Christian who finds it difficult to forgive others, plead with God for this grace and remember you have been forgiven much. God does not expect less from you. May we all live to daily please Him who loves us beyond measure.

---

48 Sandeep Poonen, Sermon: *Forgiving like Jesus Christ. Christian Fellowship Centre, India.*

CONCLUSION

There are essentially two ways of responding to life's unfair experiences. The first and natural response is to become a debt collector. We set out to make the offender pay for what he has done. This is the pathway ofresentment and retaliation— getting even, exacting payment for what they did. But the problem is that being a debt collector does more than keep our offender in debtor's prison; it puts us in prison.

But there is another way. As an alternative to being a debt collector— the pathway of resentment and retaliation—God calls us to the pure, powerful choice of forgiveness—and to pursue, wherever possible, the pathway of restoration and reconciliation.

Actually, the latter approach is not presented in the Scriptures as an option, but a mandate for every believer. Apostle Paul said to the body of Christ, "Bear with each other and forgive whatever grievances you may have against one another. Forgive as the Lord forgave you" (Colossians 3:13). So you must also forgive.

So many people today harbor ill will, grudges, and animosities toward others. Some are in the bondage of not even being able to forgive themselves. We are all full of weaknesses and errors; so let us pardon one another for our follies. We are all on a lifelong journey and the core of its meaning, the terrible demand of its centrality, is forgiving and being forgiven.49

---

49 Martha Kilpatrick "Forgiveness" http://www.tentmaker.org accessed March 2010.

No offence is too great; no offender is beyond the boundary to which our forgiveness must extend. Our fellowship with God requires it and as well depends on it.

I realize that this journey into forgiveness may require you to delve into areas of your life that are highly sensitive and still hot to the touch. But I am also aware that our natural way of handling these hurts only results in keeping them sore and inflamed. However, to whatever extent you may have been imprisoned by your response to wounds inflicted on you by others, I assure you that embracing this truth is the starting place in your journey to freedom. When we as God's children realize that His grace is sufficient for every situation, that by the power of His indwelling Spirit we have the ability to respond with grace and forgiveness to those who have sinned against us—at that point we are no longer victims.[50] Once again, I want you to know that unforgiveness is a seed from the devil. Do not let him plant it in you because it is a killer disease. It kills the body gradually, and as well kill the soul in hellfire!

Will you choose to forgive today?

> ***Unforgiveness is a seed from the devil.***
> ***Do not let him plant it in you. It is a killer***
> ***disease. It kills the body gradually, and***
> ***as a well kill the soul in hell fire!***

---

50 Nancy Leigh DeMoss, Will You Choose to Forgive? in Life Action Ministries: Online Resources accessed Saturday 9 2011.

Action

1. I shall not be ashamed to take the blame for peace to rain

2. I choose the right way to handle others' people offenses. I choose to let go!

3. I am ready to fellowship with my brothers/sister as a complete mark of forgiveness.

4. I receive the grace to sincerely pray for the well-being of all my offenders and enemies in Jesus' name.

5. Lord, at no time shall I withhold any good in my care from my offenders and enemies in the name of Jesus.